"We the jury find the defendant, Lewis T. Graham, Jr., guilty as charged of second-degree murder."

Graham was stunned. He could hear his youngest children crying in the seats behind him, but he didn't have the courage to turn and face his family. All he could think of was "guilty as charged."

BLOOD EVIDENCE

BLOOD EVIDENCE

CRAIG A. LEWIS

BERKLEY BOOKS, NEW YORK

This Berkley book contains the complete text
of the original hardcover edition. It has been
completely reset in a typeface designed for easy
reading and was printed from new film.

BLOOD EVIDENCE

A Berkley Book / published by arrangement with
August House, Inc.

PRINTING HISTORY
August House edition published 1990
Berkley edition / July 1992

ISBN: 0-425-13212-9

A BERKLEY BOOK ® TM 757,375
Berkley Books are published by The Berkley Publishing Group,
200 Madison Avenue, New York, New York 10016.
The name "Berkley" and the "B" logo
are trademarks belonging to Berkley Publishing Corporation.

PRINTED IN THE UNITED STATES OF AMERICA

10 9 8 7 6 5 4 3 2 1

For my mother, Velma Collom

Contents

Introduction

To people who haven't spent much time in this state, Louisiana means New Orleans. That's easy to understand, considering that New Orleans is the home of Bourbon Street, Mardi Gras, wonderful Cajun and Creole cuisine, and what can only be described as a N'Awlins attitude based on the south Louisiana motto *"Laissez le bon temps rouler"*—"Let the good times roll."

And in addition to New Orleans, Louisiana also means Cajun country—the poor, rural, waterlogged expanse of a dozen or so parishes near the Gulf of Mexico. The picture many out-of-staters have of Louisiana is that of a large Cajun family gathering around the porch, with kids and dogs running wild in the swampy yard and Poppa sitting next to a big pot of boiling shrimp, crab, or crawfish. Accordions and fiddles are in the background, screeching out a tapping, yelling dance call in bastardized French. People may think all of Louisiana fits that description, but that's not the way it is.

There are actually two diverse, distinct Louisianas which live in curious coexistence—held together by geography, but as different as sand and mud. The Cajun image has little in common with life in north Louisiana (by north, I mean everything above the geographic midpoint, where the base of the "L" juts out). North and south are divided by more than distance.

Just as New Orleans reigns in south Louisiana, north Louisiana is dominated by Shreveport. Creating the second largest metropolitan area in the state, Shreveport and its sister city, Bossier City, had a combined population of about 300,000 in 1980, when the Graham murder occurred. The two have separate municipalities and are spread across a geographic area as large as the city of Pittsburgh.

South Louisiana is a Catholic stronghold, and the Archdiocese of New Orleans is one of the most powerful in the country. But while the Shreveport-Bossier City telephone directory lists fourteen Catholic churches, Catholicism is not the principal denomination here. North Louisiana—Shreveport in particular—is the home of the Baptists—130 Baptist churches in all, including American Baptists, Independent Baptists, Missionary Baptists, Reformed Baptists, and not surprisingly, Southern Baptists.

One should never generalize about large segments of the populace, but it is almost a given that the people who make their home in Shreveport are of a different mind-set than those who choose to live in New Orleans or the bayou country. For one thing, Shreveport is largely conservative, one of the few Republican strongholds in the state. Shreveport business people and politicos like their government lean, composed of just the basics—roads, bridges, and okay, if you must, a little government assistance to the needy. Even in the black community, which makes up over forty percent of Shreveport's population, a cautious, middle-of-the-road political view prevails. Among whites, conservative Democrats are tolerated, conservative Republicans preferred.

Culturally Shreveport has more in common with east Texas and the conservative work ethic than the south Louisiana "good times" view. Though it is primarily a white-collar town, its biggest employer in 1980 was Western Electric, the manufacturing subsidiary of AT&T. In March 1980 employment at the plant was about seven thousand. Around that time General Motors announced that it would build a new facility on the western edge of the city to manufacture small pick-up trucks, the Chevrolet S-10 (S stands for Shreveport).

Another magnet to the Shreveport area around that time was the Louisiana State University Medical Center, which employed hundreds of people at a combined hospital/medical school complex. In addition to the hospital and teaching personnel, a large medical research staff worked under the center's umbrella. A state-owned and -managed facility, LSU Hospital was the only charity hospital in town. With faculty and research scientists recruited from all parts of the country, the facility's brain trust was a source of city pride. More and more, the center was gaining a reputation as a regional medical mecca, drawing patients and referring physicians from across the South.

No longer just an oil and gas town, Shreveport was beginning to attract workers from other states, many following the new plants, some coming for the mild climate (humidity and all). The majority of these new transplants were buying homes and creating neighborhoods in the southwest section of the city, an area known as Southern Hills. Rather than stemming from one neighborhood or one developer's plan, Southern Hills was actually a cluster of several areas offering medium-priced homes to the growing middle class. It was almost completely white, Protestant, and crime-free—the kind of area in which the police themselves might choose to live, far from low-income sections that spawned the most violence. Emergency medical technicians called to check on a deceased person in Southern Hills would generally find an elderly man or woman who had died peacefully during sleep. Murder didn't happen in Southern Hills.

It was in this atmosphere, in this neighborhood, in this city that the Graham murder case unfolded. During the sixteen-month period between the crime and the trial, more articles were written, more stories were aired, more gossip and speculation were released than with any other crime in the history of Caddo Parish, Louisiana.

Today, almost nine years since Dr. Lewis T. Graham, Jr., went on trial, the mere mention of his name elicits an instantaneous, emotional affirmation of the hearer's belief in his guilt or innocence. Lew Graham, and his sensational murder trial, are now an indelible part of the psyche of this city.

THE COPS

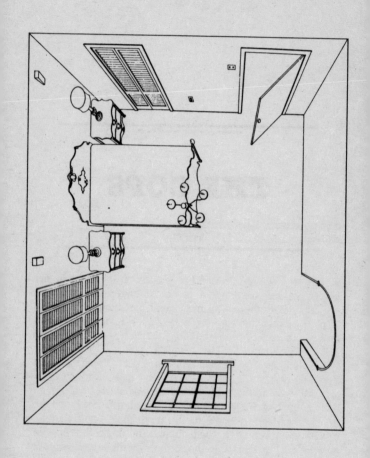

1

CAROLYN Godwin cleaned her glasses on the front of her housecoat and tried again to see if anything was moving outside. Nothing—no movement, no sound. The house directly across the street, 2033 South Kirkwood Drive, looked undisturbed on the outside. But she knew there was trouble inside.

Carolyn ran her tongue across her teeth, realizing that she hadn't taken the time to brush. Her hair was disheveled and she wore no makeup—she'd been awakened at such an early hour. It was a few minutes before sunrise, with just the first hint of light outside, hardly more than a streetlamp's reflection. A heavy fog had trapped the damp darkness at ground level and added to the eeriness on the normally quiet street. Four police cars were parked across the street, and while Carolyn watched, occasionally officers would come outside and walk around the exterior of the house. A chill ran up Godwin's spine, and she shuddered as she retreated from the front window, backing into the two boys standing behind her.

"There's really no sense in looking out there—can't see anything except the police cars," she said.

Naturally nervous and high-strung, she wasn't cut out for this. Fearing the worst, she hoped that when the time came she could hang on and be strong for these kids.

David Graham was the oldest—at sixteen and almost six feet tall, he was more a man than a boy. Eric was just reaching puberty, and little Katie was in the second grade. Katie had fallen asleep on the couch.

Carolyn pulled David aside and whispered, "Did your father say anything about the people who broke in?"

David Graham was tall and blonde, a quiet boy who was polite to adults and popular in school—a star on his high school basketball team. "All he said was that someone came in and attacked him and Mom. What's taking them so long? Why don't they bring Mom out?"

Carolyn didn't want to think about it. "Maybe they're still giving her first aid. Did you see your mother at all?"

"No. Dad and Mr. Siragusa woke me and Eric up and told us to grab Katie and come over here. Dad said he'd been stabbed, there was blood all over his shirt. He said Mom was hurt real bad," David said.

Carolyn remembered an uneventful shopping trip she'd taken with David's mother the day before. Her chin quivered, and she had to look away and take deep breaths to keep from breaking down in front of the children. She had never been so frightened—hoping that Lew and her own sense of foreboding were wrong, that somehow her neighbor was not that badly hurt. She wondered if a crazed attacker was still lurking around outside.

She walked back over to the window in time to see another team of Shreveport police officers arrive. She jumped when David spoke over her shoulder.

"More cops. There must be ten policemen over there. Where's the ambulance? Where's Mom?" David asked.

Carolyn shook her head. "I don't know, David. I'm sure they're doing everything they can."

•   •   •

DETECTIVE Frank Lopez stood on the sidewalk in front of 2033 South Kirkwood Drive. He had never been to this neighborhood, not on business anyway. In the pre-dawn glow it had a quiet charm about it, a neat and tidy ambiance that had little in common with the dirty business of murder. And Lopez was in a position to know what to expect. He'd spent the last twelve years looking at the butt end of life, in a job filled with crooks and killers, punks and prostitutes. He was a burly Hispanic who could have taken off his coat and tie and easily gone undercover. He had extra wide shoulders, a noticeable paunch, and a scraggly dark moustache that hid a thin upper lip.

Lopez's trained eye took in the limited view from the front of the house. It was brown brick, surrounded by a well-manicured lawn, with a heavy dew undisturbed and glistening across the cut grass. If it hadn't been for the police patrol cars parked in the driveway, Lopez would have thought the dispatcher had given him the wrong address.

He walked up the driveway to the front door and nodded to the patrolman in the foyer, glancing past the officer into a living room, nicely furnished in early American style.

"Morning, Frank," the officer said. "Shit, this is a bad one. The lady's in the back bedroom—that's the husband over there sitting next to the fireplace. He's the one that called."

Lopez looked across the living room and saw a small man in a white T-shirt talking to two uniformed officers. "Anybody call for an ambulance?"

"They're on the way. Not that he needs it—and neither does she."

Lopez walked a few steps into the living room. He saw a pile of liquor bottles on the floor a few feet from the man in the T-shirt. "Where's the body?"

The officer indicated a hallway. "Back bedroom. Worst I've ever seen."

Frank Lopez turned and headed out of the living room. "Lieutenant Coker will be here in a minute. Except for him, no one else gets in the crime scene." The patrolman knew the routine. "Sure thing, Frank."

• • •

LT. Dan Coker was eight minutes behind Detective Lopez, and he had to park down the street because of all the police vehicles in front of 2033 South Kirkwood. Coker had viewed some bloody scenes in his nineteen years in the department and he thought he had seen it all. Not yet.

He was the commander of the night-shift detectives, and he took his responsibility seriously. He was wearing his favorite gray sport coat and kept his curly hair regulation length. He believed that in order to get respect, you had to deserve it, and a professional appearance was important.

Dan Coker had a deep, gravelly voice, and delivered commands with a bark only a little softer than a drill sergeant's. He located one of the patrolmen on the scene, Officer Harold Patterson.

"Patterson, you want to tell me why half the uniformed officers in the Shreveport Police Department are standing around our crime scene?" Coker asked.

Patterson shrugged. "It's a homicide in Southern Hills. Nothing much ever happens in this neighborhood. They're curious."

Coker frowned. "Well, I don't care how curious they are, I don't want them getting in the way. I've already called for the Identification Bureau. You know what that means. I don't want your guys stomping around playing grab-ass, screwing up my crime scene."

"I'll keep 'em in line."

"If you want to do something helpful, check around the outside of the house and see if you can find a point of entry," Coker said.

Detectives tend to hang together, removed from the duties of uniformed officers and unconcerned with their opinions. The styles of the two detectives at the Graham house were very different. Lopez, a quiet loner, kept his observations to himself and refused to get in a hurry. Coker was a take-charge guy who wanted everything done right away, his way.

"Lieutenant, you ready to see the body?" Lopez asked.

"I guess. The question is, Frank, is it ready to see me?"

• • •

THE detectives stepped slowly through the bedroom door, stopping next to one another at the foot of the bed. Coker looked at his partner and shook his head.

The bedroom was average in size for a neighborhood such as the Grahams'. The furnishings were typical, too—gold shag carpeting on the floor, off-white walls and ceiling—except that they were now stained with the smears and spots of human blood. As the detectives stood in the doorway, the headboard of the bed was against the right hand wall. There were nightstands on either side of the headboard, a lamp on the left nightstand, a princess telephone on the right. A closet door was just a couple of feet farther right from the telephone. Across the room, a small, round table was turned on its side, papers which had been on top now lying in a neat pile on the floor. Against the wall opposite the headboard was a chest of drawers, standing near an archway leading into the master bathroom.

The woman's body was lying face-up on the bed, on the left side to the detectives standing at the foot of the bed. The ceiling and three of the off-white walls were bloodstained. Through all the blood and the hair, it was hard to tell how many times she'd been hit or even, at first, if the victim was black or white. Long streams of dried blood had crusted over her face and neck, leaving maroon trails down her neck, flowing underneath the top of her red nightgown.

In the middle of her forehead, almost dead center between the eyes, was a gaping hole over two inches in diameter, obviously quite deep. Her arms were resting at her sides, her hands almost crossed at the waist. Her right wrist was severely bruised. Looking at her wrist, Coker could finally tell she was Caucasian.

Dan Coker took out a small notebook and quickly sketched the position of the bed and body. As his eyes took in the crime scene, he began making notes. After a few moments, Coker stepped gingerly around the end of the bed over to the side nearest the body.

The sheets and bedspread, crumpled and bloody, were pulled halfway up the bed, and held streaks and pools of dried and drying blood. On the floor, next to the bed, lay a short-handled sledgehammer. Coker could see blood drying on its head.

Coker looked at Lopez. "A sledgehammer?"

Lopez said nothing, moving to the opposite side of the bed to inspect the louvered doors of the closet.

On the floor next to the sledgehammer was a hunting knife, about six inches long, with blood noticeable on the first third of the blade. An alarm clock, the time stopped at 4:12, lay face-up next to the knife. Coker could see two orange-sized dark stains, no doubt blood, in the shag carpet near the clock.

His eyes were drawn back to the sledgehammer.

After a few more minutes of inspecting the bed and body, he walked to the far side of the room. He glanced up and noticed several photographs of children—their posed, smiling faces staring out at the blood and gore in the room.

Coker pointed at the pictures. "Hey, Frank, where are the kids?"

Lopez was now inside the closet. "Across the street, with a neighbor. Haven't talked to them yet."

Coker went back around the foot of the bed, to an area midway between the bed and the nearer wall. Blue and bloodstained ladies' bedroom slippers were on the floor at the end of the bed, on the side opposite the dead body. The pillow across from the corpse had an indentation where someone had lain and bled. The beige princess telephone, its formal design in stark contrast with the gory scene, sat unmarked on a nightstand.

Coker leaned down and saw that the headboard displayed a large group of bloodstains, many of them tiny droplets no bigger than a pinhead. The wall behind the headboard held more droplets, some tiny, some as big as a penny, as did the ceiling and the other two walls closest to the bed.

Lopez came out of the closet and moved out into the hallway. Coker used his pencil to shut the closet door, noticing a woman's handbag hanging from the closet's outside doorknob. Looking closely, he could see an extremely fine spray of dried blood clinging to the side of the leather purse. Down and to the right of the closet, about a foot off the floor, the textured white wall was stained with a smear, what looked like a bloody fingerprint or two.

Coker knew that the blood evidence was very important, so he instructed one of the uniformed officers to call for a team of investigators from the crime lab.

He walked through an open archway into the adjoining master bath and noticed a couple of red stains still clinging to the side of the lavatory. There were water spots on the sides of the sink and pools of water in the bottom of the shower stall.

"Lieutenant, the ID officers are here," a patrolman called from the hallway.

Coker leaned over and looked at the sink again. "Send them on in, but everyone else, stay out."

An identification officer appeared at the doorway. In addition to doing photography and fingerprint work, the ID staff was expected to collect the evidence—bag it, mark it, and save it for court.

Coker stood up and backed away from the bathroom sink. "Looks like somebody washed up in here. Make sure you get plenty of pictures of these spots, and see if you can capture a sample for the crime lab. There's a couple of stains on the bedroom floor that look like blood—cut the carpet up. And see about taking some samples of the blood on that wall near the door."

Out in the hallway, next to a bedroom decorated for a little girl, Coker saw an empty leather sheath, probably for the hunting knife found near the bed. He walked past several officers in the living room and stopped near a set of built-in cabinets. In front of the cabinets several liquor bottles were laid out in a strangely symmetrical pattern. Next to the liquor bottles were a pair of expensive-looking binoculars and a color television and videocassette recorder on a stand. To Coker this area of the living room looked especially odd: why had someone gone through the cabinets while leaving valuable electronics untouched? If it was a robbery, he thought, then why wasn't this stuff taken?

Walking towards the kitchen, Coker saw a bath towel

on the floor near a green wall telephone, looking out of place. When he reached down and felt it, it was damp, and he wondered if there was a connection to the water he'd noticed in the bathroom. The kitchen was clean and tidy, and he turned and walked through a laundry room to a door leading out into the garage. The back door was ajar, keys still hanging on the inside from a deadbolt lock. The bolt was out, in the locked position, keeping the door from closing shut. Just outside the garage door was a long, black crowbar. A number of scratches and indentations in the wood surrounding the lock looked as though they might match the crowbar's teeth. The garage itself was too cluttered for cars, with a ping-pong table and a workbench surrounded by a large number of tools. Coker could see a space where a tracing for a crowbar was drawn on a pegboard.

The big, sliding garage door was up three or four feet, and Coker ducked underneath and walked outside. In the back yard, the Grahams' dog was scurrying around, confused by the presence of so many strangers. Outside the chain-link fence surrounding the back yard was a blue flashlight and a can partially full of dimes and foreign currency, gleaming in the dew-covered grass.

Coker walked back through the garage, came in the rear laundry-room door and called to Lopez, who was talking to a patrolman in the living room. "Frank—you got the names?"

Lopez had written them down. "The victim is Kathleen Graham; they call her Kathy. That's her husband sitting next to the fireplace in the living room. Lewis Graham. Dr. Lewis Graham."

Three uniformed officers were standing in a semi-circle around Graham, asking questions, making notes. From the kitchen, Coker and Lopez watched the officers question the man, the detectives looking for signs of pain on Graham's calm face.

"What does he say?" Coker asked.

"He told the uniforms that somebody broke in and did all this. I don't know; it don't make sense. Somebody's gonna hammer the wife like that and barely touch the husband?"

Coker grunted. "What do we know about him?"

"Just what I got from the uniforms. His name is Dr. Lewis T. Graham, Jr. He works at the med center—says he's a teacher and assistant dean. He's thirty-nine years old, his wife was thirty-eight. Got three kids, two boys and a girl; boys are sixteen and twelve, girl's eight. He said he sent the children across the street to stay with a neighbor lady, a Mrs. Carolyn Godwin. The uniform said the bedroom door was locked when he got here—had to kick it open. Graham said he locked the door to keep the kids from seeing their mother."

Coker eased back into the living room, just far enough to get Graham in view. What he saw was a smallish man who looked to be in his early forties, with short, ash-colored hair and watchful eyes behind wire-framed glasses. Graham was wearing a plain white T-shirt and jeans, and was holding a bloodstained area on his left side.

Coker had learned a long time before the value in going with his instincts. "Look how calm he is. Ever see a man that calm right after his wife got murdered?"

Frank Lopez smiled. "He's not very big."

"How big you gotta be if you're swinging a sledge-hammer?"

The detectives walked over and joined the group of cops around Graham. The patrolmen automatically stepped back when the detectives walked up, and Graham gave Coker and Lopez his full attention.

"Mr. Graham, I'm Lieutenant Dan Coker, and this is Sergeant Frank Lopez. Can you tell us what happened here?"

Graham spoke slowly. "I was asleep, and someone came in and attacked us. I was pulled out of bed, stabbed, and then knocked out. When I woke up, I found her."

Coker exchanged a glance with his partner. "Can I see where you're hurt?"

Graham gingerly pulled up his T-shirt to display a small stab wound high on his left side, up near the armpit.

"It doesn't look too serious. Did you say you were knocked out?"

"Yes. I don't know how long I was unconscious. Could have been minutes, or hours."

Coker wrote what Graham said in his notebook. "Just to be on the safe side, why don't we put you in the ambulance and get you checked out at the hospital. Someone will catch up with you down there."

Graham nodded, and one of the uniformed officers escorted him out the door to the waiting ambulance.

Coker watched him walk away and looked back down at the disarray in the living room. "Has anybody called the coroner?"

"Yes sir, they're on the way."

"Okay, I want everybody to stay out of the bedroom. Frank, I'm going to radio downtown. I'll be right back."

As the ambulance made its way through the neighborhood just after 6:00 a.m., Lew Graham noticed people out everywhere, in their yards and in the streets. His side was throbbing, and he had a chill and shivers. He noticed camera crews from two television stations, and saw what he assumed was a group of journalists talking to patrolmen in his front yard.

Gary Hines, a *Shreveport Journal* reporter, sweet-talked his way past several uniformed officers and got a close-up tour of the murder room. The Caddo Parish Coroner's Office officially pronounced Kathy Graham dead at the scene, covered the body with a sheet, and loaded it up for transport to the morgue.

The emergency room at the Louisiana State University Medical Center was quiet early in the morning, but Graham's presence caused a flurry of activity. Dr. John Menard, an intern and former biochemistry student of Graham's, took the first brief look at his stab wound. Because of Graham's position at the medical center, a senior resident was called in to consult with the nervous intern.

The doctors sutured the stab wound with one stitch, and applied antiseptic and a bandage to a minor slash on the palm of his hand. Graham told the doctors that he'd been knocked out, and they spent considerable time inspecting a small red area on his forehead. Even though he seemed clear-headed, X-rays were ordered to make sure there was no skull fracture.

Throughout the medical exam, Graham remained calm and cooperative, if a bit subdued, and his remarkable composure surprised the medical team just as it had the police investigators.

DETECTIVE John Brann was a whistler. He whistled in his car, in the office, every place he went. He was whistling on the way to work when his car radio spit out an order. "Proceed to the LSU emergency room and interview a Lewis T. Graham, Jr., in a homicide. Graham and his wife were attacked, and she is deceased. He's in the hospital with undetermined injuries." Brann wrote down the name and changed lanes to get off the interstate.

Brann had a disarming, good-ole-boy manner about him. His hairstyle was out of date—a sixties-style, slicked-back pompadour—and he spoke with a thick Southern accent that made him sound like a country bumpkin. But beneath his facade was an intelligent, wary investigator.

He had been a cop for a dozen or so years, had paid his dues working his way up from patrol duty. He had earned a reputation among his peers for effective interrogation. Brann didn't believe in playing games with a suspect; he liked to tug the truth calmly out of someone who had made the mistake of underrating him.

He flashed his badge at a duty nurse and followed her pointed finger down the hall toward a room in the rear of the emergency wing. He stopped outside, pausing to slip on his work face, and prepared to meet the hysterical man who'd just lost his wife.

Brann knocked on the door and opened it to see a quiet, serene man lying on a gurney.

"Excuse me. I'm looking for Mr. Graham?"

"I'm Lew Graham."

This guy didn't look hurt at all, but Brann shrugged his shoulders and walked inside. "I'm John Brann, a detective with the Shreveport Police Department. I've been sent here to take your statement about what happened this morning."

Brann was poised, holding a clipboard to take down Graham's statement. He was experienced in talking to victims, and he was ready to pull back immediately if any of his questions brought on a rush of tears. He was grateful that Graham was looking him in the eye. He hated people who wouldn't maintain eye contact.

"You look like you're feeling okay. Uh—they said you'd been hurt?" Brann asked.

Graham showed him the stab wound, pointed out a raised, red spot on his forehead, and held out his hand, showing the bandage across the knife wound on his palm.

Brann had expected a bit more trauma from someone who had been attacked. He'd seen more serious injuries from someone who'd fallen off a bicycle.

"Well, where do you want me to start?" Graham asked.

"How about the beginning?"

"Okay. Uh, this is not the first time we've had someone break into our house. About this time last year, my son Eric came home early from baseball practice and found the back door open and—"

John Brann interrupted. "Wait a minute—this is something that happened a *year* ago?"

"Yeah, well, that's the beginning."

"Tell me what happened last night, today, this morning."

"All right. I was asleep—I don't really know what time it was, but I had gotten up earlier, between two and three, 'cause my wife woke me up and said she heard something. I got up, checked the house, the doors and stuff, didn't find anything, and came back to bed. Sometime later, after I'd fallen back into a deep sleep, the first thing I remember is the bed lurching, like something hit it. I think I heard a scream . . ."

2

LIEUTENANT Donnie Nichols was pissed. Pissed at himself for just now finding out about the biggest murder case of the year, and pissed at the perpetrator for committing the crime during the night shift.

It was easy to tell when Nichols was upset. He stood well over six feet tall and had slicked-back auburn hair, a loud voice, and a complexion that always gave away exactly how he felt. Right now, his tomato-red face told the world of his excitement over the Kirkwood Drive homicide.

Donnie Nichols stormed down the hall and burst into the office of the Chief of Detectives, Sam Burns. Burns was on the telephone talking to the detectives at the Graham house.

" . . . and make sure we get a written consent to search the premises—no one walks because of a technical goof. Yeah, okay, so send Lopez to meet him at the hospital, and see if he'll come to the station." Burns motioned for Donnie Nichols to have a seat. "What about the ID team—are they there yet?"

Nichols made himself look around the room, not wanting to stare at the chief but absolutely dying to know what was being said.

" . . . Sure, we can handle that. I'll call the D.A.'s office and get someone over there. No, that's fine. If he won't come downtown willingly, then go ahead and arrest him. But go easy on this one: no mistakes."

Burns hung up and Nichols leaned forward across the desk from his superior. "What's the deal? Did he do it?"

"Don't know. Coker and Lopez are at the scene, and they're suspicious. Coker said the living room looks like a bunch of kids rifled through it."

"Maybe I'll drive out and see if they need a hand," said Nichols, trying to sound casual. "I just came down from the detective office, and my whole day shift is chomping at the bit."

"Do what you want. Just remember that we've got a nice little backlog of burglaries, armed robberies, the usual, that needs attention too," Burns said.

"Sure, Captain."

Donnie Nichols was a senior detective, in his eighteenth year with the SPD, and he was proud of the fact that he'd personally investigated more than two hundred homicides. He was driven by emotion, prone to leap before he looked, and not known for being particularly shy. His outspoken and aggressive manner rubbed many of the other detectives the wrong way.

There's an unwritten code among police investigators that says the first detective on the scene of the crime remains in charge of the investigation. Since Coker was the night-shift commander and had arrived at the Graham house very early, there was absolutely no reason for Nichols to think about working the case.

But Donnie Nichols didn't believe in unwritten codes: diplomacy was for diplomats. He wouldn't let a little thing like case assignments stand between him and the biggest murder of the year. A doctor's wife murdered in her bedroom with a sledgehammer—what a case!

He stuck his head into the detectives' office and motioned for his crew to follow. Detectives Nichols, Pittman, Shields, Campbell, G.C. Smith, and Al Smith loaded into their unmarked cars and made a straight shot for 2033 South Kirkwood Drive.

• • •

DONNIE Nichols and Dan Coker went way back. Nichols was the commander of the day-shift detectives; Coker had the same job at night. They'd worked off and on together since the early sixties, running down shoplifters and interrogating rapists.

There was a grudging friendship between them, more of a mutual tolerance than anything else. Their relationship was based on an untiring desire to work for law and order, and fueled by a difference of opinion on how best to achieve it.

While he was a hotheaded, tough-guy cop, Donnie Nichols was also the epitome of a family man. He had divorced his first wife in 1968 and immediately filed suit for custody of their three small children. In the sixties, in the deep South, it was almost unheard of for a father to sue for custody, but Nichols was convinced that he would make the better parent and eventually got his way. Together with his second wife, he was raising a total of five children, ranging in age from twelve to twenty.

Lieutenant Coker looked up when Nichols walked through the front door of the Graham house. "I told Frank you guys would be showing up. We've got the house under control, Donnie, but we could use some help organizing interviews in the neighborhood."

Nichols was thinking more about the master bedroom. "What's it look like? Did he do it or not?" he asked.

"Maybe—it looks a little fishy, but it's too early to know much. You planning on making a day of it?"

Nichols walked around the living room while the other day-shift detectives inched into the house.

"ID just left," Coker said, "and I've called the crime lab. They should be here any minute. Frank and I have to go meet Graham and take him downtown for a statement."

"Don't worry about anything out here. We'll poke around a little and let you know what we find."

Rolling his eyes, Coker headed out the door. He stopped and looked back over his shoulder just as Nichols and a couple of day-shift detectives started down the hallway.

• • •

"RIGHT through here, Dr. Graham. If you'll just have a seat over there, I'll run get a tape recorder and we can get started. Can I get you a cup of coffee?" Lopez asked.

"Please."

Coker walked in and sat behind his desk opposite Lew Graham. His mind kept jumping back to the crime scene, trying to remember all the details he could use to help formulate his questions. It bothered him that Graham hadn't shown any evidence of sadness or hysteria from the time he'd first seen him till right now. Coker was looking for a sign, something to tell him if his growing uneasiness was a justified suspicion or just a vague apprehension.

"So you're a doctor at the medical center?" Coker asked.

"I'm a teacher—a Ph.D., not an M.D. I teach biochemistry and do research. I'm also the Assistant Dean for Student Affairs," Graham said.

Coker nodded. "Did your wife work?"

"Not really. She did a little substitute teaching at Forest Hills Elementary School, but only when they called and then only when she felt like it."

"Uh-huh. How long were y'all married?"

"Let's see—David is sixteen, so I guess it must be seventeen years," Graham said.

Lopez came back in with a tape recorder and handed a cup of hot coffee to Graham.

"Coffee's black. Hope that's okay," Lopez said. He sat down next to Graham and set up the recorder, taking his time to make sure everything was just right.

Coker wondered if he could make Graham nervous. "Now, what we do in an investigation like this, Dr. Graham, is to take a look at everybody who was at the scene at the time of the murder, and work backwards from there to eliminate suspects."

"That makes sense."

Lopez took out a card that contained a typed version of the Miranda warning. Coker knew that the familiar *You have the right to remain silent* takes on a different aura when it's first read to someone, and he watched Graham closely as Lopez went through the formality.

Without turning the tape recorder on, Coker began painstakingly going over Graham's recollections of what happened.

" . . . All I know is that I was asleep, then all of a sudden they pulled me from the bed and threw me on the floor. There was some minor scuffling around there, and that's about when I was stabbed. Then they grabbed me . . ."

"Wait—you keep saying 'they'? I thought you didn't know how many of them there were," Coker said.

"Well, I don't, really. I didn't see them—it's more like a feeling, like there were too many hands to be just one person," Graham said.

Coker wasn't happy with what he was hearing. "You didn't see anybody? Not even a glimpse?"

"Nothing. And when I waked up, after being out, there was no one there. I didn't see anybody, and I didn't hear anything."

"Y'all have a dog?" Coker asked.

"Yeah—Candy."

"Do you remember hearing the dog bark?" Coker asked.

"No, but I sleep pretty hard sometimes. She could have been barking and I just never heard it."

"You remember what I told you earlier, Mr. Graham, about how we first have to rule out the people in the house? That's why I'm asking you this: did you and your wife get along? You know, was there ever any trouble over another woman?" Coker asked.

"No. A couple of years ago, we had some problems, but that had to do with our relationship and interactions, and we worked them all out. We even went to a marriage counselor for a while, and this last year's been really good between us."

Lopez spoke up for the first time. "Dr. Graham, do you have any idea what your wife was killed with?"

"No, I have no idea. When I woke up, the light was turned off. I turned it on just for a second, just till I saw her lying there, then turned it off again. That's when I left the room—shut the door behind me so the kids wouldn't see," Graham said.

After conversing with Graham at some length, and enduring several interruptions, Coker reached for the tape recorder.

"Okay, I think we've gone over this enough. Let's see about getting something down on tape."

DONNIE Nichols was mesmerized by the number of bloodstains scattered around the bedroom. No doubt about it, this was a wider distribution of stains than he had ever seen. Nichols was sorry he hadn't arrived before the coroner had taken the body away. The ID officers had already gathered most of the physical evidence, including the sledgehammer, clock, knife, and even the sheets and bedspread. Nichols had to be satisfied with only a bloody mattress while he worked around the crew from the crime lab.

The Northwest Louisiana Criminalistics Laboratory was an independent entity which performed technical forensic work for law enforcement agencies in a 26-parish area of northern Louisiana. Under the direction of Ray Herd, the Crime Lab could marshal expertise that the Shreveport Police Department simply didn't have. Herd and his top serologist Pat Wojtkiewicz had made their trip to Kirkwood Drive in 30 minutes, beginning their detailed look at the physical evidence inside the master bedroom. They made a videotape record of the scene, then started documenting the distances between where Kathy Graham's head had lain and the various small and large drops of blood from around the room.

Two of Nichols's detectives returned to the house after interviewing the Graham children at the Godwins'.

"Lieutenant, we talked to the kids, and apparently all this stuff belongs to the Grahams."

Nichols wondered if the kids knew anything. "What do you mean?"

"We asked the oldest boy, David, about the evidence you were wondering about. Okay, the blue flashlight and the piggy bank that we found out by the fence, he said both those items are theirs and are normally kept in the father's desk in the living room. The hunting knife, which he said also sounds like his father's, is stored in a tool box in the garage. He also said they do own a sledgehammer— it's normally on the workbench in the garage. The crowbar is kept on the pegboard in the garage."

Nichols nodded. "So everything we found is from the premises?"

"Yes, sir."

Nichols checked to make sure the crime lab guys were set, and decided to leave the scene in time to attend the autopsy. As he walked to his car, one of the day-shift detectives was escorting a man to the house and stopped Nichols in the driveway.

"Lieutenant Nichols, I think you know Bennett Kitchings. He used to be a deputy at the Sheriff's Department, and he's a friend of the Graham family. Bennett, tell him what you were telling me about the woman you saw with Mr. Graham."

Nichols turned his attention to Bennett Kitchings.

"It was last summer, I think. I was on patrol and stopped for lunch at the Ramada Inn out near the airport. As we were parking, I saw Lew and this woman, looking like they were together, checking into the motel. He was by his car, writing down his license number, and she was sitting in the passenger's seat. He went into the office, then came out and drove around the building. It bothered me, you know, because Lew and Kathy were such good friends of ours, to think he might be fooling around. Anyway, he's a big shot at the med school and all, so I thought maybe they were at the motel for a meeting or something. After we ate, I drove around the building, and sure enough, his car was parked in front of one of the rooms on the side," Kitchings said.

Nichols was happy to turn up some new information. "Do you know who the woman was?"

"No, but I'd recognize her if I saw her again. She was dark-haired, kind of slim, attractive, with a tanned complexion."

Nichols thanked him and spent another hour at the house,

going over the bedroom, looking through the kids' rooms, even checking out the attic. He decided to go back downtown, curious to know how Coker's and Lopez's interrogation was going.

Back at the station, Nichols paced the floor of the detectives' office, and he engaged several other day-shift investigators in an animated conversation about the case. They were so loud that Coker could hear Nichols's booming voice inside his office. Several times during the interview with Graham, Coker had to step outside and tell Nichols and his bunch to hold it down.

IT was 11:00 a.m. before Graham's official rendering of the night's events was given to the tape recorder. He had little idea that the investigation had already centered on him. Though Coker and Lopez were harboring suspicions of their own, Nichols and the day shift, making a play to take over the investigation, were already working under the assumption that Dr. Lewis Graham was the killer.

Through the hours he spent at the police station, Graham remained calm and cooperative, even in the face of repetitious questions and never-ending interruptions. By the time the statement was taken, he was bone tired.

In between the police interviews, several colleagues from the med center dropped by to check on him. Dr. Robert Smith, a friend who worked with him in biochemistry, came in and took a prescription for pain medication to the drugstore. Smith brought the pills back to the police station and offered to hang around and give Graham a ride home. Dr. Guilford Rudolph, the head of biochemistry, stopped in and expressed his condolences. Dr. Jim Smith, a friend who'd met Lew and Kathy during the early seventies when they lived in Indiana, spent a few moments visiting with Graham.

Ike Muslow, the dean of the medical school, was disturbed by Graham's subdued demeanor, and he talked with the other faculty members about their impressions of his state of mind. Muslow asked Jim Smith to contact the head of the school's psychiatry department and arrange for him to visit with Graham about his quiet reaction to his wife's violent death.

AT 11:40 a.m. Dr. Robert Braswell, the Caddo Parish coroner, began his clinical investigation into the death of Kathy Graham. Braswell had performed more than one thousand autopsies in the subterranean offices of the parish courthouse. He maintained a full-time medical practice and handled his duties as coroner at nights and on the weekends.

Donnie Nichols left the detective offices to witness the autopsy. In the presence of Nichols, assistant coroner Terry Franklin and Pat Wojtkiewicz from the crime lab, Braswell began.

"This is a well-nourished, well-developed white female," Braswell dictated. "She weighs approximately 135 pounds and is 167 centimeters in length. She is dressed in a red nightgown, wearing a sanitary napkin, and has blood spatters and markings on her face, neck, and upper chest area."

For the next hour, Kathy Graham's lifeless body was cut, probed, inspected, and analyzed. Braswell's surgical gloves snapped sharply when he removed them. The results were not surprising.

"Cause of death is massive trauma to the head, from a series of fractures associated with the head wounds. It's likely that any one of the fractures would have ultimately brought death, most certainly the major wound to the forehead. There is no evidence of any significant amounts of alcohol or drugs in the bloodstream, but there are some additional conclusions of note. Blood was found in the esophagus, stomach, and lungs, and in the tubes of the chest cavity. Since the involuntary reflex of breathing ends with death, it's apparent that she lived for several minutes after being struck."

3

DONNIE Nichols took the verbal report from the parish coroner, along with a few crime scene photographs he'd hurriedly had developed, and drove across the river to Bossier City. There was no love lost between the Shreveport detectives—especially Nichols—and Dr. Braswell, the Caddo Parish coroner. Whenever there was a big murder case, Nichols and his associates liked to get a second opinion from the Bossier Parish coroner, George McCormick.

A very broad five-foot-two, McCormick was almost as wide as he was tall, with a handlebar moustache and goatee reminiscent of Prince Albert on the tobacco cans. Though he had an ego as big as his waistline, it took nothing away from his impressive credentials as a forensic pathologist.

As a youngster, McCormick had been a voracious reader and mystery buff. While attending medical school in Memphis, he became friendly with a professor who also served as the Tennessee State Medical Examiner. McCormick was on hand for the autopsy performed on Dr. Martin Luther King, Jr. He was hooked.

Nichols liked McCormick personally, admired his forthright, supremely confident manner, and respected his knowledge of the intricacies of the human body. Though there was no question about what had caused Kathy Graham's death,

Nichols wanted to get more details as to the number of hammer blows and the order in which they came—maybe even whether the killer was right-handed or left-handed.

Shortly after lunch, Nichols and McCormick met in the conference room at the Bossier Medical Center, where Nichols laid out a dozen or so photographs just developed.

"These are all from the killing we got this morning out in Southern Hills. I don't know if you've even heard about it," Nichols said.

McCormick picked up the first photo, a close-up of Kathy Graham's head, and let out a grunt. "Good God, talk about overkill," he said.

Nichols nodded. "Exactly. Ever seen a killing done with a sledgehammer before? We found the hammer on the floor next to the bed, along with a hunting knife and some other stuff. The husband says he was asleep in bed, got jerked off onto the floor, and was stabbed. His only wound is a small puncture up under his arm near his left tit. The doctor in the emergency room only put in one stitch. He says that after he was stabbed, he was picked up, thrown across the room, where he hit the wall and was knocked out—"

"And when he came to, he found his wife hammered to death?" McCormick interrupted.

Nichols smiled. "That's about the size of it. What do you think?"

McCormick's eyes wandered over the crime scene photos. "Looks like someone was mad as hell. Anybody else at home when it happened?"

"Three kids asleep across the hall. We talked to them very briefly, and they said they didn't hear a thing."

"Nobody heard him hit the wall?" McCormick asked.

"That's what I was thinking. I'm sure this guy's feeding us a line of bullshit, but it might be hard to prove. If you ask me, I'd just as soon arrest him now, but we need some evidence that'll stick. I want you to perform a second autopsy, and see what you can find."

"No problem. Just get the D.A. to clear it with his coroner."

"Sure. Oh, by the way—the guy's some kind of doctor, a dean at the medical school."

"Really? I know a lot of those guys. What's his name?" McCormick asked.

"Lewis Graham. I think he goes by Lew."

"Holy shit—Lew Graham, the one that teaches biochemistry? I don't really know him, but I know who he is. How much of this has the D.A. seen?"

Nichols stood up to leave. "I don't know. I'm going over there in the morning. Right now I've got to get back out to the crime scene."

"Eventually I'll need to see the house."

"No problem," Nichols said.

BENNETT Kitchings was standing in the Godwins' front yard when Graham got back from the police station. Kitchings had told his wife that he suspected Lew had killed Kathy. Alice Kitchings didn't want to hear that; she didn't want to believe that a friend—the father of a close friend of their son's—could be a murderer.

Bennett Kitchings was a big man, with a wide, square face and a slow Southern drawl. He and his wife had spent a lot of time with Lew and Kathy, sharing jokes in the stands while David Graham and Stephen Kitchings excelled in high school sports. Kitchings knew a lot about the Graham family, about their ups and downs during their years in Shreveport.

His suspicions had been aroused during a brief visit with Graham early that morning. Knowing that Kitchings was not only a friend, but also a former deputy sheriff, Carolyn Godwin had called him to Kirkwood Drive shortly after the Graham kids arrived at her house and before the police got there.

When Kitchings saw Graham in his living room, the widower's calm attitude made alarms go off in his head. He asked the uniformed officers if he could peek into the master bedroom. The image of bludgeoned and bloody Kathy Graham was something he would never forget. By the time

Detective Nichols and the day shift arrived, Kitchings was certain that Graham was guilty.

He decided that he could keep a close eye on Graham, paying attention to how he talked to his children and to the people gathered to offer condolences. He hoped that, since Graham didn't think of him as a law enforcement professional, he could learn something that would aid in the investigation.

By this time the Godwin home was filled to overflowing. It had become the temporary headquarters of the bereaved family, since at their house the police were still very much in the middle of their survey. Dozens of friends, relatives, acquaintances, and well-wishers were milling around the Godwins'; an atmosphere of tension and sadness filled the rooms. Already, before noon on March 31, a number of people believed Lew Graham was the killer.

Lew Graham's younger sister, Elizabeth Ancelet, from the south Louisiana city of Lafayette, had driven in while he was at the police station. Kathy Graham's mother and father, who were divorced, had each been contacted and were arriving later in the day.

David, Eric, and Katie Graham rushed to greet their father when the car came to a stop in front of the Godwin house. Graham's wound made him grimace when he embraced his children. They hugged one another in the front yard, while police officers watched from across the street. "It's just us now," Graham told his three children.

Kitchings watched the reunion with a lump in his throat. He stood by silently as Graham and his kids passed through a throng of greeters and stepped inside the house. Part of Kitchings felt sorry for Lew Graham—the widower, the single parent who would have to raise those children by himself. The other part of him seethed with anger, anger over his belief that this quiet, unassuming man might have picked up a sledgehammer less than 24 hours before.

Kitchings followed the father and children through the Godwin home, anxious to see his reaction as he was confronted with wall-to-wall people. A lot of these people would be strangers to Graham. He watched the crowd press forward, patting Graham on the back, expressing condolences, making so much polite chatter it was hard for Graham to acknowledge everyone. By that time, Carolyn Godwin had taken him by the hand and was leading him toward the back of the house, to a private study where he could be alone with his children.

Kitchings stood behind her when she pulled him aside and whispered, "Lew, do the police know anything? Have they said anything about who did it?"

"Not really, Carolyn. They're just beginning their investigation. I told them everything I could think of, everything I thought might help."

"Does that mean the murderers might still be around here?"

Kitchings could see she was really afraid. "I'm sure they're long gone by now," Kitchings said.

"Lew, is there anything I can get you?" Godwin asked.

"I'm all right, I guess. It seemed like I was at the police station a long time."

"Here. I'll fix you a sandwich. You and the children have a lot to talk about."

David, Eric, and Katie were waiting, watching their father from the floor of the study.

"Someone told you what happened?" Graham asked.

David gestured toward Kitchings, his eyes swelling up with tears. "Mr. Kitchings. He said Mom was beaten to death."

Graham glanced at Kitchings. "They're doing everything they can to find who did this. Why it happened, we don't know. It looks like robbery or something—they took some stuff," Graham said.

"One of the detectives came over and talked to us. I told him we were all asleep and didn't hear anything. He asked me about a blue flashlight—sounded like the one in the garage. He also wanted to know about a can— you know, the one you used to keep all that change in?" David said.

"That's fine," Graham said.

Kitchings kept waiting for some sign of emotion from Graham.

"Why, Dad—why would anyone want to kill Mom?" David asked.

"I don't know, son. I just don't know."

RUSSELL Ancelet, a state trooper from south Louisiana, had been married to Lew Graham's younger sister, Elizabeth, for about fifteen years, though they were now separated. After receiving an early morning call from Carolyn Godwin, he had arrived in Shreveport about the time his brother-in-law was giving his recorded statement at the police station.

When Ancelet pulled to a stop on South Kirkwood Drive, he spotted an old college buddy, Shreveport police officer Terry Shields, standing in the Grahams' front yard. Ancelet walked over to say hello and, after making small talk for a few minutes, told his acquaintance that he was Graham's brother-in-law. Ancelet asked if the police had any leads on the killer. Shields gave him a funny look and said, "We're taking a long, hard look at Lewis Graham."

Shields introduced Ancelet to Donnie Nichols, who invited him on a quick tour of the crime scene. Nichols told Ancelet that he had no doubt Lew Graham was the murderer and that it was only a matter of time before he was arrested.

Several hours passed before Ancelet had a private moment with Graham, but later that afternoon he told him what Nichols had said.

"Lew, everything could have happened exactly like you said it did, and they can still drag you into a homicide investigation. You know a good lawyer? I think it'd be a good idea if you talked to somebody," Ancelet said.

"That's ridiculous—absurd. That's just one detective, not the whole police force. Somebody broke into *my* house, attacked me, and killed *my* wife. I'm going to do everything I can to help the police find out who did it. I haven't done anything, and I don't need a lawyer," Graham said.

KATHY Graham's mother and stepfather, Ray and Bobbi Parish, were visiting relatives in Mississippi when they heard the news of her murder. Arriving in Shreveport late in the afternoon, a distraught Bobbi Parish joined Graham in the Godwins' study.

After Bobbi Parish divorced Kathy's natural father, she had lived with Lew and Kathy in Indianapolis for several years. There she met and married her current husband. Like her daughter, Parish wasn't one to hold back her feelings. "Tell me it didn't happen—tell me it's all a mistake and my Kathy's not dead!" she said.

Her son-in-law put his hand on her shoulder. "It's a terrible, terrible tragedy, but we all have to face facts and pull together."

Bobbi Parish cried against his shoulder. "How? Why?"

"The police don't know who did it—I spent all morning at the police station telling them everything I could. Someone broke into the house last night, stabbed me, and knocked me out, and when I woke up, she was dead. I'm sorry—I wasn't able to protect her," Graham said.

"Did you get a good look at them?" Bobbi asked.

"No. It was so dark, and I was asleep. I told the detectives that I thought it was more than one guy. I guess they were going to rob us—I haven't had a chance to look around and see what's missing. Maybe they knew I worked at the med center, and they were drug addicts. They might have thought I had some dope in the house. That's all I can figure," Graham said.

Parish's tears flowed unchecked. "She was so kind and loving. You know that, don't you, Lew?"

"Yes, she was. It's a tragedy, a real shock."

Mike and Marsha Stringer, friends and neighbors of the Grahams, lived down the street on South Kirkwood Drive. They loaned their house to the Grahams so they would have a comfortable, private place to stay nearby, in case the police needed to talk to them.

David, Eric, and Katie were frightened that the family might be attacked again, and their father agreed to share the Stringers' king-sized bed with all three of them. The Parishes spent the night in one of the other bedrooms, while Elizabeth Ancelet bedded down at the Godwins'.

Tuesday, April 1

"I'VE been thinking. You know, the police didn't ask me a single question about what was missing from the house," Graham said to his brother-in-law. "I don't know what they might have taken. I remember there were some liquor bottles scattered on the floor in the living room. I guess they got drunk and just lost control of their senses."

"Lew, the cops were telling me that they couldn't find any evidence that the house had been broken into. There was a crowbar out in the garage, but apparently the door wasn't smashed up like it would have been if someone had pried it open. So how did they get inside?" Ancelet asked.

David Graham walked into the kitchen. Of the children, he had seemed the most visibly disturbed by Kathy's murder, making little conversation and looking a bit dazed.

"Is it okay if I join y'all?" David asked.

"Of course. We were just talking about how they could have gotten into the house. The police told Russell that there were no signs of a break-in," Lew Graham said.

"What about the back door? Eric picks the lock all the time," David said.

"That's right! Eric comes through whenever he's locked out."

"Wait a minute, Lew. If that's true, then we ought to tell the detectives about it," said Ancelet.

"Let's go over there and see. I need to compile a list of what's missing anyway," Graham said.

Graham, Ancelet, and Cliff Hall, Kathy's uncle from Mississippi, walked across the street and up to the front door of the house. David and the others stayed at the Stringers'. No one else was very anxious to go inside the house.

Graham checked with the uniformed officer at the front door, who cleared them to come inside. The house was a wreck. The investigators had strewn papers around the living room, black fingerprint powder was still clinging to several pieces of furniture, and the living room carpet showed the trampled signs of more than a few police feet.

There weren't any other people inside, and Graham took his relatives into the garage. Checking the back door from the outside, they found several things of immediate interest.

For one thing, the hinges were on the *outside* of the door, and one of the locks had been improperly installed. There was a gap of at least half an inch between the edge of the door and the jamb, giving a clear, inviting view of the deadbolt. Ancelet took out his pocketknife, sent Graham inside, and told him to lock all three locks on the door. Using only his knife, Ancelet had the door open in less than thirty seconds.

"This is very important, Lew. I think you ought to call the detectives back out."

FRANK Lopez had given Graham his business card the day before, and he pulled it out now to find the number. Coincidentally, Donnie Nichols was sitting at the front desk in the detective offices and answered the call. He listened in open-mouthed excitement as Lew Graham invited him out to 2033 South Kirkwood.

Nichols grabbed John Brann and ran to his car. "I know that little son of a bitch killed his wife. I just *know* it!"

"He may have done it, Donnie, but he's too cool. He'll never tell you in a million years."

"You're wrong, buddy. Here's what we'll do. We'll go out there and listen to whatever it is he wants to tell us. We'll be very polite, and when he's through, I'll ask him to go back to that bedroom with me. He probably won't go, but I'll ask him anyway. You make sure it's just him and me back there, and I guarantee he won't leave that room till he tells it like it is!"

Nichols and Brann parked in the driveway and came in through the front door. Graham and Ancelet were still in the garage.

"Dr. Graham, I'm Lieutenant Donnie Nichols, and I'm in charge of the investigation into your wife's homicide. Now, what was it y'all wanted to show us?" Nichols asked.

Graham and Ancelet took the detectives over to the back door and showed them the faulty locks. Brann and Nichols were attentive and made notes about the deadbolt and the other locks.

"Listen—Detective Nichols, did you say? When do you think you might be through with the house? I'd like to see about getting all this cleaned up. My children and I need a place to live," Graham asked.

Nichols was surprised that anyone would want to bring children into that house, but he answered, "We're just about through. How about tomorrow?"

"That's fine. I'm going to have the bedroom painted and recarpeted."

Nichols turned his head and winked at Brann. "Dr. Graham, we appreciate you calling this door and these locks to our attention, and I can promise you we'll look into this right away. As you might expect, it will be several more days before we can get a laboratory analysis of all the physical evidence."

He walked around the living room, glancing at the remnants of the investigation. "At this point, we're still talking to the neighbors, people in the area, trying to find out if anyone saw or heard anything. Now, we know you've been through a terrible shock, but could you spare me a few minutes? I'd like to go back over what you can recall from last night, and see if we can help you remember more detail."

"If you think it would help, of course."

"I do, I really do. Before we can ask you anything, as a kind of formality, the law says we must advise you of your rights."

"I understand."

Brann pulled a card out of his sport coat pocket and walked over to Graham. Brann held the card in front of him, but he didn't have to read. "You are under arrest for your part in the crime of first-degree murder. I hereby notify you that you have the right to remain silent, and you are not required to make any statement unless you decide to do so voluntarily. Anything you say can be used against you in a court of law. You have the right to consult with an attorney, and to have him present with you. If you cannot afford an attorney, one will be appointed to represent you. While you are not required to make any statement, you may waive those rights just explained to you and you are given the privilege of saying anything you want to about this case. Now, waiving those rights, do you wish to make a statement?"

Nichols had kept his eye on Graham the entire time, looking for some sign of trepidation. He never saw any.

"Yes, of course, I'll tell you anything I can," Graham said.

Nichols stepped in. "Of course, Dr. Graham, you aren't really under arrest; we'll just scratch those words off. If you wouldn't mind, could you just sign and date this card?"

Nichols watched as Graham signed the card with the relaxed expression of someone writing a check.

Nichols led the way, and Graham, Brann, and Ancelet followed down the short hallway to the master bedroom. The grisly scene belonged in darkness. In the full light of day, with the bed linens and body taken away, there was a strange, sickly aura left behind.

Nichols and Brann had seen plenty of homicides in their day. It was nothing for them to spend several hours going over details of murder in a still-bloody room. But Ancelet, though he was a state trooper, worked in white-collar crime and had never seen a homicide scene before. He was visibly shaken by the sight of the naked mattresses, still bloodstained with a rough outline of where the corpse had lain.

Nichols looked at the good-sized hole cut out of the wall near the closet. He noticed two pieces of carpet gone near the left side of the bed. He let a moment pass, expecting that the quiet might unnerve Lew Graham, here in the room where his wife had been murdered.

"Dr. Graham, exactly what is it you do at the medical school?"

"I'm a scientist, a Ph.D. I do basic research, I do a little teaching, and I'm the Assistant Dean for Student Affairs," Graham said.

"Sounds like an important position. About what time did you and your wife go to bed Sunday night?"

"Oh, I don't know for sure. The usual time, I guess, between ten-thirty and eleven."

"Were the kids still up?" Nichols asked.

"Maybe the oldest—David."

"All right, now tell me everything you can remember, starting when your wife woke you up and said she heard something."

"Well, I'm not sure of the exact time, but sometime between two and three . . ."

BRANN nodded to Ancelet, and they backed out of the bedroom. Nichols wanted to isolate Graham, and Ancelet seemed to understand the strategy.

"You're putting him one-on-one with your lieutenant. I know what Nichols thinks—what about you? You believe my brother-in-law's a killer?" Ancelet asked.

Brann made sure he kept his voice down, and stood near the fireplace in the living room.

"It doesn't add up. The scene, it just doesn't match up to his story," Brann said. He offered a cigarette to Ancelet and took a deep drag off his own.

"I hear you. I know the story sounds strange, but not half as strange as you telling me Lew Graham is a murderer. Why? Why would he do it?" Ancelet asked.

"I was kind of hoping you could help with that. What about marriage problems? Did he and his wife fight very much? Did they argue?"

"Who doesn't argue with his wife? Hell, I'm separated from his sister right now—we're getting a divorce. No, I think they had some trouble a couple of years ago, went to a marriage counselor and everything. But as far as I know, everything was okay. Even if it wasn't, he sure didn't have to kill her to get out of the marriage," Ancelet said.

"What about the rest of the family? His parents still alive?"

"Both died in the last few years. And that's another thing, see, there's an inheritance. I know Lew and Kathy couldn't have had any money trouble. I'm sure he's getting the same amount as Elizabeth. They got some farmland down south, oil and gas royalties. We're talking, like, ten thousand dollars a month . . ." Ancelet paused, reflecting. "I'm telling you, you fellows don't know this guy. There's no way he could get mad enough to pick up a hammer," he said. "Want to hear a Lew Graham story?"

"Sure."

"One time Lew and Kathy were visiting our house in Lafayette. Our house backs up to the river, and there's this big oak tree back there, probably a hundred years old, that stands at least thirty feet tall, and several of the branches reach way out over the water. Lew and Kathy's youngest boy, Eric—he must have been about six or seven when this happened—climbed way the hell up this tree, out onto a limb over the water. Elizabeth saw him up there and screamed. Kathy came outside, looked up, and almost had a stroke. Ole Lew strolls up, totally calm, and in the softest voice you've ever heard just says, 'Okay, Eric, come on down, son.' And the boy climbed down. That's what I mean. This man is cool. He'd never get mad enough to kill, never in a million years!"

Brann checked his watch. "You wait here. I'm going to see how things are going in the bedroom."

BRANN tiptoed down the hall and stopped just out of sight in the hallway next to the bedroom door, where he could clearly hear the conversation going on inside.

" . . . so *you* normally sleep on this side of the bed, the side where she was lying? Well, how did she get over there—did you turn her over, or push her?" Nichols asked.

"No. When these intruders came in, I was on my side, and they pulled me off onto the floor, over here somewhere, I guess. Maybe she moved over here to help me, or they moved her. I don't know."

Nichols was getting frustrated, mostly because he hadn't been able to get a reaction out of Graham, whom he had hoped to reduce to a sniveling, emotional wreck. He couldn't ever remember interviewing anyone who had displayed this much control at the scene of a homicide.

"Okay, Dr. Graham, so you were over here on the floor, around where this carpet was cut up, and this is where you think you were stabbed?"

"Well, it was dark in the room, but that seems about right, if someone were to drag you out of bed . . ."

"After you were thrown onto the floor, then you're saying you were picked up and physically thrown across the room? Through the air?" Nichols asked.

"Yeah, kind of. It's hard to be precise. I don't remember actually hitting the wall, but I must have. Because when I woke up, my head was right up against the baseboard, and there was a bump on my head."

Nichols glanced at Graham's forehead, looking for a bruise or a bump. "And that's all you remember. That's all that happened up until you got up and found your wife dead?"

"Best I can remember."

"Did you wash up? You know, wash your hands, take a shower, anything before the patrolmen got here?"

"Nope. I got up, turned on the light, saw my wife, turned the light back off, and left the bedroom."

Nichols decided it was time to turn the screws. "Okay, I'm going to ask you some pointed questions now: if you were in bed, at the time your wife was first hit with the hammer, why is it that these burglars or whatever they were—why would they hit her a bunch of times, and not hit you, the man of the house, even once?"

"I don't know. Maybe there were several of them, and like some of them came over on this side after her, and some others came over here with the knife after me. Maybe she waked up when they came in—maybe she saw them coming."

"But you said yourself that it was dark! If it's so dark you can't see, how is it light enough that she can? See what I'm saying? You can't have it both ways."

"I don't know. You've got to understand, I was being attacked, after coming out of a deep sleep—"

Nichols interrupted. Large veins stood out on his neck. His tone was argumentative. "Well, how do you explain the fact that there was a pretty good spot of blood over here where you said you were stabbed, but no blood over here, where you said you were knocked out? If you lay over here unconscious, on your stomach, you should have bled on that carpet."

"I'm not sure. Maybe—"

Nichols didn't let him answer. "Would you mind showing me the exact position you were lying in when you first came to?"

Graham shrugged his shoulders and lay down on his stomach, on the floor, about a foot past the end of the bed. "This is how I was lying, with my head right up against the baseboard."

Nichols towered over Graham, looking down at him. "Why wasn't there any blood over here, then?"

"I don't know. Maybe it just didn't bleed that much."

"We've got some very serious problems here—a whole lot of things that don't add up to what you've been saying." Nichols moved back to the other side of the bed and turned his back to Graham. "If your wife were startled by the presence of a burglar, if she saw enough to know to scream, how is it that *you* can't remember a damn thing? Not a shadow, not a silhouette, nothing!"

"You're trying to make it sound like—"

"Look around here. Look at all the blood in this room! There's blood on three walls and the ceiling. You know, we have experts who can look at these drops of blood and tell us a hell of a lot about the way things happened. We think your wife started out on the other side of the bed. She was there when she was hit the first few times. Then somebody rolled her over to the other side of the bed and cold-cocked her that last time. They beat the living hell out of her and never *once* hit you. Come on, Dr. Graham, you're an intelligent man—it just doesn't make any sense!"

"So what are you trying to say?" Graham asked. His face was flushed.

"I'm saying this: you've got blood spatters all over your shirt. Now, we could possibly explain the ones on the back, if you were over here, because there were some spots on the wall like those. But can you explain to me how you got spatters on the *front* of your shirt when, according to you, you were over here lying on the floor?"

Nichols thought Graham was surprised by the tone of the questions. "I, uh, maybe if—"

Nichols put on his most sympathetic face. "You know, Doctor, in the eyes of the law, there's a difference between first-degree murder, and, say, manslaughter. You know what I'm talking about? Legally, manslaughter is when somebody does something that makes you so mad, you lose all control of your senses. Like, for instance, in the heat of an argument, you hit somebody—something that ordinarily you wouldn't do. I think we're looking at a case of manslaughter here, not murder."

"B-but I was s-s-stabbed."

"Give me a break. You know as well as I do, that little wound of yours—well, it's just the sort of cut in just the right place to do the least amount of damage. We believe that stab wound was self-inflicted," Nichols said.

"Self-inflicted!"

Nichols was watching Graham's eyes, and for an instant he thought he saw tears forming at the edges. Then, as quickly as they came, they went away.

"I didn't do it," Graham said.

"You didn't do it?"

Graham's voice was low. "That's what I said, Detective. I didn't kill my wife."

"Then who did?"

Graham shook his head. "I don't know. Just like I don't know why my wife was killed. Or why you don't believe me. I don't have all the answers. I wish I did."

Nichols walked out of the room. Brann was waiting for him in the hall, and Nichols gave him a thumbs-up signal as he walked by.

The detectives went to the living room, shook hands with Ancelet, and said their goodbyes. Graham shuffled out of the back bedroom, obviously pondering the accusations that had been made to him. He followed the detectives down the hall.

"Is that it? Is that all you want to ask me?"

Brann and Nichols started for the front door, then Brann turned back to Graham. "Excuse me, Doctor, there *is* one more thing I wanted to say to you. We know all about your girlfriend."

Nichols saw the color fade from Graham's face.

"That—that doesn't have anything to do with this, nothing at all. Besides, it only lasted a few weeks, and it's been over a long time," Graham said.

Nichols nodded his head. "Uh-huh, yeah, well, whatever you say."

Nichols and Brann walked out the front door to their unmarked car. Nichols felt like he was walking on air.

4

SINCE Coker was on the graveyard shift, he normally didn't report to work until well after dark. But today he came in early, curious to see what Nichols and the day-shift boys had done on his murder case.

Nichols was keyed up and breathless when Coker found him. "Donnie, they just told me you've been out there talking to Graham. They said you were called out to the house. What's the deal?" Coker asked.

Nichols smiled. "He invited us out to show us the locks on the back door, but I got him back in the bedroom."

"And you told him all about our suspicions, didn't you? You told him everything?"

"We went over his story from top to bottom. It doesn't hold water," Nichols said.

"So now you're just taking over my case?"

"What difference does it make who gets credit for the arrest? The important thing is to not let this guy get away."

"It makes a hell of a difference if you go busting in there and tip him off! You go out there, stick your nose where it doesn't belong, and tell the guy everything we're thinking about him. All you're doing is giving him a chance to make up a better story!" Coker said.

Nichols waved Coker's comments away. "You and I have

different ways of getting to the truth, but it doesn't matter, as long as the truth is what comes out."

"You think *you're* going to get a confession out of Dr. Lewis Graham?" Coker asked.

Nichols nodded. "I sure do."

"Never in a million years. For one thing, Donnie, he's smarter than you. He can stand one-on-one with you and win every time," Coker said.

Nichols's face turned red. "Yeah, well, we'll see."

"What if you're wrong—what if he didn't do it? Where's the evidence?" Coker asked.

"Who else could have done it? You don't believe that bullshit story about a break-in?" Nichols asked.

Coker got right in Nichols's face. "I tell you what I believe. I believe you're jumping the gun and you're fixing to screw up this case! This isn't the first time you've barreled in and messed things up. Jesus Christ, Donnie, it's only been twenty-four hours since the homicide happened. We don't have to set any speed records bringing him in. Lewis Graham is not just some bum off the street. This guy has a brain, he's somebody, he's got money, influence, and you can't run off half-cocked and arrest him," Coker said.

"I don't care if he's the mayor! He killed his wife, and I'm not going to let him walk."

Nichols stormed out of the office, slamming as many doors as he could behind him.

Coker went to his desk and called the Caddo Parish District Attorney's office and spoke to Woody Nesbitt, the head of the Criminal Division.

"Here's the bottom line, Woody. This is a big case—it's going to get a lot of publicity. And there are a bunch of people down here who'll be trying to cut a fat hog in the ass. The most important thing right now is to go slow. But somebody's got to tell Donnie Nichols that. I can't do it— he won't listen to me. He's a lieutenant, I'm a lieutenant, and I've got no authority over him. It's got to come from higher up, because right now all he sees is his name on the front page of the paper," Coker said.

The prosecutor promised to place a call to Nichols and to Captain Burns in an effort to put the brakes on Nichols's arrest plans.

THE brothers-in-law didn't talk about the meeting with the detectives. Ancelet was embarrassed for Graham, and shocked to hear that he had been having an affair.

Ancelet offered to take care of organizing the clean-up of the house, and since the detectives had cleared the way, he made arrangements for work to begin the next morning. He contacted a local carpet company about tearing out the old carpet and installing new shag in the master bedroom, and hired a commercial cleaning firm to rid the room of all the bloodstains. Ancelet would personally make sure the stains were removed.

The Grahams were soon to be moving to a new home anyway. Lew and Kathy had found a large lot in a new, restricted subdivision not far from Kirkwood Drive. Construction was about two-thirds complete on a modern, 2700-square-foot brick home that would give each child a separate bedroom. The new home was full of gadgets—new appliances, a whirlpool, even a fancy security system complete with a master bedroom panic button. Graham's inheritance was sufficient to pay for the house in cash upon completion.

Graham gathered his children around him. "I'm having the house cleaned up, and we're going to move back in in a day or two. I called the builder and asked him to see if he could get us in our new house faster. I know you might feel a little nervous about going back in there. But there's no reason to be afraid of the house, and it's important that we get on with our lives as soon as possible. Uncle Cliff is going to rig up the back door so no one can come in. I promise you, we'll all be perfectly safe."

Several relatives and acquaintances were more than a little surprised to hear that the Grahams were moving back into 2033 South Kirkwood. Those same people had been similarly puzzled by the children's reaction—or rather, lack of reaction—after their mother's murder. David, Eric, and

Katie had apparently inherited their father's controlled personality, and each had displayed little of the sadness they must have felt over Kathy's death.

Wednesday, April 2

BRANN listened patiently, taking an occasional note as the woman rambled on about her "close" friendship with Lew and Kathy Graham. Like many of the other people he'd seen, she seemed more interested in getting information than giving it.

Only one part of their conversation even warranted a mention in Brann's written report, and that had to do with Lew and Kathy's marital relationship. According to what this friend told Brann, Kathy occasionally used to nag her husband, usually over something trivial, sometimes even in public. When she started complaining, Lew would usually sit quietly and take it, staring back at her without saying a word.

Brann's attention perked up as the conversation got more interesting.

"I talked to her the night before she was killed. It was Sunday night, about eight-thirty."

"What was Mrs. Graham's mood? Did she seem worried about anything?" Brann asked.

"No. She said she was tired, and she was depressed because they had been talking about having to put their children in private school. That really bothered Kathy because she did a little teaching and she was always a big supporter of public education. She also said that something was bothering her about Lew, but that she'd tell me about it later."

Several interviews had turned up reports of vague, ominous remarks Kathy had made during her last few days. Bobbi Parish, Kathy's mother, told the detectives that on the telephone the weekend before the murder Kathy had said, "There's something I have to tell you." When pressed for details, Kathy said it was something that had to do with the children. Another friend of Kathy's had called Sunday night and said that she "sounded tired, like she was a zombie."

Like the other detectives working on the case, Brann believed Graham was lying, trying to cover up his involvement in the murder. Brann didn't buy that story of a break-in, but he wasn't as completely certain of Graham's guilt as Nichols was. To Brann, the question was, "Did he do it, or is he protecting someone?"

Brann got in his city-owned Ford. He was about to head downtown when, to his surprise, Lewis Graham, obviously out for a jog, tapped on his window. Brann put the car in park.

"Listen," Graham said. "When I was talking with Detective Nichols yesterday you were there. He said if I came up with any explanations for the stuff we were talking about to get in touch. I've been thinking about it, and I'd like to maybe go over everything again."

"Fine—only now's not the time, and the street's not the place. Tell you what, why don't you come down to the detective offices about two this afternoon? We can sit down, and calmly go over everything at once," Brann responded.

Graham agreed, and went back across the street.

John Brann drove to the office feeling more than a little perplexed. Even after yesterday, when Nichols had come down hard with the accusations, Graham seemed to stick to his story and to show no fear of confrontations with detectives. Either his version of what happened was actually true—however confused or misstated—or the quiet professor had decided he could beat the police at their own game. Brann wasn't sure who would ultimately win this war of wills, but he had to smile at the contest. He enjoyed the challenge of mentally sparring with a man of such obvious intellect.

Brann knew that the Shreveport Police Department was lucky to have access to someone like Lew Graham, especially after they'd already told him he was a suspect. Usually people like Graham tired quickly of probing police questions and hard-nosed police attitudes. More often than not, attorneys were brought in to field the heat.

• • •

A man named Tim Hughes called the Shreveport Police Detective division to report that approximately eight months earlier he'd been attacked by a man wielding a ball-peen hammer. According to what Hughes told Detective C.R. Owens, his attacker was a black man, about twenty-five years of age, five feet nine, weighing 145 pounds. The attack occurred in front of a lounge in downtown Shreveport, and the attacker was driving a gold 1967 or '68 Chevy Impala.

Tim Hughes said he had heard about Kathy Graham's death and thought this incident might be related.

LEW Graham drove his brown Camaro to the City Hall building, home of the Shreveport Police Department. He stopped at the information desk and got directions to the detective offices. Brann was waiting for him.

"Oh, hello, Mr. Graham. Let's go down to the chief's office. I think we'll be more comfortable there."

The first time Graham had been here, the morning of the murder, he hadn't taken time to notice his surroundings. There wasn't much to notice. White institutional tile floors met with off-white sheetrock walls to form the ultimate in a boring, strictly functional public building. Brann opened the door next to a sign which read "Chief of Detectives" and ushered Graham into Sam Burns's office.

Burns had dark hair speckled with gray and the worst fashion sense in the SPD. His bright red tie looked like a fishing lure against a forest-green dress shirt.

"Captain, this is Mr. Lewis Graham. He's got something he wants to talk to us about."

Burns offered Graham some coffee, while Brann rigged up a cassette tape recorder. Graham and Brann sat across from Captain Burns, separated by a large desk befitting the Chief of Detectives. Graham noticed that the office itself was at least twice the size of the one he'd been in when he talked with Coker and Lopez.

John Brann turned on the tape recorder.

"This is Detective John Brann, along with Detective

Captain Sam Burns. We're in the detective division of the Shreveport Police Department. We have before us a Mr. Lewis T. Graham, Jr., who is not charged with any crime and is here at his own request, to talk about certain facts relating to the death of Kathy Graham. And for the benefit of the tape recorder, I have just given Mr. Graham a rights card, informing him of his right to remain silent, to have attorney, et cetera, which he has signed and dated."

"Right."

"And what we want to do, Mr. Graham, is to leave this recorder on during the entire conversation, so we can pick up details of what's being said. Is this in agreement with you?"

"Uh, yes, this is in agreement." Graham was ready to get on with it.

"So, you can just start with what you wanted to tell us."

Graham wasn't used to being the focus of so much attention. Kathy was the outgoing one, the one who always led the conversation, the one who everybody thought was the life of the party. But these policemen wanted to hear what *he* had to say, and Graham was ready to talk.

A native of south Louisiana, Graham had a soft speaking voice, with a Cajun accent. The Cajun lilt sounds like a cross between Brooklyn and backroads, with a slight French influence.

"What prompted this—I was talking with Detective Nichols yesterday, and he was telling me about some of the physical evidence that doesn't have a ready explanation, and he sort of said, 'If you can come up with something, we'd like to hear it.'

"I realize I'm in a bad spot, and I don't have all the answers. But off and on during the day yesterday, I tried to think of at least some possibilities that are consistent with both what you told me and what I remember."

Sam Burns had a paper and pen in front of him, poised to make a note.

"When I first described the incident . . . the best I can remember, the first thing I felt is the bed, a lurching, sudden movement. I think I heard a scream, a short one, like it was cut off. Then I was pushed or pulled or dragged or something off the side of the bed, onto the floor. Then I was lifted up, jostled around, and ended up being thrown against the wall. I don't remember actually hitting the wall, but I remember getting up from near the wall, near the door. What they indicated that they didn't have an explanation for was some blood spattering on the front of my shirt that wasn't mine, or didn't come from my wound, and some on the back. They indicated that they could explain the back, if I was on the floor, on my stomach, 'cause there's some blood spatter on the wall. This is what I thought of as a possibility. I had been up earlier, and I got back in bed on my side. My wife was pretty much in the middle, I think her back was turned to me. If she heard something, like a footstep—she sleeps lighter than I do—or if somebody partially closed the door . . . They indicated that the door had been closed, but we always leave it open."

Graham paused for a moment and gathered his thoughts. "Perhaps, when they came in, somehow she awakened and sat up abruptly. If she sat up, it would have pulled the covers off of me, and I could have gotten splattered right then. You said, 'Come up with an explanation,' and I'm trying to suggest a possibility."

The detectives sat quietly.

"We said yesterday," Graham continued, "that if there were two people on her, then there had to be three. Maybe not. Maybe one hit her and the other grabbed me, and then that one came to help this one. I don't know how many times she was hit. You asked, 'How did she get to the other side of the bed?' Y'all asked a lot of things. 'Did she gurgle?' Maybe they hit her again if she moved. Maybe she wasn't dead, and they hit her again. You know, this is hard."

Brann and Burns nodded, and Graham continued. "When I first told this story, I said, 'I got up, turned on the light, looked around, it was horrible, then I turned off the light and left.' Well, afterwards, you know, going over it, that wasn't all. I remember going over by our bathroom, looking in the mirror and seeing myself. They also asked, 'Did you touch your wife?' I seem to remember—standing by the bedstand, I reached down and touched her—but through all of this, you know, there are things I don't remember."

Graham picked a pencil up from Burns's desk and began playing with it. "Another question Nichols asked me: 'Why was there blood over here on the floor where I said I got stabbed, but none over there where I said I waked up?' Well, I thought about that a little. I don't know how big a puddle it was where I was stabbed, but I remember that the guy who stitched me up said that it was a puncture wound. I—I think punctures don't bleed very much. I don't know how big the knife was—from what I gather, it was my own knife, which is not that big.

"Another thing I had a reaction to," Graham went on, "was that Nichols said that the stab wound was possible to self-inflict. Okay, maybe that *is* possible. It's my reaction that, somebody can pull a trigger and shoot themselves, but to push a knife, that goes, essentially, all the way through—it just doesn't seem likely to me."

Brann interrupted. "Mr. Graham, let me just—"

"One other point I want to make. Detective Coker was the first one to ask the question, 'Did I ever have trouble in the marriage?' and I started to tell him right then. My limited, uh, involvement with this other woman, my lab assistant, was a result from, not the cause of, trouble between my wife and me. The conflicts in Kathy's and my personalities were something that had built up over a long time. My wife is very talkative, and I'm very quiet. It's kind of a long story. I can tell you who our counselor is, and you can talk to him."

Graham was looking at his feet. "Last year was a really bad time in my life. I was down, and this woman—you know, with the kind of work we do, like microsurgery—we might spend two hours at a time in the cold room, killing rats, and we'd talk. I don't know, that's been a long time ago. I just wanted to say that. But the way the question was phrased to me, it never was a problem. It never came up. My wife never knew."

Up to now, the detectives had let Graham say his piece. Now they hoped to focus the conversation on specific points of evidence.

"Okay, Mr. Graham," Brann said, "why don't we go back to the beginning. You theorized that your wife raised up in the bed because of a sound, was struck, and the blood landed on your shirt?"

"Yeah," Graham said, " 'cause that would have pulled the covers off of me, and I would have gotten hit by some of the blood."

"Do you remember wiping any blood off your neck or face?"

"No."

"Okay, if we're basing this on what you just said, then that first jolt would have been your wife being struck as you were pulled from the bed?" Brann asked.

"Yeah, I think it was that fast. My impression is that it would have to be at least two people."

"Okay, you were pulled from the bed, you hit the floor, and you were stabbed almost immediately. Is that correct?" Brann asked.

"Well, I don't know exactly. Yeah, pretty soon."

"You tell me," Brann said.

"I, uh, was coming out of a deep sleep. It seemed very soon, like I didn't have time to grab onto anything solid. I was sort of trying to find something."

"Did you ever feel any hands?" Brann asked. "Did you ever reach out and physically feel any hands?"

"An arm. I grabbed something."

"Wrist?" Brann asked.

"I don't know. Something."

"This was while, before, or after you were being stabbed?"

"Right about the same time."

"You hit the floor, you feel a burning sensation in your side. How long were you on the floor before they pulled you up?" Brann asked.

"Not too long. I just had this feeling of reaching, of someone over me. They pulled me down and then, pretty much, right back up. I was sort of pushed back and forth, and at one time, I have the sensation of being spun around. Somebody just—I don't know—like you would throw a dog out the door. I don't remember actually hitting the wall. The next thing I do remember clearly is getting up. My head was right up against the baseboard. My neck was stiff, and there wasn't anyone there when I became aware of my surroundings. Whoever had been there was gone."

Burns asked his first question. "When you got up off the floor, what was the first thing you did?"

"I think I turned on the light and turned around."

"What light?"

"The bedroom light. The switch is right there by the door. The best I can remember, I looked, it was horrible, and I turned it right back off."

"Then you went to the bathroom, turned that light on, and looked at yourself?" Sam Burns asked.

"Yeah, I think so."

"And did you wash your hands?"

"I didn't remember that at first, but maybe. If I had to say, I would say yes."

"And after you washed your hands, you went to the nightstand and got your glasses?"

"Yes. And while I was standing there, I think I touched her arm to feel."

Burns nodded. "Have you thought of an explanation for why there was no blood on your glasses, and everything around them was bloody?"

"There were a couple of spots. Why there wasn't more I don't know, unless they were behind something."

Detective Brann jumped back in. "Okay, you being a member of the medical profession—"

"I'm not an M.D."

"You're associated with hospitals and medicine. Anybody that's ever been around a hospital knows that a lot of times, once you wash the mess away the wound isn't as bad as it appears. Why did you assume, just from that quick look, that your wife was dead and couldn't be helped?"

Graham hesitated. When he finally answered, his voice was noticeably softer. "I, um, I've been trying not to dwell on that scene. Uh, it just seems like there was blood everywhere. And, um, her head was m-misshaped, like it was crushed. She was absolutely still. And I just said, she's dead. I guess that's why I thought to close the bedroom door, so the children wouldn't see. That was a real shock to see that. That must have been why I touched her. Just to verify that she was cold."

The detectives looked at each other while Graham waited for their next question.

"Okay," Brann said, "so the blood on the front of your T-shirt could have come while you were still in bed. What about the blood on the back of your shirt?"

"Detective Nichols said that it would have been possible because of the spatter marks on the wall next to where I was knocked out."

"Not consistent with what was on the shirt."

"Well, then." Graham said, "I don't know. Unless I'm just—you're asking me. Maybe whoever picked me up, and my back was turned while they were—"

Captain Burns interrupted. "Mr. Graham, let me ask you. After you did all these things in the bedroom, you went out the door. You locked the door behind you?"

"Yes. Because I was concerned about the kids coming in."

"What did you do then?" Burns asked.

"Okay, I went down the hall. I think I turned the family room light on. I went to the kitchen, got the telephone book out of a drawer under the microwave, and turned to the Blue Pages to look up the number for the police."

Captain Burns cleared his throat. "You didn't check on your children? You hadn't checked on your children?"

Graham paused. "No. I, um, locked the bedroom door to keep them out and went to call the police."

Brann jumped in. "How did you know they hadn't been hurt? I mean, your wife's been hurt, you've been hurt. The boys' door is closed. The girl's door is closed."

"I don't know. I just had the thought to—"

Brann interrupted. "To keep the kids out. But how did you know the kids were alive?"

Graham hesitated. "I don't know. I don't know what to say. I, uh, that's the two things I remember most strongly. 'I've got to lock that door and call the police.' I don't know why. Maybe I somehow optimistically assumed they were all right."

The captain leaned forward. "So that's when you went and got this telephone book?"

"Right. I called the police, and told the operator to send the police and an ambulance. I said that I thought my wife was dead, I was hurt, that somebody had broken in. I said to send the police and an ambulance. I didn't really think I was hurt that bad, and I thought she was too far gone, but I said it anyway. Then I called the neighbor across the street, Carolyn Godwin, and she said that her husband was out of town, and she would call another neighbor, Jerry Siragusa. I said okay. I turned around—I get up early in the morning, so I had my jeans and slippers on the floor there. And I put my pants on."

Brann picked up the question. "Let me ask you right here, Mr. Graham. You shut the door, you went out, called the police, then called the neighbor who said they'd get hold of Jerry Siragusa. You hung up, saw your pants, said, 'I better put them on'—"

"I figured things were going to be happening."

"All right, sir. Now that you have secured the room where your children can't see and you've got help on the way, you didn't think *then* to check on your kids, to see if they were alive?"

"Jerry came in before I could! I went and un—unlocked the front door and put the porch light on."

"That's what I mean," Brann said. "You have all these forethoughts, everyone's been attacked, you, your wife."

Graham's voice was low. "I don't know. That doesn't make sense. I mean, it sounds absurd now that you say it. I don't know. I don't have a good answer."

THE LAWYERS

5

LEW Graham walked weak-kneed into the bright sunlight outside the Shreveport Police Department. He was in shock, stunned. He felt helpless, alone, and afraid.

He sat in his Camaro for a few minutes, trying to get control of himself. In his mind he replayed everything Detective Brann and the Chief of Detectives had said to him. The day before, back in the bedroom with Donnie Nichols, he had thought it was just Nichols who didn't believe him. But today these two had echoed Nichols's accusations and ended the interview with a startling question.

"Dr. Graham," Sam Burns had asked, "I want to know how you think you'll be able to live with yourself, if you don't face up to reality and get this thing off your conscience?"

Graham's face flushed at the memory. He remembered what his brother-in-law had told him that first night after Kathy's murder: *Lew, everything could have happened just the way you said it did, and you still can find yourself in the middle of a murder investigation . . .*

He drove across town, heading home. As he pulled into his driveway, he noticed a car parked there that belonged to Johnny Harrison, an old boyhood friend from south Louisiana who worked as a patent attorney in a Shreveport law firm. He had come to the Grahams' house just an hour or so after Kathy's death and had done his best to help Graham through those first, difficult hours.

Harrison was walking out the front door as Graham came up the sidewalk. "Hey, Lew, glad I got to see you. David said you were down at the police station. Everything going all right?"

Graham felt sick to his stomach. "Not really. They think I killed Kathy. I mean, they came right out and said it."

Harrison lowered his voice. "I was afraid that might happen. I saw Donnie Nichols at your house Monday morning. Have you been talking to him?"

"At first, but today it was a detective named Brann and Sam Burns, the Chief of Detectives. Johnny, I'm scared they didn't believe a word I said. I need a lawyer. Do you know anybody who does this kind of work?"

"We've got a guy, one of the partners—he's been around a while—I think he's about our age or maybe a little older. His name is Bob Sutton, and he does quite a bit of criminal work," Harrison said.

Graham sighed. "Criminal work. Listen to how that sounds! It's amazing to me that they could even *think* I could do something like that. These detectives are serious. Do you think you could get me an appointment in the morning?"

"I tell you what. I'm heading back to the office now. I'll check with Sutton and let you know what time to come in. Listen, Lew, I know it seems like everything's going against you, but try to relax. This kind of thing happens sometimes, when the police don't have very many leads. Once you talk to Bob Sutton, I'm sure he'll know what to do."

Thursday, April 3

GRAHAM didn't know why, but he was nervous. He'd never had any dealings with an attorney, at least not one who worked with criminals.

He pulled into the parking lot of Burnett, Sutton, Walker & Calloway, a medium-sized law firm housed in a fairly large, modern Colonial-style office building on one of Shreveport's busiest thoroughfares. He hoped their obvious financial success was indicative of good legal advice.

The waiting room reminded him of a doctor's office, small but formally decorated. There were plenty of magazines, and a sliding glass window between the receptionist and the waiting area.

"I'm Lew Graham. I have an appointment with Bob Sutton."

Graham sat down and opened a recent copy of *People*. He flipped through the pages, his eyes looking at the paper, his mind unable to focus on the articles and pictures.

An attractive woman opened an inner office door and invited him back. She introduced herself as Mr. Sutton's secretary and escorted Graham down a hallway toward the northern corner of the building. He noticed a formal conference room with a long table off to the left of the hall. The secretary opened the door, and the man behind the desk ended his telephone conversation.

Until now Graham hadn't really thought about what a defense lawyer might look like. If he had stopped to take the time to consider it, he would never have conjured up Bob Sutton.

Sutton immediately gave the impression that he was all business. Appearing to be in his mid-forties, he had thinning dark hair and pointed features that made him seem lean and hard. His sharp jaw and nose gave him a hawkish look, set off by a gray, leathery complexion. He looked more like a detective than a criminal lawyer.

"Miss Ware, would you get me a cup of coffee?—Dr. Graham, something for you?"

The coffee arrived, the door was closed, and Graham was alone with this tough-looking attorney.

"I guess Johnny told you about my situation?" Graham asked.

"Mr. Harrison said that your wife had been murdered, and the police are hinting that they think you did it. I've read the stories in the newspaper. I'm very sorry."

"Thank you. But the police are doing more than hinting—they came right out and accused me! First, let me tell you, I didn't kill my wife. I don't know why these policemen don't believe that; I don't have any experience talking to detectives. And I'm not used to people I hardly know calling me a liar."

"Why don't you tell me what happened?" Sutton said.

Graham's mind was racing, remembering so many details at once he couldn't decide what to talk about first. "You want to know about the incident or about the police?"

"For now, just concentrate on telling me about your conversations with the detectives. We'll talk about the particulars of the crime later."

"This thing happened Sunday night—Monday morning actually, around five a.m. What happened was, I found my wife dead, and I called the police and asked them to get an ambulance. Then I called a neighbor across the street, 'cause I wanted to get my children out of there before they saw her. Jerry Siragusa—he's a neighbor of mine—came over and helped me get the boys up, and we told them to get their sister and go over to another neighbor's house, Carolyn Godwin."

Graham noticed that Bob Sutton was writing down the neighbors' names, and he could see, to his relief, that the lawyer was on his side.

"This was around five o'clock in the morning?" Sutton asked.

"Thereabouts. The first policeman arrived pretty soon after I called, probably only about five or ten minutes—Sorry, I don't remember his name. It doesn't matter anyway, because within fifteen minutes my house looked like a police station. There must have been a dozen officers walking around, talking on their walkie-talkies. And asking lots of questions. I remember talking to one of the patrolmen, I don't remember his name either, and this guy didn't seem especially bright. He'd ask me, 'What happened?' So I'd start telling him something, and he was going, 'Wait, wait! Slow down!' like he was trying to write down every word. So I tried to go real slow, like, 'I goot out of beeeed, theeeeeeennn I weeeeeennnnt toooo theee liiiiivinnng rooooooommm,' so he could get it all down."

Sutton smiled. "Did you say you don't remember his name?"

"There was just too much going on. Then the firemen came, and one of them looked at me—I had been stabbed, I've got a wound up here on my left side—and he bandaged my wound and put me in an ambulance and we went to the hospital."

"You didn't see any detectives at your house?"

"I think, for just a minute—two guys wearing suits instead of police uniforms. But several came by the emergency room. One of them, I think his name was Lopez, brought me this form to sign, and later took me down to the police station."

"They had you sign something?"

"Oh, I don't remember what it was called. It had to do with giving my permission for them to look through the house."

"Consent for search and seizure," Sutton said.

Graham nodded, happy to hear he was with someone who knew the procedures. "That sounds right. Anyway, while I was still at the hospital, one of the detectives said something about my attitude not being right for someone whose wife had just been killed. I guess he was expecting me to be screaming and hysterical or something. I can't help it, that's me—I tend to respond less when there's more stress. Plus, I was trying very hard *not* to lose control. I knew, or at least I thought, that the information I was giving them was very important, in terms of their ability to find the killers."

"Uh-huh," Sutton said.

Bobby Sutton was the first professional who tried to see the situation from Graham's point of view. It made Graham feel good to have him in his corner. "Okay, then Lopez took me down to the detective offices. And another detective, Lieutenant Coker, and Lopez asked me questions in this little office—it must have been Coker's office, because he sat behind the desk. We talked for a long time. It seemed like there was something going on outside the room, yelling and arguing, and every so often they would get up, saying they'd be right back, but they might be gone twenty minutes or more. I kind of got the impression that maybe they were listening to what I was saying, then calling back out to the house to see if my story fit. I really don't know what they were doing, but I was at the police station for over three hours."

Sutton looked amazed. "Three hours? What were they doing that took three hours?"

"Like I said, we'd talk for a while, they'd leave. Then they'd come back in and ask more questions, then leave again. I'd been there all morning before they even turned the tape player on."

"They recorded you?"

"Oh, yeah. It was no big deal, the whole recording probably isn't ten minutes long. It's just basic stuff, what time my wife woke me up, what side of the bed we slept on, that kind of thing."

"Did they ever offer you the chance to talk to a lawyer?" Sutton asked.

Graham shook his head. "He read me my rights, but you see, I knew I hadn't done anything. And to me, that meant that I was supposed to do everything I could to help. It never occurred to me that they might really try to turn this stuff around and use it against me," Graham stopped talking and watched Sutton, curious about what the attorney was thinking.

Sutton put down his pen and leaned back in the chair. "Why do you think they don't believe you?"

"I don't know. I've thought about that a lot, in between all the family and people hanging around. I honestly don't know. All this time they've wasted, running around trying to get me, they could have been out there looking for the real killers." Graham glanced out the window. "Talking about my lack of emotion. I remember, Detective Brann was the one in the emergency room. He said, 'You're telling me this story as if someone just stole your hubcaps, not murdered your wife.' And later one of them said something about it to my brother-in-law, and he just told them that's the way I am. I guess ordinarily they see people out of control in this situation, and when I kept my cool on the outside—inside I was a wreck, you know—it didn't sit right with them."

"Which of the detectives appeared to you to be in charge?"

"Like I said, that first day, it was this Lopez and Lieutenant Coker down at the police station. The next day is when I met Lieutenant Nichols. He's the one that first said he didn't believe me, and I think he told me he was in charge. In fact, if you want to know what I think, Nichols probably talked to the others and convinced them I was the main suspect."

"I know Donnie. He has the tendency to jump in with both feet," Sutton said.

Graham leaned forward. "I saw Nichols for the first time on Tuesday. We had gone back over to my house, and after looking at the back door, the utility room door, I called the detective office and Nichols came out. He was very nice and polite, and asked me if I would go back over everything with him, and I said, 'Sure.' We went back to the bedroom—"

"Did they read you your rights?" Sutton interrupted.

"That's one thing they always did. Anyway, we went back to my bedroom, and I walked through the room, showed him where everything happened, and he asked me about a hundred questions, the same things over and over again. Then finally he says, 'Well, if what you say is true, then how do you explain such-and-such?' That's what it came down to, he wanted *me* to explain everything, all the evidence and stuff. Well, Mr. Sutton, I'm not a policeman, I'm a scientist. I don't know diddly about police stuff. Then Lieutenant Nichols says that he doesn't believe me, and starts talking about manslaughter versus murder. Oh, and I said something to him about being stabbed, about my stab wound? Nichols just kind of grinned and said, 'Yeah, well, we kind of think that the type of wound you have, it is possible to self-inflict.' "

Sutton nodded. "It's all in your point of view. It is *possible* to self-inflict anything, except maybe a gunshot wound to the center of the back."

Graham smiled. "I like that."

"The truth is, Dr. Graham, this is not that unusual. Police detectives are all pretty much alike. They're paid to be extra suspicious of everything. They all have what we call a prosecution complex. That means, to them, even if you're not guilty of whatever it is they're accusing you of, they figure you're bound to be guilty of something."

Graham laughed. "Like I said, at first I thought it was just Detective Nichols who didn't believe me. I really wasn't very worried about it; I didn't think one guy could shade the whole departmental effort. But maybe I was wrong— I mean, yesterday with the Chief of Detectives, they really put a scare in me . . . I've always believed in the American system, and maybe I'm naive, but I still do. It seems pretty obvious that I need some professional help with all this. Mr. Sutton, I am not a criminal, I'm the victim. My wife's been killed, the mother of my children was murdered, and I didn't have anything to do with it."

Sutton nodded as if he'd heard it before.

"Once the police focus their investigation on a single person," Sutton said, "it's almost impossible to convince them that they might be wrong. They've obviously made up their mind that you are it."

Graham thought about the way the police officers had dealt with him, and he knew Sutton was right. "Oh, there's one more important thing I wanted to tell you. I've mentioned this to the detectives a couple of times, but they always just shrugged it off. Last year, in the spring, we had an incident at our house involving my youngest son, Eric. Eric is twelve now, and one day after school, around five o'clock, he came home early from baseball practice, and when he walked in the door, there were these two men in our house. He described them as older teenagers. Eric said they took him by the neck, threw him up against the wall, and demanded that he show them where I kept my gun. From my closet, they took my .22 rifle, and they also grabbed my old Boy Scout knife and threatened Eric with it. They had to go up in the attic to get the ammunition— I always kept the bullets in a different spot away from the gun—and then they took Eric out into the woods behind the house. He said they shoved him around a little—his clothes were torn when we saw him—and eventually let him go. At the time, I called the police, and a patrolman came out and talked to us and took down the information. By the time we got through talking with the policeman, it had gotten dark and was starting to rain. The policeman didn't seem that interested anyway.

"A friend of mine, Bennett Kitchings, who is a sheriff's deputy—he's a close friend of ours and might be someone you'd want to talk to—he came by and talked to Eric that day. Eric gave him a description of the two men, and even later, Bennett brought out some pictures of some crooks he knew about, but Eric didn't recognize them. The next morning, Eric and I retraced his steps in the woods and found the rifle lying on the ground. I took it to the police station, but it had rained all night, and the man said it would have washed away any fingerprints. Anyway, I don't know if this is important or not, but it seems to me here's a situation where two men broke into our house once before. I don't know if it was the same two guys or not, but it's certainly something to look into. And when I told the detectives, it was kind of like 'ho-hum, yeah, sure.' They didn't seem to pay too much attention."

"That's a perfect example of what I'm saying," Sutton said. "Once the police lock onto somebody, it doesn't matter what happens; it's almost impossible to deflect their focus. Fortunately, the judicial system is set up in such a way that the Donnie Nicholses of this world don't have the final say. If the police continue to direct all their attention at you, eventually it will end up in the hands of the district attorney. And he has to go on facts—*provable* facts—in a court of law."

"Well, what's going to happen next? Are they going to come arrest me or what? And if they do, can I get out on bail? I know it sounds silly, but they were actually pretty civilized about the whole thing. Even when they were saying they didn't believe me, it was a very calm conversation."

"If they didn't arrest you yesterday, they probably aren't going to today or tomorrow either. And yes, even if they did arrest you, we could get you out on bond. The detectives are probably waiting for some kind of go-ahead from the D.A., and he'll be taking this case to the grand jury. What that means is, if they do finally come after you, we'll have some warning. A grand jury would probably take several weeks to return an indictment, if it happened at all. For now, try not to worry too much about the police. Just go back to work, try to be a good father, and quietly go on with your life. In the meantime, I'll see what I can find out. Sam Burns is an old friend of mine, maybe he'll tell me something. I'm also going to pay a visit to the D.A."

Graham smiled. "I really do feel better, just getting all this off my chest. I haven't told my children or any of my family about this yet."

"For now, why don't we keep this visit to ourselves. There's nothing anyone can do about it anyway, and there's no sense in worrying them needlessly."

"This is all so different from what I'm used to . . . By the way, what's all this going to cost me?"

"We can talk about money later, after I find out what's going on. It may take me a few days, but don't worry. In the interim, if you do happen to hear from the police again—or the press—just politely tell them I'm representing you and you have nothing to say. As soon as I find out anything, I'll call."

Graham stood up to leave and offered a handshake. "Thanks." For the first time in several days, he thought he could see some light at the end of the tunnel.

6

PAUL Carmouche smiled at the receptionist and walked back toward the crime lab's conference room. He knew very little about the Graham homicide, not much more than what he'd heard on radio station KEEL the morning of the murder.

First Assistant District Attorney Woody Nesbitt had been called to the crime scene early Monday morning. Nesbitt had listened calmly to Coker's and Lopez's initial suspicions about Lew Graham and watched over the evidence-gathering at the scene. An amateur photographer, he took several pictures of the bedroom and the distribution of physical evidence. Later that week, following an emotional telephone call from Lieutenant Coker, Nesbitt had asked Captain Burns to restrain Donnie Nichols from arresting Graham.

It was unusual for the D.A.'s office to intercede in a police investigation. Carmouche believed it was best to stay out of the day-to-day decision-making process at the detective office. His staff stood ready to offer legal advice and arrange for search warrants and such, but when it came to telling the cops how to run their business, Carmouche agreed with his predecessor in the D.A.'s job. "We're lawyers, not detectives. We'll do the lawyering and let the police do the policing."

In his second year as District Attorney for Caddo Parish, Carmouche supervised thirteen assistant prosecutors and more than two thousand felony cases a year. No one who went to work in the D.A.'s office could expect a cushy job. Sixty-hour work weeks were the norm, as were mediocre pay, a bureaucracy that often refused to cooperate, frequent personality clashes, and more than a little politics. But service in the D.A.'s office had its assets, too. Young attorneys fresh out of law school could get a decade's worth of trial experience in twenty-four months. Those interested in a career as trial lawyers knew they could put in their time, then go into private practice and cash in on their courtroom skills. The best trial lawyers usually ended up specializing as either plaintiff's or defendant's advocates in damage cases. Some ex-prosecutors found a niche in criminal work, though that field usually paid much less than commercial litigation.

Paul Carmouche was a transplanted south Louisiana Catholic Cajun who had married a Shreveport girl while attending Loyola Law School in New Orleans. After graduation, he took a job as an associate with a small Shreveport firm and moved to north Louisiana. He had three very lean years in private practice before being recruited as the eighth of eight assistants in the Caddo D.A.'s office.

Anxious to gain trial experience as quickly as possible, dreaming of collecting multi-million-dollar tort judgments, he told all the other assistants that he would go to court on anything. His battle cry was, "You got a case that you don't want to prosecute? Give it to me—I'll handle it!" He learned the hard way how to prepare a case for trial, and more importantly, how to know when to prosecute and when to say no.

In the next two years, Carmouche handled more than thirty jury trials. A bit shy in front of the jury, he developed a conservative, plodding, but consistent trial technique. Over time, particularly after watching defense lawyers take potshots at his cases, he developed a special knack for effective cross-examination. Carmouche liked the idea that he could show a group of average citizens why they'd be better off with a defendant behind bars.

With his confidence and courtroom successes growing, he was appointed the administrator of the local Indigent Defender Board. The I.D. Board, as it was known, was formed after the U.S. Supreme Court's *Miranda* decision established everyone's right to an attorney—meaning a free lawyer to those who couldn't afford to hire one themselves.

Carmouche spent two more years working the other side of the table, representing defendants in a wide range of criminal matters. But he never really felt comfortable defending people he knew to be guilty and kept his eye open for a chance to go back to work for the state.

In 1978 Carmouche ran for Caddo Parish District Attorney, backed by a large group of fledgling politicians, many of whom were also running for public office for the first time. He had put his boyish good looks on the line, and found an easy charm that translated well into effective campaigning. He was elected, and in his first year as D.A. he tried several high-profile cases. He recognized the importance of good media relations in politics and made it a point to keep himself well-informed on the day-to-day operations of the office. To the reporters who covered the courthouse beat, Paul Carmouche was always accessible.

Easygoing, a kidder and fun-loving troublemaker, he had a disarming manner which appealed to his constituents. He was clean-shaven, with straight brown hair which he kept cut short. Sometimes he wore contact lenses, sometimes stylish, round glasses, and his face often bore a mischievous smirk. At lunchtime, he could often be seen jogging shirtless through the downtown area, where his athletic physique drew wolf whistles and appreciative stares from many of the high-rise man-watchers.

Carmouche didn't yet know very many details about the Graham case, just that the police detectives were uniform in their suspicions about the quiet medical school scientist. He had been told that there had been little police effort to look elsewhere for suspects, and he decided he would

reserve judgment on whether or not he agreed with the
police position.

Carmouche walked into the crime lab conference room
and found Donnie Nichols preaching his gospel about Graham. Brann and Burns, together with Wojtkiewicz and Herd
of the crime lab staff, sat around a large table across from
First Assistant Nesbitt. Nesbitt and Carmouche had been
invited to get a full briefing on the physical evidence gathered from 2033 South Kirkwood.

" . . . and I tell you, he was absolutely the coldest man
I've ever seen. We stood right there next to the bed where
his wife had been hammered, blood still on the mattress,
and he never *once* showed the first sign of emotion."

As Carmouche sat down, Burns chimed in. "John and
I interviewed him yesterday for over an hour, took him
through his story step by step. He never batted an eye."

"That's all well and good, people, but we don't go to court
and ask a jury to convict someone of murder just because
they don't cry when they're supposed to," Carmouche said.
"Especially someone from his side of town. Besides, we
won't get the chance to talk to him any more. I just got a
call from Bobby Sutton. He's working for Graham now."

Nichols slammed his fist on the table. "Damn!"

"Let's get this show on the road," Carmouche continued.
"What about it, Ray? What do you have for us?" he asked
the crime lab director.

A soft-spoken man, Ray Herd was in his fifties, gray-
haired and balding. He stood up and pulled a box out
from under the conference table. He moved down to one
end and began unloading the contents, arranging them in
a neat grouping so everyone could see: the sledgehammer,
the hunting knife, about two dozen photographs, an alarm
clock, two pieces of shag carpeting, and a man's T-shirt
and boxer underwear.

"Pat and I spent the day at the house the morning of the
murder. We documented all the bloodstains, took several
samples, even videotaped the whole room. Y'all can see
that tape later if you want."

He indicated the physical evidence. "All this came from

the Graham house. Blood tells the story of this crime. If you follow the story the blood tells you, you won't have any trouble proving this case in court," Herd said.

Carmouche knew it was never as easy as the criminologists thought.

Herd passed around the photographs, which showed several wide shots and some close-ups of the body and bed. Carmouche found himself in the grip of some of the most gruesome pictures he'd ever seen. He passed the photos on, deciding to look at them later when he could be alone.

"We found two blood types, primarily concentrated in the master bedroom. The first thing we had to do was try to go through and establish whose blood was where. Obviously, ninety-nine percent of this blood came from the lady, but don't forget that Graham had a stab wound too. Pat and I took samples from several places. This carpet was on the left side of the bed, and it was soaked through with a pretty decent quantity of blood. We were able to take two cc's out of the carpet. Considering what had dried and soaked in, there was probably ten cc's total. That blood belongs to Dr. Graham," Herd said.

Carmouche was taking notes, anxious to keep it all straight in his mind.

"On the bed—this is an awful lot of blood, and you won't be surprised to hear that this is her blood. We took three samples from different places on the sheets and bedspread, even the headboard, and it's all her blood type. Pat took a couple of samples from some of the larger blood spatters on the wall—one over near the bedroom door, and one right up next to the closet, and they both matched her."

Carmouche walked over to the display of evidence and tried to imagine how these items had looked in the bedroom. It was one thing to see pictures of a crime scene and quite another to actually experience the room. The brutality of the murder continued to eat at him, and he made a mental note to arrange for a tour of the victim's house.

" . . . and the strange thing about the blood on the bedroom door is that we found spatter on *both* sides. Now, in order for that to happen, one of two things had to occur. Either there were two separate beatings, one with the door open and one with the door closed, *or* the door was cracked open slightly, at precisely the perfect angle to allow the blood to land on both sides. Pat and I think the odds of that happening are astronomical. We believe there were two beatings," Herd said.

Carmouche interrupted. "Which door are you talking about?"

"The door leading from the bedroom into the hallway."

"What do you mean, two beatings?" Carmouche asked.

Wojtkiewicz answered. "Look at the photo taken with the wide angle from the foot of the bed. You can see that she's lying to your left, but just to the right of her head is another pillow, that obviously someone was lying on. There's no doubt she was on the right side. She had to have been hit over there and lain there a while for all that blood to collect. I'd say she was there, unconscious and bleeding, for at least five minutes. Wouldn't you, Mr. Herd?"

"Probably longer. So the first beating is delivered when she's on the right side of the bed. Then, several minutes later, she is moved to the other side and hit in the forehead."

Wojtkiewicz continued. "Over here in the first position, there is one area of blood spatter that's different from all the others. It is a stream of blood and came *after* she was hit with the hammer. Looking at this line, it looks to us like she either coughed or sneezed. The force from that cough shot a line of blood down the sheets."

Carmouche was confused. "She coughed after being hit with the sledgehammer. *After* she was unconscious?"

Herd nodded. "Coughing and sneezing are involuntary reflexes. You don't have to be conscious for the body to automatically expel something clogging up the air passages."

No one said a word. The two crime lab technicians were matter-of-fact in their explanation; they were merely relaying scientific facts established by physical evidence. The detectives, while curious and attentive, were equally detached from the emotional effect of the crime lab analysis. Paul Carmouche, the politician, trial lawyer, and chief prosecutor, couldn't take his eyes off the pictures of Kathy Graham's body.

Carmouche cleared his throat. "Still—it's one thing to know how the crime was committed, and another to prove who did it."

Herd agreed. "Along that line, there's one other area of the house where we found bloodstains: in a bedroom, straight across the hall from the murder room. It looks like the boys' room. This bedroom had bunk beds in it, and up on the sheet, near one of the pillows, we found a small amount of blood. Detective Brann said the bed belonged to David Graham, the oldest son."

Carmouche looked at his assistant prosecutor. "The teenager?"

Saturday, April 5

OVER seven hundred people came to the Summer Grove Baptist Church for Kathy Graham's funeral. The crowd was a strange mixture of relatives, friends, acquaintances, co-workers, and busybodies. There were a number of close friends of the Grahams who, despite their appearances to the contrary, were privately talking about the cloud of suspicion that had fallen on the widower. That concern added to the sadness of the moment and created an undercurrent of tension that could be felt in the packed church.

Lew, David, Eric, and Katie sat on the front row nearest the pulpit. For obvious reasons, the casket remained closed. Some parts of the congregation buzzed with whispered expressions of a macabre curiosity about how the body might look prepared for burial.

Summer Grove Baptist was a unique mixture of the fundamental and the progressive. The sanctuary was a modern, semi-octagonal, two-story blend of rough white walls, offset against deep wood paneling around the hundred-seat choir section. Outside, a forty-foot-tall concrete sculpture in the front of the church suggested a stylized, abstract interpretation of the Trinity.

Rodney Thomas, the acting pastor, had visited the Grahams earlier in the week, and had borrowed Kathy's Bible to look up her favorite scriptures. Thomas was a barrel-chested man with bright orange hair and a moustache to match. He had a soft, crisp evangelical lilt in his voice.

"Kathy Graham is not hungry, because the Lord preparest a table for her in the presence of her enemies; he anointeth her head with oil, and her cup runneth over. His goodness and mercy followed her all the days of her life, and she is dwelling in the house of the Lord forever."

Thomas stepped down from the pulpit, walked over to where the Graham family was sitting, and reached down to hand David the Bible. "I give you, as the oldest son, your mother's Bible," he said.

For the first time since the murder, one of the Grahams showed sadness in public. David cried softly.

Thomas returned to the pulpit. "I'd like to share with you a special group of quotations that I found tucked away in Kathy's favorite Bible. It is fitting that Kathy Graham, a wonderful mother, a wonderful teacher, would have kept something like this over the years. It's called the Ten Commandments for Teaching Children."

Thomas paused dramatically, and leaned close to the microphone, speaking in little more than a whisper.

"Thou shalt love thy children with thine whole heart, for truly they are the children of God. Thou shalt lead thy children into paths of righteousness, by thy example, for verily, what ye do speaks so loud, they cannot hear what ye say.

"Thou shalt be a Christian teacher worthy of thy name, and great will be thy reward in heaven. Thou shalt continuously train and improve thyself, in Christian maturity and understanding, always studying to show thyself approved unto the Lord. Thou shalt teach by parables in words familiar to thy children, and they will surely learn. . . ."

Thomas looked down at the three Graham children. "And finally, thou shalt recognize the differences in thy children's personalities, remembering always that each is as unique as flakes of snow."

• • •

THE cemetery at Forest Park West sat atop a small knoll across the highway from the Shreveport Regional Airport. The family had requested a brief service, and their wishes were respected. Except for David's momentary tears in the church, the Graham family remained stoic. Lew Graham was very proud to see their control; he considered it a sign of emotional strength.

At the burial, Graham had considered removing his own wedding ring and, as the casket was being lowered, tossing it into the grave. His intent was to symbolize the fact that part of his life was over. At the last minute, a little concerned that the gesture might be misunderstood, he decided to forgo any public display.

Graham was right, though. Part of his life *was* over: the part that existed before he was accused of murder.

7

IT took a week for Bobby Sutton to gather enough information to warrant another office visit with Lew Graham. Sutton had been frustrated in his attempts to find out the details of any evidence against his client. Until Graham was formally charged with a crime, the authorities were perfectly within their rights to refuse to discuss the matter with Sutton or anyone else. Sutton got the impression that it was only a matter of time before Carmouche called for a grand jury to look into the death of Kathy Graham.

In the meantime, Sutton's only source for information about the case was Graham himself. He called the biochemist in to the office, handed him a pocket dictating machine and several tiny cassettes, and instructed him to make a recording of "everything that might possibly be relevant. Tell me all about your relationship with your wife, as well as every detail you can remember, from the night of the murder until the day you walked into this office."

Graham sat down alone at the end of a long conference table in the law firm's offices. Feeling a little silly to be asked, in effect, to talk out loud to himself, he took several minutes to gather his thoughts.

"I'm going to ramble for a while about events that have happened, and I would like to talk a little bit about my relationship with my wife, Kathleen or Kathy Graham. Probably increasing over some number of years back, we've had some difficulties in our marital relationship—mainly on the basis of differences in our personalities. Some of the problem is, I don't talk enough. I'm very tuned inward. I find it difficult to relate feelings verbally. I would like to touch, or hug, for example, instead of saying 'I love you,' and even though that was my way, she would like to hear things. Probably somewhat to attract attention, or get a response, she would resort to sarcasm. Verbal exchanges are the kinds of things I would tend to avoid or want to withdraw from.

"Our family backgrounds are quite different. Emotion, or the expression of emotion, was really suppressed in my house. Kathy was raised in sort of a volatile Cajun household, where loud discussions or shouting arguments were just typical. That's the way she was—everybody got it out and shouted a while until it all cooled off.

"I certainly learned to deal with disagreements by withdrawing. I found her fluctuations in mood were up and down much more so than mine. My range of emotions was much narrower, up and down.

"We finally got to a point, building up over several years, that I began to be really uncomfortable in the relationship. I felt like I was holding too much in, when what she wanted was for me to talk to her. I probably did more in the way of household chores than most husbands, and that was sort of the way I was trying to express that I wanted to help her, to reach out and touch her. But we were not utilizing the same wavelengths in communication, and we just weren't getting along very well.

"I think it was in the fall of 1977, there was a seminar at our church about marriage and family. It was several hours long, and was conducted by a clinical psychologist who works out of a psychiatrist's office. My wife brought it up and said, 'Why don't we go?' and I said, 'Yeah.' I think she was sort of surprised," Graham said.

He glanced up at the wall, trying to visualize that day.

"The psychologist had a lot to say about interaction and people being different. It sounded good, so we decided that we could make things better in our relationship if we'd go talk to him. Over the next few months, we had several sessions together. And it seemed like our relationship was better for a while. We managed to get some things out into the open, what we like and what we don't like, but somehow, during the year, it kind of wore off. I felt like I was acting—that I was saying things I was supposed to say—and I didn't really feel as close as I was trying to sound.

"I was a whole lot less interested in sex. Early on, in the early years of our marriage, I was more interested in sex than she was. More recently, I became less interested and she became more interested. It wasn't like impotence, in the sense that if I was inclined to perform, there was no problem, it was just that I wasn't interested in initiating anything, like I had in years past.

"During 1978 and through the fall, I was really feeling uncomfortable and it gradually got to the point where I felt it was almost intolerable. I believe strongly in family groups staying together, in children having two parents. But the situation got to the point where I felt I could just not live with her. We had a few discussions, and it sort of came to a head during the Christmas holidays. We talked about how maybe I should live somewhere else.

"Fortunately, a year or two before, my mother had passed away and left my sister and me a rice farm in south Louisiana, that had oil and gas royalty income. I was thinking Kathy could stay in the house, and I could go live in an apartment or something. I was going to give her like twenty-five hundred or three thousand dollars a month, just to make sure there would be no financial burden," Graham said.

"New Year's Day, 1979—we had had a long talk that night, most of the night in fact, and early in the morning I said, 'As difficult as it's going to be, I just can't stay.' I packed up what clothes I could get into the Camaro, a few belongings like my tool box, deer rifle, jogging shoes, and I went to a motel. I was trying to think of what to do, and I thought that maybe I could buy a mobile home, so I rode around. It was New Year's Day, and everything was closed. I went back to the motel, and I called her and told her where I was.

"She called me around suppertime, and asked me to come back, drink a Coke, and talk to the kids. I wasn't bitter or angry—I wanted to have a friendly, civilized separation—so I went and visited for a while, and I left. Later, she called again and said she didn't feel good, and she thought she was getting dizzy. She had had some problems with anxiety a year or two before, and I was reasonably certain that this was an anxiety-provoking situation. She said she was uncomfortable and could I please come back. I packed up and went back to the house.

"We talked for a while, and we finally decided we'd go see a different counselor and try to work things out. We had too much going for us over the years to just throw it out. So I agreed. The main thing was that I was interested in leaving the difficult interactions; it wasn't that I disliked her. So we had a long talk, and we ended up getting hold of another counselor, Milton Rosenzweig. The separation was only a matter of hours, probably less than twelve hours.

"We started seeing Milton Rosenzweig, and he was really good. We got into the differences in our background, how one thing is not right or wrong, just different. We went to see him every week for a couple of months—this is in the spring of '79."

Graham smiled. "Kathy changed the most, in terms of her attitudes and behavior toward me. She became softer, a little quieter, letting me take my time about getting something out when I had something to say, appreciating that I will *never* react to things the way she does. It was really a very, very good experience for us. This is probably the best year we've had in many, and this coming August will be eighteen years."

He hesitated for a few seconds, and his voice softened. "During January of 1979, after I had decided to leave and we hadn't begun to talk to a counselor, there did occur, I guess you would call it, an affair. It was still a bad time in my life. I was down. I was not enthusiastic about my work or about life in general. I ended up talking more and more to my research associate, Judith Carson. She's worked with me since I came to Shreveport in 1975. We became good friends.

"Judith's very different from my wife, in the sense that she's quiet, soft-spoken, a good listener. One thing led to another, and, it's hard to explain—how can you be in love with two people at the same time? I'm not sure exactly what her relationship is with her husband. It's not that she wanted to get out of her marriage any more than I did. We just needed something that we weren't getting from our other relationships.

"We went to lunch, or went for a ride, and I guess, like they say, one thing led to another. We ended up in a motel several times during 1979, in fact up until recently, like a month or two ago.

"On the weekend of March twenty-eighth, I went with the LSU Medical School Faculty on a faculty retreat. We went down on a Friday afternoon and stayed through Sunday morning. I got home Sunday the thirtieth, while the rest of the family was at church. We had lunch, I don't remember exactly what we did—I think I worked in the yard—just an ordinary family Sunday afternoon. Sunday night, we watched a little TV and went to bed around the regular time, between ten and eleven.

"The next thing I remember, between two and three in the morning, my wife waked me up and said she heard something. Now this is not unusual—she's done it ever since we've been married. And I found out a long time ago that it's easier to get up and make a round through the house and go check whatever it is—a faucet dripping, a noise in the closet—than it is to try and tell her she didn't hear anything. And since we've been in this house, my son has a hamster, and the hamster has gotten out sometimes— the dog will bark. Anyway, I got up, and I went into the family room and turned on one lamp, a wall lamp, and looked and I could see the front door is closed and the patio door is closed. I went into the kitchen and looked, and the utility room door is closed, the door leading into the garage, the hamster was in his cage—everything looked okay. I went back to bed.

"The whole time I was up, I was trying not to get too wide-awake, so that as soon as I hit the sack I could go back to sleep. As I remember, my wife was in the middle of the bed, on her side facing away from me, and I got in on my side of the bed and turned over up close to her. She pretty well sleeps in the middle of the bed, up close to me, and I sleep on the edge. As best I can remember, this is how we got into bed.

"Now, the next thing I can really remember is being awakened by a violent movement, a lurch of the bed, the bed shook suddenly, and all of this happened practically simultaneously—I heard a short scream, that seemed to be sort of cut off. Somebody or something grabbed me—I was coming up out of a deep sleep and I was pushed or pulled or dragged off the bed. I remember hitting the floor, on my back. I was sort of struggling, then a sharp pain in my side, under my arm, and I kind of grabbed and I got a pain in my hand, and it turns out I was stabbed. All of this is going on too fast, and I don't know exactly what was happening, but it hurt, and I didn't seem to be able to get ahold of anything—I felt sort of helpless. Somehow, I got the impression that there were two people in the room— I don't know if that's from seeing silhouettes—then I had the feeling that I was picked up, sort of jostled around, and it seemed like there were too many hands just to be one person. I was pushed back and forth or something, then flung against the wall by the door to the bedroom. I don't actually remember the impact of hitting the wall, I remember some time later waking up with my head up against the baseboard, the right side of my neck was a little strained, stiff. I definitely had the feeling that I had been unconscious, I don't know if it was twenty seconds or twenty minutes.

"I remember pushing up, getting up, turning on the bedroom light, turning around, and it was a horrible sight.

There was blood all over, that's the first impression I got: blood all over the bed, the bedding, it seemed like all over the wall, and my wife was laid flat on her back, and somehow, I just sort of knew she was dead. All of this didn't take very long to take in, and I turned the light off."

Graham talked into the recorder about going to the lavatory in the master bathroom to wash up. He described touching his wife's body, leaving the bedroom, and locking the door behind him.

"I did leave the room and locked the door behind me, thinking, *I can't let the children see this, it's terrible, I've got to call the police and an ambulance immediately.* I don't know why I said ambulance—I was sure my wife was beyond help, and I didn't seem to need one badly, even though it hurt."

Graham described calling the neighbors and putting his pants on while waiting for help to arrive. "Jerry Siragusa came running in, saying, 'What happened?' and I told him briefly that the door was locked and I had to wake the children up and get them out of there. He went with me, and I went to my oldest son . . ."

Graham described in detail getting the children out of the house. He talked about the arrival of the police patrol officers, going to the hospital, and each of his conversations with Shreveport Police detectives.

Then Graham explained his theory concerning the murder. "I think these two guys came into the back yard, into the patio, and maybe the dog barked. It's not much of a dog, but maybe that's what my wife heard the first time. They opened the [garage] door and either sweet-talked the dog or the dog just ran out so as not to be cornered. My crowbar was found on the [garage] floor by the door, so apparently they used that to break into the door. When I finally did get back to my house Tuesday, I found my tool box in disarray. I have an old hunting knife that was out of the sheath on the workbench, which it never is—my new hunting knife is missing, gone completely. Apparently that is what I got stabbed with—I got stabbed with my own knife, but I didn't know that at the time.

"Anyway, these guys found this knife, and the sledge-hammer—a four-pound, short-handled sledgehammer—on the shelf right over the tool box, and why they took it I have no idea. They opened the back door, which didn't take a lot. There were some marks where they jimmied around and they must have come in and gone right around the corner and started opening cabinets in the first place they came to, my desk area. There were bottles spilled out; maybe they started taking swigs of vodka or gin or something like that. I think perhaps they were taking some sort of drug which interacted with the alcohol and they went berserk.

"Then, I think they got this idea, 'Let's go check out the bedroom,' and they came down the hall, they peeked in one door and saw it was just a child's room, and closed the door so as not to wake them up and went to the master bedroom. Maybe they figured they could get in and get around and nobody would wake up—who knows if they were taking drugs or had drunk from my bottles or both? Maybe they came in with the intent of killing the adults in the house so it'd be easier to search. Again, I have no idea about motives. Maybe they knew I worked at the medical school, and they thought I was a doctor and had drugs in the room. Anyway, when they came in my wife heard them, sat up suddenly, and screamed and one of them hit her. The other came around the bed, the one that hit her had the hammer, and the other came around with a knife to me, dragged me out of bed. I don't know how many times my wife was hit—I gathered more than once—several times maybe. Maybe he just kept swinging when the other guy pulled me out of bed. At some point, both of them—there were too many hands— I got thrown up against the wall and knocked unconscious. Now why they didn't keep stabbing me or begin beating me, I don't know. Maybe the first one thought I was stabbed in the chest and hurt much worse than I was; then when he threw me I was limp. Maybe the one that grabbed me first was more coherent than the other one. Maybe the other one who was swinging the hammer was the most berserk, and the other one, the one who grabbed me, convinced him,

'Look, let's get the hell out of here,' and they took off.

"I don't know how long I was out. I don't know how many times my wife was hit. Maybe they just took off running then.

"The things I found missing were a flashlight that's normally kept where these whiskey, vodka, and gin bottles are, and I have a can, a baby-food can, that I have kept dimes in for years. I had a hundred and fifty dollars in paper rolls and then a handful more of loose dimes as well as some foreign money. . . ."

AT the request of Paul Carmouche, Shreveport detectives interviewed neighbors, friends, co-workers, and acquaintances of the Grahams. The conversations were condensed and sent to the D.A. in a large file that contained police reports from the first seven days following the homicide.

Carmouche had been anxiously awaiting the arrival of the material, hoping to find enough to take the case before the grand jury. The first batch of police interviews resulted in a number of interesting comments.

Mike and Marsha Stringer, who had loaned their house to the Grahams the first night following the murder, talked for more than an hour with Detectives Pittman and Ogburn. Marsha told the investigators that she and Kathy were very close and that she knew about Lew and Kathy's earlier marital problems. Kathy told Marsha that during the period when she and Lew were having the most trouble, Lew had said he didn't love her. Kathy had said she didn't understand how Lew could be so unemotional.

Down the street from the Graham house, at 2022 South Kirkwood, investigators interviewed Mr. and Mrs. Ron Rak. The Raks said they didn't know the Grahams very well, but on the night of the murder, something unusual happened at their house. The Raks' son, Mike, who was about Katie Graham's age, told them that at about 2:30 a.m. he was awakened by a noise. The boy said that he went to the rear door leading into the garage and saw a man standing outside in the carport. The man was white, with dark hair and a moustache, and he was wearing a tan leather jacket, blue jeans, and a black hat with ear flaps. Mike also said the man was tall and thin and had a black eye.

Mike Rak told Detective Ogburn that he turned on the light, and the man ran as soon as he saw Mike. Mr. and Mrs. Rak said that their son had never told them anything like that before, but that they weren't sure he was telling the truth. They also mentioned that Mike was on medication for being hyperactive.

Immediately next door to the Raks, Mr. and Mrs. Watts told the same detectives that their son, aged four, had come into their room that night at two or three o'clock, saying he had had a bad dream. The Watts boy didn't mention seeing or hearing anything unusual.

Carmouche couldn't help but be struck by the coincidence in the time of these occurrences and Graham's early statements about when his wife had first awakened him, saying she heard something.

NESBITT and Carmouche both spent a lot of time wondering whether one of the Graham children might have had something to do with their mother's death.

David, Eric, and Katie had given only very brief statements to the police, and Carmouche wanted to find out more about their recollections of March 31. In preparing a list of witnesses to be subpoenaed before the grand jury, Carmouche added the Graham children to the list below their father's name.

Sutton smelled indictment in the air and asked one of his law partners, Glenn Walker, to help him organize Lew Graham's case.

Walker worked frequently with Sutton on trial matters. Preparation is the key to effective courtroom advocacy, and Walker had an almost photographic memory for statutes and rulings that the lawyers might use in arguing the case before a judge. Walker was shorter and meatier than Sutton, with a trimmed white beard that gave him a professorial air. He and Sutton worked well together, with Walker handling most of the writing and case research and Sutton concentrating on the courtroom action.

Sutton and Walker met privately with District Attorney Carmouche in an attempt to convince him that he would be wrong to seek an indictment against Lew Graham. It was obvious to Carmouche that Sutton and Walker truly believed in their client's innocence, but that had little to do with the prospects for the grand jury.

"Hey, Bobby, Glenn, I gotta do what I gotta do. I respect your opinion, and I know you guys are sincere in your beliefs," Carmouche said. "But the truth is, I've got a whole police department that is convinced your client killed his wife. I'm going to let a grand jury hear it, and we'll let the chips fall where they may."

ON the evening of April 18, 1980, a deputy served subpoenas on Lew Graham, commanding his and David, Eric, and Katie's appearance before a grand jury. Though Sutton and Walker had told Graham that the children might be called to testify, he was still surprised to see the D.A. actually do it.

"It's silly, and I think it's asking too much to get the kids involved in all of this. They're reaching far enough to try and say that I had something to do with this, but to make the children come in . . . I just wish there was something we could do about it," Graham said.

"Maybe there is. Glenn and I have an idea. Give us a day or so, and we'll be in touch," Sutton said. He told Graham that a Louisiana grand jury was little more than an inquisition, in which the children would be led one at a time into a closed room where, sitting in front of the members of the grand jury, they'd be forced to respond to any question put to them. According to Sutton, the entire session would be one-sided and completely orchestrated by the D.A.

"It's pretty antiquated. No attorneys but the prosecutor are allowed into the grand jury room—no spectators, no nothing. And the jurors hear only the D.A.'s side of the story; there will be no defense. It's much more intimidating than testifying in court, and for a child who's recently lost a mother, it's just unthinkable," Sutton said.

With Graham's consent, Sutton and Walker filed a motion to quash—a challenge to the District Attorney's subpoenas, hoping to prevent the Graham children's compulsory appearance before the grand jury.

Carmouche was surprised, and impressed, by the defense motion. He and his first assistant spent long hours researching the law, looking for statutes to reinforce their contention that the children should be required to testify.

In an emotional clash between the D.A.'s office and Graham's legal counsel, District Judge Gayle Hamilton agreed with the defense contentions and canceled the grand jury subpoenas. Angry at the ruling, Carmouche appealed to the Louisiana Supreme Court. It took several weeks for the high court to agree with an amended version of the original ruling.

The grand jury investigation into Kathy Graham's death went on without the children's testimony. In late April witnesses began appearing.

One of the first was Lew Graham, whose testimony was confined to a prepared statement. "The District Attorney has advised that he is going to indict me in this case. And because I'm innocent, I'm not going to help him do that. Accordingly, upon the advice of my counsel, I would like to assert my Fifth and Sixth Amendment rights and refuse to answer on the grounds that these answers may tend to incriminate me."

Several friends and neighbors were also called as witnesses. As all grand jury testimony is secret, it is not known what testimony they gave, though it most likely corresponded with the statements they gave to the police.

Ray Herd represented the Northwest Louisiana Crime Lab and likely described the various blood types found throughout the house. The coroners, McCormick and Braswell, went over the results of their respective autopsies.

Judith Carson, Graham's lab assistant and admitted former lover, came in twice before the grand jury. Through an attorney she had been negotiating for amnesty, but that request was in limbo during her first grand jury appearance.

Since she stayed in the jury room for only about one minute, it's assumed that Carson also took the Fifth. At a later appearance, testifying under a D.A.'s grant of amnesty, she was in front of the grand jurors for almost an hour.

Graham's legal counsel was completely shut out of all the information gathered by the grand jury. They were hard-pressed to develop a defense strategy, since they knew little more than what Graham could tell them. They did tell their client to expect an indictment and contacted a local bonding company to prearrange a bail bond.

On July 15, 1980, over three months after the violent death of Kathy Graham, a "true bill" was returned by the grand jury. Judge Hamilton issued a bench warrant, and Sutton and Walker brought Graham to the judge's chambers for a formal arrest. After fingerprinting and processing, Graham posted a $200,000 bond and, within an hour, was back home with the kids.

The case of the State of Louisiana versus Lewis Texada Graham, Jr., had begun.

8

July 28, 1980

Mr. Paul Carmouche
District Attorney
Caddo Parish
Shreveport, Louisiana

Honorable Sir:

I have great respect for the office which you hold, and for you whom the people have elected. I respect any honorable man who gives up so much to pursue justice. However, as the grieving aunt of Kathleen Graham, I feel that I have the right, and that I must for my own conscience' sake, object to the indictment of Lew Graham.

Kathy's mother, her grandmother, and myself (her mother's only sister) are all in accord and believe this man to be innocent.

The fervent prayer of the grieving family of Kathy is that the real criminal will be caught and an innocent father will be left in peace to bind up the wounds of himself and his children.

If justice is to prevail, the three elder women who

loved Kathy so dearly feel the trial should be moved
from Shreveport.

Dolores Hall
Homestead, Florida

Graham's daily routine changed radically in the weeks that
followed his formal murder charge. He and the children had
moved from 2033 South Kirkwood to their new home in
Chasewood Estates.

It didn't take long for the murder charge to affect his
work, in more ways than one. Soon after the formal indictment, Graham heard through the grapevine that he was to be
relieved of his duties as Assistant Dean for Student Affairs.
He called the dean of the Louisiana State University system
in Baton Rouge to verify the rumor and learned that in addition to losing the assistant dean's position, he would also
have to give up all teaching duties. The decision irritated
Graham, as he believed the school was choosing to convict
him before he ever received his day in court. He politely
requested a formal, written ruling on the decision. He got it.

Because he was tenured, the Shreveport medical school
was obliged to keep him on staff. He was reassigned to
work full-time as a research scientist.

Without mentioning any details, Graham quietly recommended to his immediate superior that Judith Carson be
transferred to another position. That request was immediately granted.

Now Graham spent most of his time at work trying to
finish writing a few research papers, but he wasn't able to
concentrate well. The combined responsibilities of being
a single parent, living under the pending indictment, and
trying to build a defense drained him of energy. It didn't
take him long to lose all enthusiasm for his work.

Walking the corridors of the medical center, he couldn't
help but wonder if people were whispering about him behind
his back. Conversations sometimes came to a halt when he
walked into a room, and he got the feeling people were
watching him, asking themselves, "Did he kill her?" Some

days it was all he could do just to make it to work.

One way Graham dealt with the stress was to increase his daily exercise regimen. He'd been a jogger for several years, and neighbors around Kirkwood Drive had gotten used to seeing him out for early-morning runs. But now he attacked his running with renewed vigor. Al Vekovius, a gregarious, Nordic-looking computer mathematician, got into a habit of running with Graham near the medical school at lunchtime. Vekovius had met Graham during the faculty retreat the weekend before Kathy's death. He thought the murder charges were preposterous—a prime example of a miscarriage of justice. Vekovius and Graham ran together several times a week, and their jogging became a catalyst for a number of detailed conversations about Kathy's death.

Vekovius used to kid with Graham. "So, Lew, you want me to put you on an airplane?" he would ask—in jest, though he was interested to see his friend's reaction.

Graham would always smile. "No, that's okay. Sutton says we have a real good case. He says there's nothing to worry about."

The faculty members at LSU Medical School were divided in their opinions about their colleague's guilt or innocence. Medical schools and hospitals are known for being gossip centers. The campus rumor mill worked overtime coming up with new and more exciting tidbits about the Graham family.

One rumor was that Graham had taken out a million-dollar life insurance policy on his wife, then bumped her off for the money. Virtually no one at the medical school knew about Graham's inheritance, which provided him an outside income of over $100,000 annually.

A lot of people thought Graham might be protecting one of his children—making up a story to hide the fact that one of them had committed the murder. One very juicy rumor was that David Graham was a down-and-out drug addict who owed a lot of money to a local pusher. The pusher, according to this rumor, had murdered Kathy Graham in an attempt to frighten David into paying up. The truth was, David Graham was a very straight kid, totally clean, and had never even smoked marijuana.

Lew Graham and his younger sister, Elizabeth Ancelet, grew close, much closer than they had ever been. They saw each other almost every week, either in Lafayette or Shreveport. The Ancelets managed to get a friendly divorce, and Graham and Elizabeth took their kids to Disney World in Orlando. Not only Elizabeth but the entire family on both sides had supported Graham strongly since the murder, frequently telling him that they believed in his innocence, confident that everything would turn out all right.

There was talk that Graham had become a "free spirit" after his wife's death—even going so far as to buy a flashy sports car. The truth was, Al Vekovius had offered to sell him his white 1968 Porsche 912, on the condition that Graham give the classic car a good home. Graham was a tinkerer anyway and enjoyed the challenge of trying to keep the sports car running. Graham paid $6,000 for the car, which had well over 100,000 miles on it, and the Porsche spent as much time up on blocks as it did on the street.

SUTTON and Walker spent untold hours going over every aspect of the Grahams' lives. Their frustration was building, and they repeatedly met with Graham to gain insight into his marriage and work and to rehash the events of March 31, 1980.

The lawyers knew that to defend Graham properly, they had to have a clear understanding of every aspect of the crime scene. Although they frequently told Graham how much better it would have been if the bedroom hadn't been cleaned before they had been retained, they recommended that he hire his own group of experts to look over the evidence. Technical forensic experts from Dallas were hired and came to Shreveport to inspect the scene at 2033 South Kirkwood. Dr. Charles Petty, a nationally known forensic pathologist, was retained to study the two autopsies of Kathy Graham and to develop his own opinions about the manner in which she was killed. The experienced criminologist Dr. Irving Stone spent a full day inside the house looking for bloodstains and other evidence which might have been overlooked by the police and the clean-up crew. These two professionals gave the defense team the same kind of expert analysis that the District Attorney received from the crime lab.

Sutton and Walker canvassed Kirkwood Drive, speaking to everyone they could find. Some neighbors were hostile, openly expressing the belief that Graham was the killer. Others had significant information, and the first lists of potential defense witnesses were drawn up.

Sutton and Walker interviewed virtually everyone who had ever known the accused man and his wife. When they finished with the present, they started on the past, tracking down old high school and college chums of Lew Graham's, in hopes of putting together an impressive group of character witnesses. They also spent a lot of time talking strategy, trying to anticipate what kind of case Carmouche would present and planning their response and counter-arguments.

During a long meeting with Graham, Sutton went through their strategic options. "When you are preparing to defend a charge, you want to use everything at your disposal," he said. "The way we see it, you really have three distinct defense strategies."

"Three? That's great."

"You may not think so when I tell you. One defense would, of course, be your story about what happened. We've been able to come up with several things that can support the contention that there were people running around the neighborhood. In addition to the evidence at your house, where the back door was pried open and such, we've located several neighbors who will testify that they had had strange occurrences at their homes. There's a kid up the street who saw someone in his garage; we've got dogs barking and the like. Anyway, that's defense number one."

"Sounds good."

"Defense number two," Sutton said, "is simply to try to shoot holes in the D.A.'s case. Whatever evidence he puts on, whatever his witnesses say, we try to tear down their credibility with strong cross-examination. In effect, we'll say that he hasn't proven his case."

Graham nodded. "And number three?"

"That's the tricky one. We need to be prepared in case the jury doesn't believe your story about someone coming in. If they start to think, for example, that somebody inside the house was involved, then we have to convince them that there are really three suspects, and they can't say for sure which one did it."

Graham looked puzzled. "What do you mean?"

"What I'm saying, Lew, is simply that we need to show, however subtly, that others in the house that night *could* have done this, and that there is evidence inside that house that doesn't have a specific name on it."

"You want to suggest that David or Eric might have killed their mother?"

"Only that it would have been possible," Sutton said, "and that the jury can't determine, beyond a reasonable doubt, which one of the three did it."

"That's crazy. It's crazy to think they could have been involved and crazy to want to imply that. I won't allow it. No, sir, not under any circumstances."

"I realize that it sounds strange, but Glenn and I feel very strongly that this is in your best interest."

Graham was adamant. "How can it be in my best interest to suggest that one of my children is a murderer? First of all, it isn't true. Now, I have a great deal of respect for you and Glenn. But this crosses the line. No, sir, I can't go along with this."

"I understand how you feel, Lew. But we just don't know how a jury is going to see all this. The correct defense strategy is to use every tool at your disposal. If we aren't able to prove your innocence, then we have to put doubt in the minds of the jury. And the sort of subtle things we're talking about will feed that doubt."

Graham shook his head. "Forget it. You are not to hint, imply, or otherwise suggest that those boys had anything to do with this. We'll have to do the best we can with what we've got. Which is the truth—that someone broke into my house, attacked me, and killed my wife."

• • •

SEVERAL months after the murder, Bennett Kitchings was named the Liaison Officer for the Caddo Parish D.A.'s Office. Officially, his job was to keep track of the flow of paperwork between law enforcement agencies and the prosecutors. Unofficially, he became Carmouche's personal investigator on the Graham case. By now he and his wife were convinced of Graham's guilt, and he spent hours running down rumors, following up leads, and trying to piece together the details of the Grahams' life.

The D.A. sent Kitchings around the medical center, looking for any other girlfriends Graham might have had. None turned up.

The whole time Kitchings was working for Carmouche, he would periodically run into Lew Graham at school functions or social events. He was always friendly and never let on that he thought the other man a murderer.

IN August, Sutton met with Graham about an idea that the defense team had.

"Lew, I want to run something by you. You've heard of hypnosis, but have you ever heard of using hypnosis for memory enhancement?" Sutton asked.

"What do you mean?"

"The classic example of enhanced memory is like when someone witnesses a bank robbery and sees the getaway car. Sometimes, under hypnosis, they can be helped to remember the license number," Sutton said.

"You want me to get hypnotized about that night?"

"Right. We need every single shred of information we can get our hands on. The D.A. may have all the physical evidence, but we've got you, if we can pull all your memory to the surface," Sutton said.

"I'm game."

"I know a psychiatrist who does hypnosis. I think I'll send you over to see him. And I want him to give you a complete mental examination too. I believe in you, and Glenn believes in you, but there's always the slightest chance that somebody could do something and have abso-

lutely no memory of it later. I want you to go see Dr. Paul
Ware," Sutton said.

"What you mean is, you want to make sure I'm not
crazy?"

"We both know you're not. But when we go to court, we
can use Dr. Ware's testimony that you're calm and sane to
help convince the jury that you are innocent."

"Fine. Set it up, and let me know when you want me to
go. You might want to talk to Milt Rosenzweig too; he was
our marriage counselor. He probably knows more about me
and Kathy than anyone."

"I'd already planned on it. We'll get hold of Ware, and
either Glenn or I will be in touch before the week's out.
Give my love to the kids," Sutton said.

GRAHAM'S first meeting with Dr. Ware was on August 4.
After a very brief physical, the psychiatrist took a family
medical history, then told Graham that he needed the benefit of a number of psychological tests. Since Ware didn't
do his own testing, he arranged for Graham to go see a
psychologist the next day. The psychologist gave Graham
four separate tests designed to develop an in-depth profile
of his personality. The tests indicated that Lew Graham was
highly intelligent, with an IQ of 132, placing him among the
top two percent of the population. There were no signs of
schizophrenia or other serious emotional imbalances, and
the psychologist's report essentially gave Graham a clean
bill of health.

On August 15, Dr. Ware hypnotized Graham in his office.
As is standard procedure for hypnosis in a clinical setting, the
entire session was videotaped with Graham's consent. Under
hypnosis, Graham "re-lived" the night of March 31. In full
and great detail, he went over his complete remembrance
from the night of the murder, and though there were a few
additional recollections, he told essentially the same story
he'd been telling all along.

Ware was convinced Graham was telling the truth, and
reported that opinion to Bobby Sutton.

9

IN late August, Paul Carmouche and Ray Herd flew
to Evansville, Indiana, to meet with Professor Herbert
MacDonell. MacDonell was a former chemist with the
Corning Glass Company who in the early sixties had begun
a career in an unusual area of forensic science.

MacDonell was a criminologist who described himself as
an expert in the unusual field of bloodstain pattern analysis.
A blood spatter expert, it is said, can look at the size, shape,
and distribution of bloodstains in and around a crime scene
and come to specific conclusions about the circumstances
surrounding the bloodshedding. Herd, himself recognized
in district court as a blood spatter expert, had gotten to
know MacDonell during his travels to various criminology
seminars and had convinced the D.A. to try to recruit the
professor as a prosecution witness.

Carmouche was convinced that Lew Graham was a murderer, but he had serious doubts that he would be able to
prove it in a court of law. "We can say all we want to about
Graham's quiet nature," he told Herd, "and the fact that he
didn't seem upset on the day of the murder. We can play
the tape recordings of his interview with the police. But
what I don't have is very strong, believable evidence that
will prove that he swung that hammer. You say that blood

101

spatter proves it—well, let's just see."

MacDonell was in the midst of delivering one of his seminars on blood evidence to a group of law enforcement officers from Indiana. Carmouche and Herd sat quietly in the back of the room for an entire day's lecture.

After the session, Carmouche admitted that he still didn't completely understand the intricacies of the theories, but he believed that MacDonell was the witness who could connect Lew Graham to the murder.

Herd had brought along the sledgehammer, Graham's T-shirt and boxer shorts, and the hunting knife. The three men went up to MacDonell's hotel room to go over the evidence. MacDonell was an experienced traveler and rather thrifty. Carmouche noticed an ice chest filled with soft drinks and snacks sitting on the dresser inside the room.

"Professor, we want you to come to Shreveport and testify at the trial. And we'll pay your normal professional fee."

"That's all well and good, Mr. Prosecutor, but what are you going to do if I don't see what you want me to see?"

Carmouche smiled. "What do you mean?"

"If I look at this evidence and think you've got the wrong man, you should know that I'll be making myself available to the defendant's lawyer," Professor MacDonell said.

Carmouche nodded. "If you can convince me I've got the wrong guy, you won't have to give it to them. I'll do it myself."

Spring 1981

IN April it became obvious that Graham's trial was about to be postponed again. Already it had been set and re-set on the court docket three times, and predictions were that it would be June or July before it began. If anything, the delays served to whet the public's appetite about the Graham case.

Until the trial began, neither the state nor the defense released much information at all about its case to the other. Ordinarily the defense team in a criminal case files a motion for discovery, a legal tool that allows the accused to learn about the key elements of the prosecution's case. But a defendant's discovery request triggers a reciprocal arrangement for the prosecutor. Sutton and Walker didn't want Carmouche to know anything about the findings of their expert witnesses, so they took a calculated risk in not asking to see the D.A.'s material.

In addition, a gag order was in effect, and none of the participants discussed the case with the media, except to say that preparations for trial were continuing. The local news media, shut out of all the pre-trial maneuvering, ran the same basic stories over and over again.

Graham tried to shield his children from the constant coverage of the case, making it a point not to leave the newspapers lying around for them to see. He himself watched the six o'clock news and thought if he heard the word "bludgeon" used one more time he was going to throw up.

Carmouche had personally managed the state's case after the grand jury indictment, responding to the high-profile status. Although he was totally confident in his experience as a trial lawyer, he recognized that he had an extremely complex, circumstantial case on his hands. So far, it looked as though the prosecution would call at least 40 witnesses, and would likely introduce more than 150 separate pieces of physical evidence—everything from photographs to fingerprints to samples of hair and bone tissue. Carmouche started looking around his office for the perfect co-prosecutor. He didn't have to look very far. He picked an up-and-coming young assistant district attorney named Jim McMichael.

IN Jim McMichael's eighteen-month career with the D.A.'s office, he'd already earned a reputation among the staff for his fierce attention to detail and thorough trial preparation. McMichael took his responsibilities as a lawyer very seriously. He tended to shrug off the hard, tough attitude that most of the young prosecutors developed and remained rather idealistic.

Physically, he was hardly impressive. Short, chubby, with fat cheeks and a baby face, he could easily pass for sixteen. In fact, he looked more like the manager of a Baskin-Robbins than a successful prosecuting attorney.

McMichael was a lifelong Shreveporter. His father had retired after forty years with a local construction company; his mother was a librarian with the public school system. In high school McMichael was a conscientious student, garnering all A's and B's. His interest in government had led him to the law. His parents had saved for his college education, and he entered Northeastern Louisiana University.

Jim McMichael's college grades didn't live up to the high marks he'd received in high school, but he held onto a C+ average and was able after graduation to enter LSU Law School.

After receiving his law degree, he went into practice with a college buddy, opening a small firm in an older downtown building. Out of necessity, they made themselves available for work through the Indigent Defender Board, which at the time was under the direction of Paul Carmouche.

McMichael's work as a court-appointed lawyer usually involved small misdemeanor cases in the city court. Often he found himself defending street people and transients. Once, after successfully defending a man on a shoplifting charge, McMichael was pleased with his victory—until he saw his client exit the courtroom in a pair of slacks that still had the store tags on them. The man had apparently stolen the clothes he wore to court.

McMichael's experiences as a fledgling attorney had given him a taste of the real world—a world far removed from the abstract theories taught in law school. Carmouche hired Jim McMichael as an Assistant D.A. shortly after he was elected and was pleased to see him take to prosecuting like a duck to water. After only ten months, McMichael was named a Section Chief and put in charge of several other assistants.

Late one afternoon in April, Carmouche strolled into McMichael's office.

"How would you like to co-prosecute the Graham case?"

McMichael was thrilled. The biggest case to come along in years! "Shit, yeah—what do you want me to do?"

"It's going to be a tough case and a long trial, probably two or three weeks. Get somebody else to handle your other cases. This will take all your time. I'll send down the file—you look it over and help me start organizing it," Carmouche said.

McMichael was at his best when he could drop everything and concentrate on a single case, something he rarely got to do in the frantic pace of the D.A.'s office.

A day or two later, having cleared his calendar, the young prosecutor sat down with a three-foot-thick accordion file. He rubbed his hands together like a starving man in front of a feast. His eyes were wide with anticipation as he opened the file and began to read. "Okay, Dr. Graham, tell me your story," McMichael said.

THE TRIAL

10

THE blue station wagon turned left onto Milam Street four blocks from the courthouse. Graham was in the back seat with his three children; Bobby Sutton, Glenn Walker, and Sutton's secretary, Debbi Ware, sat up front. The car was crammed full of all the support material the defense team would need—mountains of documents, files, and copies of statements they'd collected during the year-long preparation.

It was unusually quiet in the car and Graham assumed that the others were mentally steeling themselves for the big event, as he was.

Being in the headlines was foreign to Graham. All his life he had been a very private person. He didn't mingle well in crowds; it took him a long time to get to know someone, to feel free to make small talk and chat about the trivia of life. Now the most intimate details of his life and marriage would be exposed under the glaring light of public opinion. Graham already had an inkling of what he could expect from the news media. To him, they were responsible for creating the circus-like atmosphere of sensationalism and high drama. He thought the news accounts of his accusation had gone beyond the bounds of good taste.

But here he was, the center of attention.

All of his life he had been quiet and unassuming, content to be a player and not the quarterback, not especially concerned with how he was perceived by people. His married life with Kathy was no different. She was the leader, the outspoken one who made the decisions, herded the kids, ran the household. People gravitated toward her, not him.

It wasn't that he was shunned or disliked by their friends and acquaintances. Kathy Graham was just so outgoing, so vivacious, so in love with life and people and living, that she naturally stood out in a crowd. Lew Graham was intimidated by his wife's superior social skills and her dominance in social settings. Mostly, he recognized that the force of her personality required that he take a back seat when they were in the company of others.

But today, this morning, right now, the spotlight would be on him. Kathy Graham would be there in memory only, nothing more than the tragic victim in a scenario played out on a public forum. The lawyers, spectators, media, and jury would never get to know her. She had been relegated to second string, and now Lew Graham would be on the playing field. To be sure, he didn't relish the role, he didn't want it, and even now, just minutes away from entering the arena, he was more than a little surprised to be standing trial for murdering his wife.

It was 96 degrees—even hotter in the concreted downtown area. A throng had begun to gather outside the courtroom in the Caddo Parish Courthouse around 7:30 a.m. Court bailiffs kept the spectators lined up in a hallway. No one except the lawyers and the defendant would be allowed inside until just before court opened. The people waiting for a chance at one of the precious seats were as diverse as America itself. Right up at the front was a group of elderly ladies, each carrying a sack lunch and attired in a flower-print dress. They looked organized, as if they'd done this before. Behind them was a group of four men, each wearing the standard legal uniform of dark suit, light shirt and bright tie, perhaps hoping to pick up pointers on how to handle a big case. Still more people, young and old, from all walks of life, stood patiently, anxiously, outside Courtroom F. For many, it was the first time they had ever seen the inside of the six-story, white-granite courthouse that took up an entire block of downtown Shreveport.

Presiding in the courtroom was Judge C.J. Bolin, Jr., the gray-haired, wide-faced senior judge for the First Judicial District Court. Sutton had told Graham that Bolin "ran a tight ship and didn't make many mistakes." Graham was happy to hear it, because he wanted nothing more than a fair trial. Judge Bolin had made it clear he would just as soon not have the crowds and hoopla that came with the high-profile case.

Before the trial, the *Shreveport Times* asked the judge to consider moving the trial to one of the larger courtrooms within the courthouse. Courtroom F had seating for maybe seventy-five spectators, which would only accommodate about a third of the number waiting for a seat. Bolin sternly refused to move to the bigger setting, antsy over all the fuss and attention inside his normally quiet, controlled courtroom.

Graham, dressed in a conservative dark-blue sport coat and matching vest, sat stone-faced in a chair, a couple of feet back from the lawyer's table. It was a small table, small for four lawyers, a legal secretary, and a mountain of paperwork. Graham's children had accompanied him inside the courthouse, though they would not be allowed to enter the courtroom and watch the proceedings. David Graham was scheduled to be a defense witness and, along with all the other prosecution and defense witnesses, was barred from the courtroom except during his testimony.

Immediately behind the counsel table, covering the first two benches in the spectator section, just about every radio, television, and print medium in the region was represented. Two reporters who covered the court for rival daily newspapers—the morning *Times* and afternoon *Journal*—called a truce for the Graham trial, teaming up to save each other's place on the crowded media bench.

The audience fell quiet as court clerk Dianne Ellzey stood up to read the charge. "Ladies and gentlemen, the accused stands charged as follows: The State of Louisiana versus Lewis T. Graham, Jr. To which the accused pleads not guilty and places himself before a jury of his country. If you find him guilty, say so. If you find him not guilty, say so and no more. Now, stand together and hear the evidence."

Graham was nervously optimistic about his chances. It had been a long road, getting past the initial police suspicions, finding himself alone against his accusers. When he found Sutton and Walker, everything had changed. He trusted their judgment.

He smiled when he remembered Sutton's lecture about how to look "right" in the courtroom. Graham didn't have to wear a coat and tie at the medical center, but Sutton had cautioned him that conservative attire during the trial was essential. The suit didn't bother him as much as having to wear dress shoes instead of his usual well-worn pair of Hush Puppies.

PAUL Carmouche stood and faced the jury. He was very different from the easy-going, jovial man most people knew outside this environment. This was war, and Carmouche was serious and subdued.

The week-long jury selection had been the most tedious in Caddo Parish legal history. More than four hundred people had been queried as potential jurors. There were seven men and five women, and practically every member either had or did work in a white-collar job. Only one juror was under the age of forty, and in spite of the fact that some forty percent of Shreveport's population is black, there was only one black on the jury.

Dorothy McClamroch, who worked with her husband in the family business, occupied seat number one, in the front of the jury box, closest to the witness stand. Next to her was Reverend David Laverty, a Presbyterian minister. Laverty had already spent a week sequestered away from his family. The rest of the front row consisted of Jean S. McKinney, a white, 54-year-old employee of one of Shreveport's largest banks; 51-year-old James Reeves, a self-employed marketing consultant who had two sons attending the LSU Medical School's New Orleans campus; Clara Irvin, a retired nurse, a Catholic, the mother of three and grandmother of six; and Barney Burks, the oldest juror at age 70.

Behind them sat 68-year-old Marvin Kennedy, a retired cafe-owner from Vivian, Louisiana, a small town about twenty miles north of Shreveport; Robert Etheridge, an executive with International Paper Company; and Thomas McDonald, 62, the second juror with a child at LSU Medical School. The youngest juror, Masie C. Edwards, 37, worked for the Caddo Parish School Board and attended Summer Grove Baptist Church, where the Grahams had been members. The rest of the jury was made up of Pauline Blount, 55, a former garment factory supervisor, and Charles Berthelot, a 46-year-old meter man for the local electric company. Marjorie Oney, a Lutheran grandmother, and Harry Loving, an employee of a pharmaceutical business, were selected as alternates.

For the remainder of the trial, the twelve jurors and two alternates would be kept away from any kind of contact with the general public. They would not be allowed to see or talk to even their closest relatives. Messages between jurors, friends, and family would be passed through court bailiffs, who'd read the messages to make sure there was no mention of anything pertaining to the Graham trial. All news of the case would be cut out of the daily paper before it was given to the jurors to read. They would eat every meal together, mostly in the Holiday Inn where they were staying. There were no telephones in their rooms, and they were not allowed to watch television or listen to the radio. Each morning, the jury would board a chartered bus outside their motel and be driven to court, escorted by two bailiffs. Each evening they would be returned to their motel and fed their evening meal.

Bennett Kitchings sat inside the railing, in a special seat allowed by Judge Bolin. As the liaison to the D.A.'s office, Kitchings was something of an unofficial scorekeeper for

Carmouche and McMichael, ready to pass notes and make comments as the trial got started. A few days before, Sutton had told Graham that all this time, ever since the day Kathy was killed, Kitchings had been against him. Sutton had called Kitchings a "Judas" when he gave Graham the news.

Carmouche paced slowly in front of the jury box.

"May it please the court, ladies and gentlemen of the jury: in this case, the defendant is charged with second-degree murder. During the course of this trial, the State will offer evidence to prove to you, beyond a reasonable doubt, that during the early morning hours of March 31, 1980, Kathleen Thibodeaux Graham was viciously beaten to death by her husband, Lewis T. Graham, Jr.

"The evidence will show the death blows to Kathleen Graham were made by a four-pound sledgehammer, which was left on the floor of the bedroom. The sledgehammer belonged to the defendant.

"The evidence will show the police were summoned at approximately 5:09 a.m. A call was made to Carolyn Godwin, a neighbor, who in turn called another neighbor, Gerald Siragusa. Mr. Siragusa found the defendant and noted he had blood on his T-shirt. Mr. Siragusa then checked the bedroom and found it to be locked by the defendant. Mr. Siragusa assisted the defendant in waking his three children, asleep across the hall from their dead mother. The children were sent across the street to a neighbor's house."

Carmouche paused and looked at the jurors one by one.

"The evidence will show that shortly thereafter, Officer T.H. Willis, the first of the police officers, arrived at the Graham residence. He checked the bedroom door and found it locked and decided to kick it in. Once inside, he found Kathleen Graham in her bed, dead.

"Officer Willis called for additional officers to come to the scene, and Officer Patterson arrived. He checked the bedroom and saw the scene. He checked the entire house, inside and out, and doors, windows, and other entrances in an attempt to find a sign of forcible entry. He found none.

"These officers and other officers found, in the bedroom next to the bed, a sledgehammer, a hunting knife, and a clock that had been knocked to the floor. They found the bed and body of Kathleen Graham covered with blood. Many of the items in the room, and three walls, were spattered with blood."

Carmouche cleared his throat.

"The evidence will show that the defendant was taken to LSU Medical Center by ambulance, where he was treated for a superficial wound to his left palm and a bruise to his forehead. The treatment to a wound on his side required one stitch. The body of the victim was taken to the morgue, and at the morgue autopsies were performed by Dr. Braswell, the Caddo Parish Coroner, and Dr. George McCormick, the Bossier Parish Coroner. Those autopsies confirmed the cause of death was a beating by a sledgehammer.

"During the course of this investigation, the defendant's T-shirt and undershorts were taken to the Northwest Louisiana Crime Lab for testing. The officers gathered other evidence, including bed linens and a lamp that was in the room. They took parts of carpet that contained blood and a piece of a wall that contained blood. They took the headboard off the bed and the clothing of the victim.

"The evidence will show the blood spots found on the defendant's shirt matched the blood type of his wife. The bloodstains on both the front and back of his T-shirt are typical of 'cast-off' from an instrument used to administer a beating. Bloodstains from his undershorts indicate he was within two to four feet of the impact of the blows.

"This evidence, and other evidence that we will introduce during the course of this trial, will prove to you beyond a reasonable doubt that on March thirty-first, 1980, the defendent, Lewis T. Graham, killed his wife, Kathleen Graham."

BOBBY Sutton stood up to take his turn. When Carmouche and Sutton performed, each took on a persona exactly opposite from his usual demeanor. Carmouche, normally so laid-back, almost happy-go-lucky, became rather staid and plodding as he worked the jury. Sutton, normally restrained, quiet, and almost without emotion, brought forth an impassioned presentation much different from his natural disposition.

"May it please the court: Mr. Carmouche, the prosecutor, has just told you what he hopes to prove, to convince each of you beyond a reasonable doubt that Lewis Graham committed the crime with which he's charged. From that opening statement, the evidence would seem to indicate this is a simple case of a beating of the wife by the husband with his own tools. The police performed an efficient investigation. The husband is here now on trial."

Sutton's voice got progressively louder as he continued.

"I will reiterate one thing mentioned to you in the prosecution's opening statement. He said that neither anyone they talked to, nor any of the neighbors, heard or saw anything unusual that night around the Graham home. The defense will prove to the contrary. The defense will prove the neighborhood that night was very, very busy between the hours of three a.m. and five a.m. The defense, as you know, is not required to put on *any* evidence, but it will do just that. It will present evidence sufficient to show that he is, in fact, not guilty of the crime.

"The defense will offer evidence of who and what Lewis Graham is; evidence of where and how he was raised in Lafayette, Louisiana, of his family's academic background and influence in his life, church, and marriage with Kathleen Graham; evidence of the three children, of their relationship with their mother and father, of his years at the University of Indiana, his years at LSU Medical School in Shreveport, and of the defendant's temperament, disposition, and capacity as a human being. In presenting this evidence to you, there will be some bad things, or things you may consider immoral or distasteful, or contrary to Judeo-Christian ethics. Nonetheless, it is our intention to bring you *all* the evidence, the good with the bad, to prove to you the accused did not commit the crime with which he's charged."

Sutton paused, and looked briefly over his shoulder at

Graham, who sat calmly, expressionless, attentive, exactly as Sutton had instructed him. Sutton turned back to the jury. "The defense will show that, as in many marriages, after seventeen years and three children, the electricity of their honeymoon had begun to diminish. Though the defendant and his wife loved each other, there was something missing from their marriage in 1978 and 1979. This was their low point. There was a lab assistant who had worked with the defendant for four years. They respected each other's professional ability. At that point in time, she also was having marital difficulties. So, there they were: at the right place, at the right time, under the right circumstances. This was not, as the prosecution would have you believe, a typical triangle situation.

"So the marriage was at a low point. The defense will show that rather than argue and bicker, as some husbands and wives do, the defendant and his wife, the deceased, the victim, both wanted their marriage to continue. They sought professional counseling. It wasn't a case you sometimes see, where the wife will drag the husband to a counselor. Both the defendant and his wife desired counseling. The reason, you will be shown, was to put their marriage in a better perspective. We will show that as a result of the efforts of both parties, in reflection upon their own attitudes and personalities, the year 1979 and the first three months of 1980 were the best years of the marriage since the honeymoon. It got to the point where the counselor told them, 'You don't need me any more.' "

Sutton turned and walked toward his client, stopping just short of the counsel table.

"And then, March thirty-first, 1980.

"We will show you a chain of events totally inconsistent with any conclusion except that the defendant did *not* kill Kathleen Graham. He did not argue with her that morning. He did not fight with her that morning. He did not strike her that morning. We will show you that in the early morning hours of March thirty-first, 1980, the neighborhood, South Kirkwood Drive, was very, very busy outside the Graham home.

"We will show you that an intruder—indeed, intruders—entered the garage of the Graham residence. There they obtained the tools of the deed—the sledgehammer, the knife. The deceased, Kathleen Graham, heard a noise, and asked her husband, 'I hear something. Will you please go and check and see if someone is in the home?' He walked through the home, checking the doors to see if they were all closed. He found nothing amiss and returned to bed. Then he went back to sleep, comfortable that he had checked his home and no one was inside.

"The next thing he realized he was physically grabbed, taken from the bed, and thrown to the floor. He fought with whomever it was, not knowing whether he was dreaming or whether this was reality. As he fought with what appeared to him to be more than one person, he was stabbed. He continued to fight and was ultimately rendered unconscious. When he awoke, he turned on the light to his bedroom and found the tragedy. He saw the tragic scene of his wife having been killed. He subsequently called a neighbor and had the children taken across the street and called the police and an ambulance.

"We will show you that within four hours after the police arrived they were letting it be known they did not believe the defendant's recitation of what happened. And the public was being told this.

"As a result of this, three terrible things occurred. Number one, the police did not investigate some things that should have been investigated, talk to some people who should have been spoken to, which wider investigation could have led to the identity of the real murderer. Second, because the public had become aware of the attitude of the police by *nine o'clock* that morning, people in the area who had very significant evidence did not come forth with it. They didn't call the police. Their attitude was, 'Well, the police say they have who they think did it, so what I saw must be of no significance.'

"Thirdly, we will show you that every act, every word uttered by the defendant was looked upon to see if it could be used as circumstantial evidence of his guilt. We will show you that, with faith in our judicial system, the defendant did not run and obtain an attorney. He did not carefully guard his every word and comment. To the contrary, he talked to the police at every instance they asked him to, and even in some instances when they did not ask him to. As he would remember something, he would call them and tell them, with faith they were conducting an investigation to find who had killed his wife. As a result of that, he now sits here before you, to be tried and judged."

Sutton looked intently at the twelve decision-makers. "We ask that you keep an open mind as the evidence is presented to you. Do not form your opinion until you have heard *all* the evidence, and I am sure you will not only reach a verdict of not guilty, you will wonder why this man was ever charged."

11

TENSION was high among the four lawyers at the counsel table as the prosecution's first witness edged toward the stand. Carmouche made a note of Sutton's comment, *You will wonder why this man was ever charged.* Carmouche said to himself, *I'll show you why this fellow was charged*!

Carmouche wished that his case had a more dramatic beginning. He realized that the jury was just like everybody else in the community—curious, anxious to hear all about it. He watched his co-prosecutor organize his thoughts as the first witness was sworn in.

McMichael's boyish face belied his intense, detail-oriented courtroom manner. This was his first murder trial, and his fresh-scrubbed appearance and soft, high voice gave no hint of the gruesome evidence to come. Neither did the first witnesses.

Police dispatcher Willie Bryant played a tape recording of Lew Graham's call for help, and in deference to a defense objection, a second tape of the confirmation call-back was also heard. Graham's voice had the same calm tone as he asked for police and an ambulance.

The two spectator benches closest to the jury box were overflowing with media representatives. Two television sketch artists brought the courtroom to life with illustrations for the six o'clock news. Radio reporters hung on every word, ready to break for the telephone—risking the loss of their seats once they got up.

The first witness from Graham's neighborhood was a very nervous Carolyn Godwin. Carmouche noticed that she was having trouble making eye contact with the jury, though she managed to smile quickly at Graham as she was sworn in.

Carmouche realized that they were dealing with a difficult situation, calling acquaintances and neighbors of Graham's as prosecution witnesses. It was unusual to see people having to testify in a criminal case against someone they knew socially. In several pre-trial meetings, McMichael and Carmouche had tried to prepare Godwin and others for telling their stories in a courtroom.

Given her fidgeting in the witness box, it was obvious their reassurance hadn't worked. Godwin's voice cracked several times.

"Mrs. Godwin," McMichael began, "can you tell us what kind of person Kathy Graham was?"

"She was a lovely person. She was kind. She was generous and loving," Godwin said.

"I call your attention to March thirty-first, 1980, and ask if you were at home at that time?"

"Yes, I was."

"Did you receive a telephone call from Lewis Graham that morning?" McMichael asked.

"Yes. It was a little after five a.m. He asked for my husband, and I told him Jerry was out of town. He told me there was a problem in his home, that he thought there were intruders."

Godwin talked in detail about her telephone conversation with Lew Graham that morning, and how David, Eric, and Katie had walked sleepily across the street to her house. She told the jury how she and the Graham kids had waited there together for news.

McMichael walked around the counsel table. "Did you see the defendant later that day?"

"Yes, later that afternoon."

"Did you make any observations about his emotional state?"

"He just looked tired, and drained. I fixed him a sandwich and took it into our office, where he was talking to his mother-in-law."

UNDER cross-examination, defense lawyer Bobby Sutton asked about the Grahams' relatives who had arrived throughout the first day. Sutton's voice and manner were gentle.

"When the Graham family moved back into their house later that week, who all was staying with Dr. Graham? Was the deceased's mother, Mrs. Parish, staying with them?" Sutton asked.

"Yes, sir."

"The deceased's father, Mr. Thibodeaux?"

"He was staying in my house."

"Dr. Graham's sister, Elizabeth Ancelet?"

"She stayed in my home one night, and after they moved back in, she spent some nights with the Graham family," Godwin said.

OFFICER T.H. Willis, the first cop on the scene that morning, had a dark, bushy moustache and a twangy Southern accent.

"I took one step in the bedroom, and I seen Mrs. Graham lying in the bed."

"Did you check the body for signs of life?" Carmouche asked.

"No, sir. I could tell from where I was standing she was dead."

"After the other officers arrived, what did you do?"

"I went and interviewed Dr. Graham. He stated between the hours of one-thirty and two, his wife woke him up, and he got up and checked the house, found nothing, and went back to bed. The next thing he remembered, he was laying on his stomach, and when he got up, he seen his wife all bloody."

Carmouche used Willis to introduce various photographs of the house and its interior. The Rules of Evidence required that any photographs offered must be an accurate portrayal of the original scene, and each picture must be identified by someone who had seen the actual scene.

"State's Exhibit 16—can you identify what that depicts?"

"That's a picture of the cabinets, just above the liquor bottles [in the den]," Willis said.

"State's Exhibit 18?"

"That's looking across the kitchen. It shows a telephone, brick wall, and a towel on the kitchen floor."

"Do you recall seeing that towel on the floor in the kitchen?"

"Yes, sir. I picked the towel up once. It was damp."

Willis identified a total of twenty-three photographs taken in and around 2033 South Kirkwood.

ON cross-examination, Bobby Sutton began to pursue the idea that the Shreveport Police had used less than perfect investigative technique.

"Isn't it true that there were a number of civilians that came to the scene and walked into the house and walked around?" Sutton asked.

"No, sir, not while I was there."

On the first row of trial spectators *Shreveport Journal* reporter Gary Hines sat staring at his feet. He knew better. He had been inside the house that morning.

OFFICER Harold Patterson, a thirteen-year police veteran, told McMichael about his arrival at the crime scene.

"Officer Willis told me to come into the bedroom, and I looked at the scene. I checked to see if the deceased was dead. I felt her pulse."

"How did the skin feel—do you recall?" McMichael asked.

"It had a cold clammy feeling."

"Did you talk to the defendant about what happened?"

"Yes, sir. He said he was sleeping and felt the bed shaking and thought he heard a scream. He said he felt himself being stabbed and rolled onto the floor," Patterson said.

"What about his emotional state?"

"He acted nervous, but not real shook up."

"After talking to Dr. Graham, what else did you do?" McMichael asked.

"I checked the outside of the house for signs of a forced entry. A screen that had been torn off, a broken window, anything."

"Did you find any kind of forced entry?"

"No, sir. There were marks on the door leading from the garage to the utility room. In my mind, it wasn't enough to open the door."

Sutton jumped all over Patterson's answer. "When you say you checked the door for signs of a forced entry, what did you look for?"

"Pry marks."

"Did you look at the locks themselves?" Sutton asked.

"Yes, sir," Patterson said.

"Did you see if the deadbolt lock actually worked?"

"No, sir."

"There's a small thing you turn [on the top lock]—did you see if it would move back and forth?"

"No, sir."

"So when they ask you if there had been forced entry, that's with all this in mind [that you didn't check to see if the locks worked]?"

"Yes, sir."

THE first day of the trial hadn't been the classic legal battle the packed courtroom had hoped to see, but at this early point, the two legal teams were merely setting the stage for the evidence to come. If anything, Carmouche and McMichael were a little edgy over the detailed, encompassing way the defense had tried to dissect each one of their witnesses.

A criminal trial is not unlike a boxing match, with quick jabs and punches, each fighter hoping to deliver the one knockout blow that stops the fight and wins the championship. The truth is, more fights and trials go the distance and are won or lost after a series of small battles.

In that sense, Round One went to Lew Graham.

Graham and his attorneys met at the law office to discuss the day's testimony. They had planned to meet at the end of each day to analyze the prosecution's witnesses, trying both to anticipate the future and to discuss any new ideas for Graham's defense.

Bobby Sutton still wanted Graham to let them open up their defense strategy. "Lew, I know we've talked about this before, but Glenn and I feel strongly about this issue with the boys. You have to let us establish the groundwork now if we're to be able to use that defense."

"I thought we had settled that. I don't want David and Eric dragged into this."

"We're not going to come out and say that one of them did it. It's more a matter of establishing the fact that some of the police never even considered them as suspects. While the D.A. is bringing in all these police witnesses, we can simply ask if they checked the boys' fingerprints against some of the evidence—that sort of thing. It'll plant an idea in the jury's mind that we can capitalize on later."

"No. Forget it. David and Eric are not to be mentioned. Just leave things like they are."

SERGEANT Frank Lopez, the lead-off witness on the second day of the trial, was the kind of soft-spoken witness who plays havoc with court reporters and jurors. He and Paul Carmouche had known each other for many years, going back to the days when Carmouche was a young assistant prosecutor and Lopez a lowly patrolman. In one pre-trial conversation, Carmouche told Lopez to be aware of his demeanor on the witness stand and to not let his relaxed manner be interpreted as boredom. Lopez must have listened; he came across as alert and cooperative.

Carmouche began by taking his old acquaintance through each of the rooms of the Graham house, giving the jury and the spectators in the courtroom their first detailed description of the death scene. A large drawing of the interior of 2033 South Kirkwood was placed on an easel, and Lopez was given a pointer to show where various items had been found.

"In the bedroom, there was a fairly large spot of blood in the carpet, where we found the hammer and knife. I instructed Lieutenant Blankenship to take this piece of carpet, and about a foot square was removed."

"Did you go anywhere else in the house?" Carmouche asked.

"Yes, sir. In the hallway, we found a sheath or scabbard for the hunting knife found in the bedroom. In the southwest corner of the den there were some cabinets, and several liquor bottles on the floor, and a pair of binoculars in front of the cabinets.

"I walked back toward the kitchen, and I observed a phone on the wall. The receiver was off, hanging on the floor. I also observed a large bath towel," Lopez said.

"Did you handle the towel at all?"

"I instructed Sergeant Derrick, a member of ID, to make a photograph and collect the towel. I felt it when he finished. It was damp."

Carmouche walked to the counsel table and picked up a cassette tape. It was the recording of Graham's statement, given to Coker and Lopez the morning of the murder.

Bobby Sutton interrupted the flow. "Your Honor, before we proceed any more on this matter, I would like to argue a point of law concerning the way this is handled."

Judge Bolin excused the jurors. In the First Judicial District Court, the judges made sure that all arguments on points of law were made outside the presence of the jury. Jurors, uneducated in the fine points of legal procedure, could misinterpret a legal discussion and form an opinion from matters not germane to the real issue of guilt or innocence. As the last juror exited Courtroom F, Sutton began.

"Your Honor, we are going to object to the playing of the tape at this time, on the grounds it is not reflective of the statement. There was discussion before the statement was recorded that is not included. I'm quite certain the prosecution is not playing the tape for its contents, but for other reasons. I strenuously object to the tape being played under those conditions."

Sutton believed the prosecution was going to introduce a large body of evidence designed to paint a picture for the jury of a cold, unemotional Lew Graham. The defense team had heard the tape in pre-trial preparations and knew that Graham's voice sounded calm and collected on the recording. They were afraid the jury might read something into Graham's relaxed demeanor.

The objection nettled Carmouche, but Sutton didn't mind irritating his opponent.

"Your Honor, I have never heard that type of objection. Obviously, every time a police officer takes a statement, they discuss the matter with the witness, or suspect. Once they get the story, they go back and record it. They do it every time! As far as we're concerned, this is a free and voluntary statement that is perfectly admissible," Carmouche said.

"The fact that a statement is partly inculpatory is what makes it evidence," Judge Bolin said. "The objection is overruled."

The tape recording was played for the jury in open court. The jury heard Graham tell Detectives Coker and Lopez that his wife had awakened him, having heard a noise in the house. Graham described being pulled from the bed, struggling briefly, being stabbed, and being rendered unconscious. He talked of finding the bloody mess, of calling a neighbor, of calling the police.

The tape continued: " . . . *later, the fire medics advised me to get checked by a doctor. I did that, and the detectives met me in the emergency room and suggested I come here. A friend of mine came along to give me a ride home.*"

"*Let me ask you this, Mr Graham, which side of the bed did you get in on?*"

"*I always sleep on the left, facing the bed. I'm sure I got back into that side when I checked the house.*"

"*Do you have any idea what your wife was murdered with?*"

"I have no idea. I had the light on, and looked at her only briefly, to see so much blood, and she seemed to just be lying there. I know enough about physiology to sort of decide that she was dead."

"Mr. Graham, this statement you have given is of your own free will?"

"Yes, absolutely, I certainly want to cooperate in any way, so the police can find whoever did this."

Carmouche turned the tape player off and put it back on the counsel table. "Detective Lopez, you indicated the time was eleven o'clock a.m. at the end of the tape. That was on the day of the murder?"

"Yes, sir."

"During any time you were with the defendant, at the house until you finished the statement, what was his emotional condition?"

"He showed no emotion. He was real at ease and cooperative."

SUTTON finished making a note, and slowly walked toward the witness stand. "Sergeant Lopez, there's just a couple of things I want to ask you to clarify. After March thirty-first, 1980, did you continue to investigate this matter?"

Lopez stole a glance at the prosecutor's table. Carmouche wondered if Sutton had somehow found out about the graveyard shift's anger with Donnie Nichols over stealing their case.

"No, sir. I didn't do anything else on it."

"You said either you or perhaps the ambulance attendant suggested this man should have some medical attention. Do you know what time it was by then?" Sutton asked.

"I'd be guessing," Lopez said.

"If I showed you a copy of what purports to be a medical report from LSU, and it shows an admission time . . ."

"It would be right."

Sutton handed Lopez the report.

"What time was that?"

"Six-thirty."

"While you were at LSU [before bringing Graham to the police station], did you have to wait for him any length of time?" Sutton asked.

"I guess I had to wait a few minutes."

"So you arrived [with Graham at the police station] shortly after seven? Is that fair to say?"

Lopez could see where the lawyer was heading, but he was powerless to do anything about it. "Yes, sir."

"I recall, Sergeant Lopez, it states on the tape that it was done at eleven that morning. Had you talked to Dr. Graham for a period of four hours before you turned the tape on?"

"Thereabouts."

"So everything he said on the tape, he had told you three or four times already?" Sutton asked.

"I don't think he told us three or four times. I disagree with that."

"My point is, Sergeant Lopez, this tape recording is not an extemporaneous first recording of what was said to the police, is it?"

"No, sir."

"Sergeant Lopez, you expressed an opinion about the emotion of Dr. Graham. Did you know Dr. Graham that day?"

"No, sir."

"Did you know anything about his personality, or stress threshold, prior to that day?"

"No, sir."

"I have no further questions."

LT. Dan Coker, now retired from the police department, and night-shift commander at the time of the murder, took the stand next. He toned down his usual tough-sounding delivery, coming across as relaxed and professional. His testimony was essentially a rehash of Lopez's, though Sutton continued to press forward his attempts to discredit the investigation.

The prosecutors spent the next two hours establishing the chain of evidence—the tedious but necessary process of verbally identifying and tracking the trial exhibits from their retrieval from the crime scene through every pair of hands that touched them on the way to the courthouse. Investigators might *point out* a piece of physical evidence, but only identification officers *collect* evidence. If a detective asked someone to collect a sledgehammer, the officer who actually did so would have to testify, "Yes, I picked it up, put it in a bag, put the bag in my car, took it to the police station, put it in a locker, and the next day, took it to the crime lab for testing." The crime lab employee would come in next, saying, "Yes, they brought it in, I took it, gave the officer a receipt, and it's been in our possession ever since."

Lt. James Blankenship was an old pro in Identification at SPD. He looked more like an accountant than a cop, though he made a good courtroom witness. In addition to photographing and collecting evidence, the ID Bureau had dusted the Graham house for fingerprints. Carmouche asked his witness about that.

"I show you State's Exhibit 15. Is that a picture you took?"

"Yes, sir, it's the den area of the house, and it shows some bottles on the floor."

"Did you or Sergeant Derrick do anything with those bottles?"

"I processed the bottles for latent fingerprints. They were dusted with graphite powder."

"Were you able to lift any prints or partial prints?"

"Yes."

"Were you able to match those prints to anybody?"

"No. We had no suspect to attempt to match the prints against."

On cross-examination, Sutton wanted to make a point to the jury about SPD's lack of effort. "Do you ever take the fingerprints you lifted and run them through some intelligence base, such as the FBI?"

"On occasion, if a print is of sufficient quality, it could be broken down into a code number. Normally we don't send latent prints anywhere. If someone needs to compare, they come here."

Carmouche used his redirect to shed light on the fingerprinting issue. "How many prints do you have on file at SPD?"

"Oh, somewhere around a quarter of a million."

"If you have no name, no suspect, you would have to look through a quarter of a million cards?"

"If you had just one print, yes sir. It's an insurmountable job if you have just one print."

Graham had to struggle to hide his irritation. He couldn't believe that the police department had failed to check the fingerprints on liquor bottles from his house. He watched as Sutton attacked again. "Lieutenant Blankenship, there's still something I'm confused about. You know we have this man charged with a crime sitting here. You obviously have his prints on file. You have one or more latent prints you lifted from the liquor bottles. Do I understand you to say you have not checked those latents against those of the accused?"

"To what purpose, to match his prints to his own property?"

Graham grabbed a piece of note paper and scribbled a note to his attorney. "*They don't even know that those are not my fingerprints!*"

MCMICHAEL took over for the prosecution and asked Sgt. Jimmy Derrick to identify a number of items of evidence. Derrick noted Lew Graham's hunting knife, found on the floor in the bedroom. He recognized the carpet cut from the bedroom floor; the linens off the bed; the bath towel, found damp on the kitchen floor; the knife sheath; the crowbar; and the flashlight, found outside by the fence to the Grahams' back yard. He testified there was water in the bottom of the tub, implying someone had washed up shortly before the cops arrived.

Sutton attacked Derrick's evidence-gathering technique. Derrick was forced to concede that there may have been some wet blood on the bed linens, and he admitted that several sheets were bagged together. Sutton asked about the damp towel, found in the kitchen. He reached down inside the bag containing the towel, pressed his hand on the bottom, and withdrew it, displaying a group of small hairs. "Would it be safe to assume these hairs came off that towel?" Sutton asked.

"I would assume that, yes, sir."

"Any idea, Sergeant Derrick, how these hairs got on that towel?"

"My first thought would be someone dried their hair with it."

McMICHAEL and Carmouche were concerned about the way things were going. They met after hours in the District Attorney's fifth-floor office.

"He's getting in some real good potshots at our police," Carmouche said. "Bobby's a smart lawyer. I think they're ahead right now."

"Maybe so," McMichael said, "but the game's not over yet."

"What about all these people from the neighborhood? You think they're going to do us any good?"

McMichael nodded. "If they do, fine, but it doesn't matter. Our really powerful stuff is yet to come. You watch, once we get into all the blood evidence, things will change. Let Graham win a few minor points right now. We'll come out on top in the end."

Carmouche was worried. "What do you think they're going to do when the defense gets a chance to put on a case?"

"Hard to say. I guess we'll find out when the jury does. Don't worry—we're gonna win."

Paul Carmouche stared out the window at the dark evening sky. "I hope you're right. I can't afford to lose this one."

12

THE third day of Lew Graham's trial offered the jury their first detailed look at the medical facts relating to Kathy Graham's death. Caddo Parish Coroner Robert Braswell led off the day for the prosecutors. He brought to court a Styrofoam model of a human head, which looked like the sort of thing used to style a wig.

Experienced courtroom observers knew Dr. Robert Braswell as the kind of witness who could "bore the hair off your head," but his testimony would be crucial in establishing the brutality of the murder. His testimony would introduce a number of very graphic photographs of the crime scene and Kathy Graham's body. In several pre-trial conferences with Sutton, Walker, Carmouche, and McMichael, Judge C.J. Bolin sided with defense objections and ordered a large number of the most explicit close-up pictures deleted from the prosecution's collection. The defense team knew that it was important to keep these photographs to a minimum and successfully argued that overdoing it would inflame the jury against Lew Graham.

Dr. Braswell looked rather intellectual with his longish, snow-white hair and fashionable steel-framed glasses. He took his time drawing circles and various other shapes on the wig stand, indicating the location and size of the wounds inflicted on the victim's head. He identified the sledgehammer as the murder weapon and discussed various details associated with his autopsy.

The prosecution team wanted the jury to understand just how comparatively minor Graham's injuries were. Dr. Braswell, who had performed a cursory examination of Graham's stab wound on the day of the murder, told the jury of his findings: "The wound was not directed toward the chest cavity. There was also a small raised area on his forehead. This was slightly abraded—just redness and swelling."

McMichael probed further. "Did the little bump on his forehead—"

"Your Honor," Sutton interrupted, "I object to that classification as 'a little bump on his forehead.' The doctor described it as abrasion with swelling."

McMichael smiled and turned back to the witness. "The wound or abrasion or swelling or whatever, did it appear to have been treated?"

"No."

"How long were you with him in your office that day?" McMichael asked.

"I'd say not more than ten or fifteen minutes."

"How would you describe his emotional state?"

"He seemed nervous and distraught, but he was calm and cooperative."

"Did he complain of any pain? Any headaches or dizziness?"

"I didn't make any notation to that effect."

During his pre-trial preparations, McMichael had spent some time in the coroner's office. During one visit to the morgue, he and Terry Franklin, the assistant coroner, turned up a potentially juicy tidbit of evidence. "Dr. Braswell, concerning the rings and jewelry you took from the body of Kathleen Graham. Did any family member ever come to claim those?"

"No."

McMichael turned and looked at Lew Graham. "Did anyone ever call about these?"

"Not to my knowledge."

• • •

FOR the time being, Sutton ignored the jewelry question. "Dr. Braswell, based on your experience as a physician, can you say whether or not the wounds to the top of the head would have rendered Kathleen Graham physically immobile, where she could not move?"

"I think the first blow, the depressed skull fracture on the top of her head, rendered her immobile. And whoever delivered the blow—she kept moaning and groaning and maybe making small sounds and small movements. I think the last blow was when she was turned face up."

"You mentioned that when you saw Dr. Graham, he was nervous and distraught, but he could still be calm and cooperative?" Sutton asked.

"Right."

"Mr. McMichael asked you about the rings and earrings Mrs. Graham had on. He asked if Dr. Graham ever came by to collect the rings, and you said he did not. Did you ever tell Dr. Graham, 'I've got the jewelry from your wife, you can come by and get these things'?"

"No."

Sutton's tone was sarcastic. "But then if he *didn't* come and get his jewelry, I guess that would indicate a lack of interest in his wife. And if he *did* come and get it, that would indicate he was only interested in the monetary aspects. Kind of damned-if-you-do, damned-if-you-don't."

"Well, I'm sure I can't answer that properly . . ."

"Have you ever had a situation before where people just didn't come and get the things of their loved ones?"

"Occasionally."

To prove Graham's story was fabricated, the D.A. would need to show that no one in the neighborhood heard anything unusual the night of the murder. To that end, prosecutors first called Jean Johnston, an older woman who lived next door to the Grahams on Kirkwood Drive and had been loving and supportive to the Grahams after the murder. She believed in Graham and was sorry that she had been subpoenaed to appear as a prosecution witness.

During her pre-trial visit with the D.A., she told him that her hunting dogs had been disturbed on March 31, 1980. Carmouche knew she would be happy to talk about her dogs. "Mrs. Johnston, where do your dogs stay at night?"

"They are on our bed, and on the floor. But mostly on the bed. We have a king-sized bed."

"These are house dogs?" Carmouche asked.

"We both like the dogs in the house, and we like hunting dogs. That's one part of our marriage that has always worked out. I spoil them, and he hunts with them."

The spectator area broke out in laughter.

"Did you ever get up at any time during the night?"

"It was exactly one-thirty. I know because I have a digital clock radio. And the reason I looked at the time— sometimes I get up and take arthritis medicine."

"So the dogs got you up at one-thirty?"

"Yes, sir. I knew they wanted to go out. They went running all over the back yard and checked to make sure everything was all right."

"Now, if someone had been by that fence at your house that night, would your dogs have barked?" Carmouche asked.

"If they had smelled—they're hunting dogs. One is a weimaraner, and one's a short-haired pointer. I didn't hear anything."

Mrs. Otto Chandler, the Grahams' neighbor on the garage side, also testified she had heard nothing unusual the night of the murder.

"WOULD you state your name for the record, sir?" Carmouche asked.

"John T. Brauchi. I'm the chairman of the Department of Psychiatry at the LSU Medical Center."

"Do you recall March thirty-first, 1980, as the day Dr. Graham's wife was killed?"

"Yes."

"Did you see Dr. Graham that day?"

"Yes, at a neighbor's house. I was asked to go see him

by the dean. The dean had seen Dr. Graham in the police station and was concerned about him."

"Was anyone else present when you talked to him?"

"Yes, Jim Smith and Bob Smith."

"Did he ever say anything concerning his emotion, or lack of emotion?" Carmouche asked.

"Yes. I was trying to get some feeling about how well he was holding together. At one point, he got up and closed the door and made the statement, 'I don't know whether you know this or not—Jim does. Kathy and I haven't been getting along very well lately, and I'm not as upset as I should be.' That is not an exact quote."

"This was on March thirty-first, 1980? The day of the killing?"

"Yes."

"DR. Brauchi, you are a board-certified psychiatrist, are you not?" Sutton asked.

"That's correct."

"When you heard that statement from Lewis Graham, do you think he said it for your benefit?"

"I think he was trying to reassure me."

"If a person is exposed to a loss, *is* there a normal reaction? Is there such a thing as 'normal'?" Sutton asked.

"Any reaction anybody has to a stressful situation is going to be based on their personality and the stresses they've been through. I would never make a judgment about someone's personality unless I had enough historical background. If I see someone cry, I don't know if it's tears of joy or tears of sadness. I don't know what a 'normal' reaction is."

"If we're talking about Lew Graham on March thirty-first, 1980, would there be any benefit for the father of three young children to make it a point to maintain a stoic personality?"

"I think he was very well in control of himself, in presenting the best picture of stability that he could."

"For the benefit of his children?"

"I believe that."

• • •

CARMOUCHE was worried that the effect of the psychiatrist's testimony had been watered down during the cross-examination. He tried to make the point on redirect. "As I understand your testimony, it wasn't until he made that statement [about not getting along with his wife] that he got up and closed the door?"

"Well, there was some noise coming from the other room."

"Did that statement surprise you?"

"No, not in my business. I know lots of people that don't get along very well."

"But that statement being made the same day as a tragic death—didn't it surprise you?"

"No. The way I was questioning Dr. Graham, I was obviously conveying to him I was concerned about his health and welfare. I think the statement was to reassure me he was not under as much stress as I might have thought."

CARMOUCHE called Dr. Jim Smith to the stand. Jim and his wife, Patti, had been close friends of the Grahams, going back to when they had all lived in Indianapolis. Now the Smiths were convinced that Lew Graham was Kathy's killer.

Shortly before the trial began, Graham had learned that Jim Smith had turned against him. Sitting at the defense table, he stewed, remembering all the times he had run into them in various settings. Though he had always detected a coolness from Patti, he couldn't recall a single time when Jim Smith had let on that he thought Graham was guilty.

"When was the next time you saw Lewis Graham?" Carmouche asked.

"Dr. Brauchi and I asked Lew if we could talk to him alone. We asked to talk because there did not appear to be the responses one might consider appropriate when someone's wife of fifteen or twenty years had just suffered a vicious, brutal death. Dr. Brauchi asked Lew how he felt, if he could describe his situation in one word. Lew said, 'Apart.' Dr. Brauchi told Lew we didn't feel he should be left alone," Smith said.

"Was there any response to that?" Carmouche asked.

"At that point, Lew got up and went and shut the door to the study. He said something to the effect, 'I think Jim already knows this, but Kathy and I did not have a perfect or good marriage. If it had been a better marriage, I'm sure I would be more upset.' It appeared that Lew sensed what Dr. Brauchi and I were getting at—that his emotional state was not reflective of the events."

SUTTON had been prepared for this line of testimony and set about trying to pick apart Smith's opinions.

"Dr. Smith, you were aware in 1979 that the Grahams were having counseling in their marriage?"

"Yes."

"I think you said Dr. Brauchi asked him for a one-word synopsis of the way he felt, and Lew chose the word 'apart.' Would that word be appropriate for someone who perhaps would be subject to a delayed reaction—he was apart, and hadn't felt it yet?" Sutton asked.

"Possibly."

"That's what a delayed reaction is, isn't it? It just hasn't sunk in?"

"Yes."

"Then he indicated to Dr. Brauchi that he was not as upset as Dr. Brauchi would have thought he was?"

"That's not what I said."

"I know it's not what you said. You didn't remember the exact wording of what was said."

"Not the exact wording, but in the spirit he presented it," Smith said.

"Do you recall, after that conversation, Dr. Brauchi said to you he thought Graham had said that for his benefit?"

"No, I do not."

DONNIE Nichols had looked forward to his day in court for weeks. He was proud to have been responsible for Lew Graham's arrest and indictment, and glad to have been the first detective to state openly that he thought the quiet research scientist was a wife-killer.

Nichols walked confidently to the witness stand, looking calmly at Graham as the clerk swore him in. He told the jury of his initial visit to the crime scene and his first suspicions.

Carmouche asked about Nichols's first contact with Lew Graham. "When you looked at the locks [on the back door], did you form any opinion whether someone had come through those locks?"

"It was my opinion the pry marks were old and had not been made in the previous twenty-four hours. In my seventeen years of policing, I've seen numerous burglaries where doors are pried open. It leaves an appearance of new marks where the pry bar pries on the two pieces of wood."

Nichols described in detail his interview with Graham the day after the murder, how the doctor had walked him through everything he could remember from the night of the killing.

"And after he finished, I then explained to him there were some fallacies in his story. I took him over to the side of the bed and said, 'Dr. Graham, can you explain to me the spot of blood on the floor [where you say you were stabbed], but no blood on the floor where you remained unconscious?' He couldn't give any explanation for that. Then I said, 'Can you explain how you got blood on the front of your T-shirt, if you were lying on the floor on your stomach?' He could offer no explanation for that. Then I took him to the bathroom, I said, 'Did you go back over to the bed?' and he said no. I said, 'Did you wash your hands in the sink?' and he said no. I asked him, 'Did you say you flipped the light on, then flipped the light out and left the room?' and he said, 'That's correct,' I said, 'At what point did you retrieve your glasses off the nightstand?' and he couldn't tell me when he got his glasses."

Carmouche sat down and exhaled audibly. He and McMichael were nervous about Nichols's testimony. They assumed that Sutton had gotten wind of the in-fighting with the police detectives, and knew that Sutton could make mincemeat out of an ego the size of Nichols's.

• • •

SUTTON took his time beginning his cross-examination. He waited until the detective lost the small grin that had been on his face.

"Lieutenant Nichols, when you arrived at the Graham residence on the morning of the murder, do you recall, about nine o'clock, opening the front door, and a lady asking for Dr. Graham, and you telling her he was going to be charged with this murder?"

"No, sir. I remember a lady at the front door. I told her Mrs. Graham had been murdered. She asked me if Dr. Graham was under arrest, and I told her it was a possibility."

"Do you remember telling Dr. Robert Smith that that morning?"

"Yes, sir, as he was leaving the detective bureau later that day."

"You know John Harrison, don't you?" Sutton asked.

"The attorney?"

"Yes. Do you remember telling him that Dr. Graham committed this crime?"

Nichols shifted in his seat, and cleared his throat. "I do seem to recall talking to John outside the house, yes."

Sutton walked toward the red-faced detective. "Lieutenant Nichols, when you were telling all these people you had come to the conclusion that Dr. Graham was guilty, did you have any information from the crime lab?"

"Not at that point."

Sutton's tone of voice was as soft as peaches and cream. "Had you received reports from the neighbors as to whether or not they had seen anyone?"

"No, sir."

Sutton turned and paced in front of the jury. "Isn't it true, Lieutenant Nichols, the investigation from that point forward was conducted with that in mind? Your mind was made up, wasn't it?"

Nichols squirmed uncomfortably in the witness chair. His face turned a deeper shade of red, and he appeared to be grinding his teeth. "No, sir, it wasn't."

Sutton took his time. He knew he was making Nichols

anxious, and that was just what he wanted.

"Detective Nichols, you said, in your opinion, the pry marks on the door were not made in the last twenty-four hours?"

"That's correct."

"What test did you run?"

Nichols frowned. "I ran no test, Mr. Sutton; it was a visual observation."

"Did you understand Dr. Graham's story to be, he was thrown to the floor, stabbed, then picked up after a few seconds?"

"That's his words."

Sutton turned on his heel and walked quickly back to the counsel table. His manner had changed now; he was a hunter, stalking, moving in for the kill. "Let's go through what *you* said were the fallacies in Dr. Graham's story."

Nichols rolled his eyes.

"After he was stabbed," Sutton said, "Dr. Graham said he was thrown across the room, and remained on the floor unconscious. I believe your first fallacy was there was a blood spot where he was stabbed, but no blood across the room in the area where he was unconscious? Lieutenant Nichols, what training do you have in the way a puncture wound bleeds?"

Nichols's irritation was obvious. "Sir, I am not a doctor. I am not a blood spatter expert. But I believe I possess an abundance of common sense, and it makes sense to me that if a man is on the floor for a few seconds, how can you explain a spot of blood that big?" Nichols held up his hands in a circle about the size of a grapefruit. "He gave me the impression he didn't lie there for a minute, two minutes, three minutes. Now, I don't know how long it takes a wound to start bleeding, or how long before the wound closes up."

Sutton looked over at Carmouche. The D.A. had his head down, as if he were praying. "Did you ask Dr. Graham if he may have been holding his left arm, holding the wound?"

Nichols shook his head. "No."

"Do you know, Lieutenant Nichols, if you have a puncture wound and you put pressure on it, it will stop the bleeding?"

"Yes."

"You asked him when did he get his glasses. He said, 'I don't know.' In your seventeen years as a detective, you've learned something about the odd little traits human beings have. Have you ever seen somebody walking around looking for their glasses, and they've got them on?"

Carmouche and McMichael looked at each other. The jaw muscles on Nichols's face were clenching and unclenching furiously. "I've heard about it."

"Now, this man, according to his story, had a knife stuck in his side, been rendered unconscious, had a contusion to the forehead, and had found his wife brutally murdered. And he couldn't remember putting on his glasses! *That* was a hole in his story?"

"In my opinion, yes, sir." Nichols's face was as red as a tomato.

Sutton paused and glanced down at his notes.

"Lieutenant Nichols, who was the investigator in charge of this case?"

"There were several detectives on the case, Mr. Sutton, following leads, talking to neighbors, things of that nature."

"Who was in charge?"

"Several detectives, Mr. Sutton."

"Who made the determination to interview all the neighbors in the area and checked to see that each one had been contacted?"

"I don't recall who made that decision. There were several day-shift detectives who went out to interview those neighbors. Basically, Mr. Sutton, I can't go out and lead each detective by the hand and say, 'You do this and you do that.' It's standard procedure to interview the people on the block."

"Then, presumably, there is no neighbor in the vicinity with any information pertinent to this case?"

"If there is evidence of someone in the neighborhood with knowledge of this homicide, I'm unaware of it."

"If the police are not working to solve a crime, if the

police are saying, 'We solved it,' then a neighbor or someone else who has significant information might not be
inclined to call?"

"I can't control the opinion of other people."

"In reciting his story to you—it had holes in it?"

"In my opinion, yes sir."

Sutton paused for several seconds, considering his next
question. "Do you remember on Friday, July tenth, 1981,
me sitting in your office at the Shreveport Police Station?"

"You mean, last week?" Nichols said.

"Yes. Do you remember me asking you if you would talk
to me about this case?" Sutton asked.

"Yes."

"Do you recall telling me that you have learned that
if you attempt to answer questions, you're going to tell
me something that's not consistent with your investigation, and I'd use it against you on the stand?" Sutton
asked.

"Just like you're doing now."

Sutton turned and walked toward the lawyer's table. He
stopped and glanced back at the detective. "Oh, one more
thing, Lieutenant Nichols, just to make it clear—you and I
are close friends, aren't we?"

"Yes."

"My firm has done legal work for you in the past?"

"Yes, sir."

"No more questions."

Nichols stormed out of the courtroom and passed John
Brann in the hallway outside. One look at Donnie Nichols's
face told Brann that things hadn't gone well for him inside
Courtroom F.

"Hey, Donnie, what's wrong? Looks like you've got
quite a sunburn there," Brann said.

RUSSELL Ancelet, now Graham's former brother-in-law,
was called as a prosecution witness. In the months since the
homicide, the Ancelets had finalized their divorce, though
everyone remained friendly.

"As I recall, the detectives were summoned by Dr.

Graham in reference to a back-door lock?" Carmouche asked.

"Yes, sir."

"You were able to enter that door with a pocketknife?"

"Yes, sir, I was."

"Now, when you were there with the police officers and Lewis Graham, was the house put back in his possession at that time?" Carmouche asked.

"Yes, the police released it on the second day, which would have been April first."

"And you had the house cleaned?"

"Yes, I took care of having it cleaned and having the carpets replaced."

SUTTON knew *this* prosecution witness could be good for his side.

"Sergeant Ancelet," he asked, "if I could ask you a few questions about that back door. If those locks had never been opened with a knife before, at least they were by you?"

"Yes, sir. I opened those doors."

"How many locks did you open?"

"Three of them."

"Did it take any special knowledge on your part, or did you just take a knife and slide them back? My question is, it wasn't because you are with the State Police and have some expertise in that sort of thing?"

"No, sir."

"Sergeant, how long have you known Lew Graham?"

"Since 1960."

"How would you describe his personality?"

Ancelet looked Graham in the eye and smiled.

"He's a very quiet, low-key person. He doesn't usually have a lot to say—no small talk. Not until he knows you, anyway."

"Is he a cold person?"

"I wouldn't—no, not to my knowledge."

"Have you ever heard him speak in anger, in a loud voice, for any reason?" Sutton asked.

"Never have."

"Have you ever heard him exclaim profanities, or express that kind of emotion?"

"No, sir, I never have."

"Were you around Dr. Graham when his mother and father died?"

"Yes."

"Did he have any outward manifestations of emotion—hysteria, sadness, that sort of thing?"

"No, sir, he didn't."

"And yet he loved his parents?" Sutton asked.

"The best I could tell, yes, sir."

Sutton walked over near the jury box. "Did you notice the police seemed to be amazed the children and Dr. Graham were not crying, that sort of thing?"

"Yes, sir, they were."

Ancelet was excused, and he gave Graham a "we're with you" pat on the back as he exited the courtroom.

In the morning, just before court began, Captain Sam Burns pulled Bobby Sutton into a private conference room down the hall from Courtroom F.

"God, Bobby, what the hell did you do to Donnie Nichols yesterday?" Burns asked.

Sutton grinned. "What do you mean, Sam?"

"All I know is, he came screeching into my driveway last night, yelling and cussing that you made him look like a dumb-ass on the witness stand. He said you kept asking over and over who was in charge of the Graham case."

For a moment the Chief of Detectives and the defense attorney looked at one another without saying a word. Then, simultaneously, they burst out laughing.

Paul Carmouche walked near the witness stand. "Could you state your name for the record, please?"

"My name is Sam Burns. I'm a captain, and the Chief of Detectives for the Shreveport Police Department. I was in charge of the Graham investigation."

Sutton and Walker barely stifled their smiles.

Carmouche used Burns's presence to introduce the tape recording of Graham's last interview with the Shreveport Police Department—the long discussion in which Graham tried to offer explanations about the crime scene to Burns and Brann. The prosecution thought that the recording was important to their case for a number of reasons. For one thing, it once again showed how unemotional Graham had seemed when he discussed minute details of the murder room. But more importantly, in Carmouche's opinion, the recording had captured the moment when Brann asked Graham why he didn't stop to make sure his children were all right before calling the police. After a lengthy legal argument, the jurors were each given a typed, transcribed copy of the interview to aid them in following the conversation.

The recording lasted about thirty minutes, and while it was playing, Graham sat quietly at the lawyer's table reading along with his copy of the transcript. The tape ended dramatically, with a flustered Lew Graham trying to explain the very significant question, "Why didn't you check on your children?"

The defense tried to gauge the effect of the interview on the jurors, but as usual, the twelve expressionless faces gave no hint of their individual or collective opinions.

13

CARMOUCHE and McMichael met in the D.A.'s office an hour before court was to begin. Carmouche was worried. "Well, Jim, is it me or is this case coming apart at the seams?"

"We've had a couple of setbacks. I don't know that I'd say it's falling apart."

Carmouche paced around his office. "I didn't expect Sutton to clean house with those first witnesses. Some of them sound like they're giving defense testimony."

"How do you see it?" McMichael asked.

"The patrolmen and the detectives were a draw. I wish Nichols had never been born. Sutton had him for lunch."

"That second taped interview was good. I saw a couple of jurors giving Graham the eye, when he said he never checked on his kids. Don't forget we still have Professor MacDonell," McMichael said.

Carmouche leaned back in his chair. "Yeah, Professor MacDonell. But is he going to be enough?"

OFF-THE-RECORD legal arguments ensued again over photographs brought to court by the Bossier Parish coroner, George McCormick. Again the defense team objected to certain explicit angles, and again Judge Bolin barred the bloodier pictures. Judge Bolin explained his decision to the jurors. "We try to reach a reasonable balance between what's required in order for the jury to makes its decision, as opposed to anything that is gruesome just for the sake of gruesomeness."

McCormick was an experienced trial witness. Despite his short, wide physique, his friskiness helped him hold a jury's attention. He had a nervous habit of twisting the ends of his handlebar moustache as he pondered an answer to a lawyer's question. To him the courtroom was a stage, and he made it a practice to look at the lawyer while a question was being asked, then turn and face the jury to give his answer. As an expert witness, he would be allowed a wide latitude in expressing opinions, and McCormick was never shy about telling people what he thought.

"Dr. McCormick, what was the general condition of the body when you first saw it?" McMichael asked.

"The body was in good condition; there was little or no postmortem degeneration. The body had been previously autopsied, and the organs had been reinstated to the body cavity, with the exception of the brain and heart."

"Would you use the Styrofoam model to explain the wounds?" McMichael indicated the wig stand McCormick had brought to use as a visual aid in explaining his opinions about how Kathy Graham had died.

"First, let me dismiss in a short period of time the part of our autopsy procedure which did not bear on the death. We examined the body through the previous autopsy incisions. We examined the organs that were present for natural disease which could have caused or influenced death, and found none. The brain was examined on the eighth of April [1980] at the Caddo morgue in conjunction with Dr. Braswell. In general, we found three areas of wounds on the body. One was a very minor wound on the thumb side of the right hand and wrist. It appeared to be a recent bruise from both its gross appearance and dissection of skin in the area," McCormick said.

"What else did you find?"

"The next area of examination was the face of the

deceased. The most obvious wound was a large, depressed laceration of the central part of the forehead. There are important points to be made about this wound at the present time. On the right side of the wound, the deceased's right, it has a tunneling effect—that is, the skin of the wound is pushed under itself. This indicates the wound came in a direction, not straight into the forehead, but from the deceased's left to her right. There are other injuries to the face, including a hemorrhage around the eyes and lids. The right eye of the deceased has two very pertinent findings. One was a large laceration of the right eyebrow, where the eyelid comes into contact with the bone of the socket of the eye. There was a smaller laceration of the lid just below the eye."

"Were there other wounds to the victim's face?"

"Further examination subsequently indicated there was a large laceration in the frontal portion of the brain, made by inward-driven pieces of bone. At the lateral aspect of the left side of the nose, there was a laceration. It was deep, as if the nose had been forcefully moved to the right, and the skin stretched and tore."

McCormick was experienced with death and autopsies, but the jury wasn't. Several jurors had wrinkled brows when the coroner was giving his testimony.

McMichael began gathering up the numerous photographs to show the jury. "What else did you find, Doctor?"

"There is a variable process by which the body responds to an injury. Anything foreign introduced to the body provokes a reaction with a liberation of white blood cells to the area of injury. Most experts agree that within thirty minutes or an hour, we see white blood cells."

McCormick had the jurors' undivided attention. "The first wound was applied to the right side of the scalp. We were able to obtain microscopic sections which showed a few [white blood] cells, suggesting but not proving that this wound was applied between fifteen and thirty minutes before the subject died. There was further evidence to corroborate that. We found she had swallowed blood into her stomach. The swallowing mechanism requires a life state: you can be unconscious, but you will still be alive," McCormick said.

"What about the four wounds to the top of the head?" McMichael continued. "Is there any conclusion you can draw from that?"

"My opinion is these four wounds were made in rapid succession. They are consistent with being made with the weapon," McCormick said.

McMichael passed photographs to the jury of the wounds and blood on Kathy's body. The jurors had been intent on McCormick, but as they saw the autopsy photographs, their faces took on a sterner, more sober expression. As the jurors passed the photographs, McCormick testified that several trails of blood on the body placed the victim first on the right side of the bed (to the viewer facing the bed), but that then she apparently moved or was moved to the other side.

Jim McMichael picked up the sledgehammer from his side of the counsel table and handed it to McCormick. The coroner held the hammer nonchalantly as he gave his testimony.

"We have two sequences of blows. The first sequence was of four in rapid succession. There was sufficient force and injury to the brain to render her unconscious. She may have moved, jerked, made some noise, but I seriously doubt she rolled herself over on to her back. I think it's more likely she was rolled over, and in that position . . ." McCormick placed both hands on the handle of the sledgehammer, and held it as if he were about to strike a blow, letting his gesture finish the sentence. "The final blow was administered with a weapon such as this, held with two hands."

"Dr. McCormick, you've stated your opinion that the wounds to the head were made with an instrument similar to this hammer. What about the wounds to the face?" McMichael asked.

"I can't give you a definite conclusion, but I have to raise a possibility. It's possible the destructive force of the hammer in the center of the forehead was enough to cause the other injuries on the face or to stretch the whole skin of the face, so the nose and lip tore. But the second possibility is that the force was made by something other than a hammer—a broad, flat object, like a fist. It is the type of injury you see in boxers when the eye is struck forcefully, and in my opinion, it was not made by the hammer striking that eye directly. I'm not saying I have definite proof she was struck by a fist twice, I simply raise that possibility."

McMichael changed direction. "Did you examine the portion of carpet that was cut up from the floor of the bedroom?"

"Yes, sir, I have."

McMichael was referring to a large bloodstain in the bedroom carpet, identified as Graham's blood type. "Can you determine how much blood may have been on the carpet?"

"I can give you an opinion. It is probably four or five cc's—to make a stain that size."

McMichael asked him to speculate about how long it would have taken to leave a spot of blood the size of a baseball. Graham had said he was stabbed and was on the floor only a few seconds before being thrown across the room and knocked out. Sutton objected to McCormick's speculation, but Bolin allowed it.

"My own opinion is it would have taken as much as thirty or forty-five seconds to do this," McCormick said.

"If a person who sustained this wound was moved to a different location, would you expect to find blood at that location?"

"Yes, sir, I would."

THE second coroner had raised some intriguing points: the possibility of a time lapse between two separate beatings, and the idea her killer had also hit Kathy Graham with a fist. Sutton believed that much of what McCormick had said was pure speculation.

"Dr. McCormick, I understand the opinions you've been giving these last few minutes were basically, roughly, observations, not scientific facts?" Sutton asked.

"Yes, they were my opinion, not fact."

Sutton picked up several papers from a large stack on the corner of the counsel table. He read for a moment. "In your [autopsy] report, you said, 'The broad area of contusion on the right eye, coupled with multiple minor surface contusions, suggested this wound was made by an application of force.' Were you talking about a black eye?"

"Yes."

"And the left eye was also black?"

"Correct."

"Doctor, can't the fractures [from the forehead wound] extending into the [eye] orbit cause the black eyes?"

"They certainly can."

"Doctor, you were talking about a bruise [to Kathy's wrist], and you said you thought you could determine the timing of when a bruise was made to within thirty minutes?"

"I like the thirty-minute time better, but I have documented cases where we see inflammatory changes in fifteen minutes," McCormick said.

"What you're saying is that it's a possibility to [time] that? We are dealing in possibilities? You're not willing to testify, within a reasonable scientific certainty, that the bruise on Mrs. Graham's wrist occurred within fifteen minutes of her death?"

"No."

Sutton sounded skeptical. "In fact, Dr. McCormick, the bottom line of what you're telling me is that you are dealing in probabilities?"

"As in all of forensic medicine, yes."

Sutton decided to challenge McCormick's theory that Kathy's face had first been struck by a fist. "You said the forehead blow could have caused it, or it could have been caused by a broad, flat instrument, which you described as a fist?"

"Yes, sir."

"So again we're talking in terms of possibilities?"

"Yes, sir."

"Could the handle of the hammer come across her face

and have caused those wounds?"

"I would admit to any possibility. It's possible the handle did, yes."

Sutton questioned McCormick's assertion Graham would have to have lain on the floor much longer than he said, in order to leave the large bloodstain.

"I believe, with that statement, we are now down from a possibility to an observation?"

McCormick nodded. "Yes, sir."

SUTTON sat down and Jim McMichael came back on redirect.

"Dr. McCormick, what is your feeling on just how accurately the hammer was used?" McMichael asked.

"I think the four blows to the side of the head were relatively accurate. They were placed within a small area in a killing portion of the body. The blow to the forehead, in my opinion, is extremely accurate. I personally would find it very difficult to apply that blow with this weapon," McCormick said.

"Particularly in a dark room . . ." McMichael asked.

Sutton objected. "I believe that's leading the witness, Your Honor."

McMichael waved his hand and went on without waiting for an answer.

"What effect would the lights being on or off have on your opinion of the accuracy?" McMichael asked.

"You could possibly hit the target without lights. My personal opinion is that it would take some lighting to see the target, because this is a short-handled sledgehammer," McCormick said.

SUTTON stood up for a final question.

"You said the four blows to the head were accurate, because they were in close proximity to each other. From what you're saying, whoever did it was aiming at the same spot every time, and hit it every time?" Sutton asked.

"Rather than just swinging and hitting the head once, the chin once, the shoulder once."

•   •   •

THE next witness, Jimmie Box Cannon, a serologist who
worked at the Crime Lab, had analyzed and typed the
various blood samples found throughout the Graham home.
She told of typing Graham's blood, found to be type O.

Kathy Graham's blood was type A.

Cannon noted the blood which saturated the bed linens
was type A. On Lew Graham's T-shirt, a large stain near
his stab wound was type O. But tiny spatters of blood on the
front of his shirt and underwear, along with larger drops on
the shoulder, were all found to be type A.

A blue bedspread, Cannon testified, taken from David
Graham's bunk bed, had a small amount of type O blood
on it.

PAT Wojtkiewicz from the crime lab finished the chain of
evidence with his identification of twenty-six photographs
from the crime scene. He told the jurors the lab staff had
collected some evidence themselves, including the alarm
clock found next to the bed and the headboard of the bed.

14

FOR sixteen months Lewis Graham had recited his story time and time again. On March 31, 1980, he told Coker and Lopez that he and his wife had had their troubles, but their problems had been resolved and their marriage was good.

Coker and Lopez were skeptical.

On April 1, 1980, Graham told Nichols that he and Kathy were getting along fine in the weeks before the murder.

Donnie Nichols didn't believe him.

On April 2, 1980, in his last conversation with the police, Graham told Captain Sam Burns and Detective John Brann that the last few months before Kathy's death had been some of the happiest times in their marriage.

Burns and Brann thought he was lying.

Convinced Graham was guilty, the prosecution looked to prove their opinion with two witnesses who'd seen and talked to Kathy Graham hours before she died. Pam Byrd, an acquaintance who taught at the school Eric and Katie attended, was first.

"Mrs. Byrd, when was the last time you saw Kathy Graham?" Carmouche asked.

"The day before she was killed, Sunday. My child Amy had a birthday party, and Kathy brought Katie to the house."

"Did you notice anything unusual about Mrs. Graham's appearance?"

"Yes. She was not smiling. Her eyes were red, and she appeared very upset—she wasn't her usual smiling, friendly self."

SUTTON was prepared for that. "Mrs. Byrd, you said Mrs. Graham wasn't smiling?"

"I guess what I want to say—expressionless, maybe, or not usually the way I saw her. She was usually a very friendly person. I feel like she would have talked to me in a different way," Byrd said.

"Do you know Marsha Stringer?"

"Yes."

"Did you know, just a day or two prior to that, she [Marsha] had a very tragic loss of a brother-in-law?" Sutton asked.

"I believe I did."

"Do you know whether or not Kathy Graham was emotionally upset over that tragic death?"

"I'm sure she would be."

"Would that explain why she wasn't smiling and happy like she usually is?"

"It might."

UNDAUNTED, Carmouche called Mrs. Arlis O'Neill, a neighbor from Kirkwood Drive.

"Mrs. O'Neill, when was the last time you saw or spoke to her?"

"I talked to her on the telephone that night about eight-thirty. She seemed irritable, and she said she didn't have time to talk. I saw her that night, between ten and ten-thirty, at the grocery store."

"Did she appear normal?"

"She was dressed, and had her hair fixed, but she was real dark under her eyes, and looked like she had been crying," O'Neill said.

"The dark under her eyes—black eyes?"

"No. Just strained and emotional, I'd say."

• • •

SUTTON was polite. He and Graham believed that the witness was merely mistaken about which night she had seen Kathy, and the attorney chose not to pursue the matter. "Mrs. O'Neill, did you consider yourself a friend of Kathy Graham's?"

"Yes."

"So when you saw this friend of yours standing there, looking like she had been crying, certainly you asked her why?"

"Well, she was about three people in front of me, and I'd already talked to her, and she seemed somewhat irritable. I just felt, you know, it wasn't my place to interfere."

Sutton pressed on. "That night, the telephone call—you said she sounded irritable. Do you know whether or not, on that particular night, Mrs. Graham was in her monthly menstrual cycle?"

Mrs. O'Neill blushed, embarrassed by the question.

"No, I, uh, n-no, I didn't know it."

"Do you know whether or not, during the early phases of Kathy Graham's menstrual cycle, her eyes were usually darker?" Sutton asked.

"I had never noticed that, no. That's a personal thing."

GRAHAM knew what was coming next, and he wished he didn't have to remain in the courtroom. She was an innocent victim, caught in the middle of something she knew nothing about.

His relationship with Judith Carson had titillated the spectators and the media. All during the jury-selection process, Sutton and Walker had asked each potential juror the same question: "If the evidence should show that Lew Graham, a married man, had engaged in sexual relations outside of marriage, would that be such an abomination, such a terrible thing, that you would think, well, he ought to be convicted of something?"

No one who had answered "Yes" was presently sitting in the jury box.

Under Louisiana law, the District Attorney is not required to address the issue of motive in a murder case. But human nature being what it is, Carmouche realized that it would help his case if he could give the jury some reason for which Graham might have killed his wife. The only thing Carmouche had was the affair.

Some reporters had heard about Judith Carson early, within a few days of the murder. The *Shreveport Times* was preparing to run a story naming Carson when Bobby Sutton stepped in and invited the reporter, Linda Farrar, to lunch. Sutton convinced Farrar that nothing would be gained by exposing the laboratory assistant to publicity at that early stage, that her relationship with Lewis Graham was totally unrelated to Kathy Graham's death, and got the paper to agree to sit on the information until later. He rewarded the reporter and the newspaper by going the extra mile to make himself available to them throughout the pre-trial effort, bending over backwards to give the *Times* extra consideration, including a couple of exclusives.

Even though Carson was a witness for the prosecution, Graham knew she was much more sympathetic to his side and believed in his innocence. She had kept her relationship with him a secret from her husband until just a few days before her grand jury testimony. Apparently the Carsons had come to an understanding about her infidelity, because Judith's husband, along with the pastor of their church, accompanied her to Courtroom F.

Knowing basically what her testimony would cover, Graham anguished about having the cold, hard, sterile aspects of his affair presented in a public forum for all the world to hear.

As the witness walked proud and erect toward the stand, she was bestowed with the sort of unabashed attention usually reserved for a processing bride.

"State your name, please, ma'am?" Carmouche asked.

"Judith Carson."

"Mrs. Carson, are you married?"

"Yes. I have two children."

"And do you know the defendant in this case, Lewis Graham?" Carmouche asked.

"Yes. I worked as an associate in his laboratory, doing tests for his research projects."

Just at that moment, Carmouche thought of a question he wanted to ask, and deviated from his planned line of inquiry.

"Did you ever do research on animals?"

"Yes, on white rats."

"Are the animals ever killed during the experiments?"

"Sometimes."

Carmouche got what he wanted: a soft murmur ran through the spectators.

"During the time you worked with Lewis Graham, did your relationship ever develop into anything other than professional?"

"Yes, it did. In the early part of 1979, we were engaged in an affair."

Carmouche walked nearer the jury. "That's a sexual affair?"

"That's right."

"How long did that continue?"

"For a year, fourteen months. It was not formally terminated in March of 1980."

"So in fact, it was still continuing on March thirty-first, 1980?" Carmouche asked.

"Could have been, yes."

"During this time, did you understand the defendant had been having some problems in his marriage?" Carmouche asked.

"For some months prior to the onset of the relationship, I was aware he was having marital difficulties."

Carmouche wished Carson could relax and quit being so stiff with her testimony. "On the weekend Kathy Graham was killed, where had you been?"

"At home with my family."

"When did you find out?"

"When I arrived at work that morning. A short while after that, we went to the residence in an effort to see Dr.

Graham and his children. [I saw him] later that day, in the accompaniment of Robert Smith and my husband."

"Have you ever spoken to Dr. Graham about the murder?"

"Yes, after he returned to work."

The District Attorney relinquished his witness, and tried to discern her effect on the jury. He couldn't tell what, if anything, they were thinking.

GRAHAM forced himself not to smile or nod or otherwise acknowledge Carson while she was on the witness stand. Sutton and Walker had told him that it was important that the jury not see any sign of deep feeling between the two of them. Sutton would be trying to use Carson's testimony to reinforce Graham's story, and the matter of love or lust had to stay out of the way of that line of questioning.

"Mrs. Carson." Sutton asked, "during the year 1979, did you become aware that his marital problems were minimizing?"

"Yes. I was quite aware he and his wife had sought counseling, and it was obvious from the things he said that things were greatly improved."

"How long had you worked for Dr. Graham?"

"Four and a half years."

Graham remembered the first time he had met Judith Carson, just after he moved to Shreveport from Indiana. She was assigned to him early in his tenure at the medical school, and their many common interests helped engender first friendship, then romance.

"During that four and a half years, was there, in fact, a friendship between you and Dr. Graham?"

"There was a close friendship, a mutual respect and admiration for each other."

"You used the word 'affair.' Did Dr. Graham buy you gifts, jewelry, things of that nature?" Sutton asked.

"No."

Graham was surprised she was so composed in this stressful setting—and sorry she had been dragged into the fray.

"Did you and Dr. Graham take any weekend trips together?"

"No."

"Did you ever go out at night together?"

"Never."

"When would you and Dr. Graham see each other on a personal basis?"

"During the day, usually around the noon hour."

"You mentioned you heard about Kathleen Graham when you arrived at work. Did you go to the Graham house?"

"Yes. I rang the doorbell."

"Did someone come and answer that door?"

"Detective Donnie Nichols."

"As a result of that conversation with Detective Nichols, did you become aware Dr. Graham was going to be charged with this crime?"

"That's what I was told that morning. He told me."

SUTTON sat down, and Carmouche fired a few more questions at his monotoned witness.

"Mrs. Carson, you indicated it was noon when you had sex with the defendant. Where would you go?"

"A motel."

"Would this be once a week, twice a week, more than that?"

"Once a week would be pushing the average."

"When was the last time you all had gone to a motel, prior to the time Kathleen Graham was killed?" Carmouche asked.

"I truthfully do not recall. It had been some weeks."

"When Dr. Graham was going through this counseling, and he indicated things were getting better, did he ever suggest that you should terminate this affair, since things were getting better?"

"He never said that, nor did I."

After excusing Carson, Judge Bolin sat quietly, glancing at a stack of papers on the bench, suspending the proceedings for a few minutes. Graham realized that Judge Bolin was giving Carson time to exit the courthouse, time to get away before he recessed the trial and the throngs of spectators went outside for lunch.

AFTER lunch, Jim McMichael called two fingerprint experts to the stand. Sgt. Jerry Wood from SPD gave a brief explanation about the limitations of fingerprinting.

McMichael handed Wood several off-white cards.

"Let me show you what I've marked as State's 165 and 166."

"These appear to be the cards I got ink impressions on at the morgue of Kathleen Graham. We had a little problem with some of them, and had to redo them several times."

"Is that unusual?"

"Not really, 'cause after a body is brought down there into the cooler, where it's kept until the autopsy, the body has a tendency to, I guess you would say, sweat. A lot of times, there's moisture on the fingers."

Wood mentioned an unsuccessful attempt to get prints off the flashlight and the can of coins found outside. Major Singleton Taylor, head of the SPD Identification Bureau, said he had matched Graham's fingerprint to one found on a vodka bottle and the hunting knife. Both items belonged to Graham, so it was hardly surprising the prints were on them.

AFTER the witness was dismissed, Carmouche addressed the judge. "Your Honor, the State has one more witness to present. We expect this witness to last a considerable period of time, perhaps an entire day."

Judge Bolin acceded to his request. "We will recess until nine-fifteen in the morning."

15

IN the months of pre-trial build-up, media reports predicting a battle of the experts had set the stage for the prosecution's star witness. Tall, confident, and cocky, Herbert MacDonell prepared to take the stand on a Saturday—very unusual for criminal proceedings.

During several preliminary conferences with prosecutors, MacDonell generated some concern in Carmouche and McMichael because he seemed so lackadaisical about the case and his opinions. The prosecutors had a hard time pinning him down, and MacDonell's normal response to a pre-trial question was "Don't worry about it, just leave it to me."

McMichael and Carmouche both realized that they might have a hard time selling the opinions of someone who called himself a blood spatter expert. MacDonell's generous ego didn't make either of them feel comfortable; McMichael especially didn't care for MacDonell's cocksuresness.

Yet MacDonell was experienced in the courtroom and an unshakable expert witness. Carmouche and McMichael were putting a lot of hope behind MacDonell's testimony. In the past few days, particularly when things weren't going their way, they'd frequently boosted each other with the rallying cry, "MacDonell is coming!"

The "science" of bloodstain pattern analysis, a field in which the only textbook in existence was written by MacDonell, was little known. Only a handful of technicians claimed enough expertise to come into a courtroom and be recognized as authorities. But the concepts and basic theories behind the study were simple enough.

Imagine an average puddle of water. If you were to throw a rock into the puddle, the water would be dispersed in all directions from the weight and force of the rock. A bigger rock would send out more water, a smaller rock less. If you threw the rock with a lot of force, more water would be displaced, with the largest drops of water traveling the farthest from the puddle. If you could somehow capture the various shapes and sizes of the water drops, in theory, you could figure out what size rock, thrown in what direction, at what angle, had caused the pattern of drops.

That premise made up the basis for MacDonell's theories on bloodstain pattern analysis. He had testified in several big cases. The trial of Joan Little, the prisoner accused of the stabbing death of her jailer, was one; another was the trial of Jean Harris, accused of killing her lover, the author of the Scarsdale Diet.

The District Attorney went about establishing MacDonell's expert credentials. "What is your occupation?"

"I'm the Director of the Laboratory of Forensic Science in Corning, New York."

"What is 'forensic' science?"

"The term is an adjective, and it might apply to any science that ends up in litigation."

"Professor, what experience do you have with human blood?"

"I began studying human blood while working as a forensic scientist at the University of Rhode Island Laboratories, where the state's crime lab is located. That was in 1954. We began studying some of the relatively simple patterns of blood in 1956. In '67 and '68, I began a study of bloodstain patterns, sponsored by the Department of Justice. It dealt with impacts of various types. For example, a low-velocity impact, such as stepping into a puddle of blood; medium-, which is a beating; and high-velocity, which is gunshot. When that work was completed, I was asked by the State of Mississippi to run a workshop, and I have done forty or so two- or three-day workshops, one of which was held in Shreveport last spring."

"Have you ever given expert testimony on bloodstain evidence?" Carmouche asked.

"Yes, sir. I've testified in twenty to twenty-five states. I've investigated homicides in forty-two states."

"Do you recall when you were first contacted on this particular case?"

"In August of 1980, yourself and Mr. Herd came to Evansville, Indiana, where I was conducting a bloodstain evidence institute for area law enforcement agencies."

MacDonell identified twenty-five pictures from the murder room, as well as the sledgehammer, clock, pillowcases, sheets, quilt, lamp, lampshade, and knife. The silverbearded professor seemed to be almost blind as he looked closely and carefully at the various photographs and room layouts.

"Using the photographs, Professor, did you come to any conclusions that indicate where the victim was when the blows were struck?"

"Yes. The photographs show two origins of spatter. There was one, possibly more, in the position slightly to the right from where the body was found. The bloodstain pattern on the left is completely consistent with where the victim was found. [For the initial beating] the person was lying more or less on their left side, facing away from the bed, facing right as you look at the bed from the bottom. At some point, after the first blows were struck, the person either rolled herself or was pulled over [onto her back]. Blood was running down the neck and upper chest and breast area. She had to be sitting up for a moment, while the blood did run down. The longest streak of blood, which is on the center of the neck and goes over the top of the left breast, is interrupted by a wiping. It has dried partially, and is wiped through. That wiping had to occur five minutes at the outset. It could have been as quick as twenty or thirty seconds. All of those things together clearly demonstrate the victim was initially face-down at the time she received some blows, I don't know how many."

Carmouche hoped the jurors would understand the technical nature of MacDonell's testimony.

"She would have been in that final position how long before the wiping took place?"

"The wiping occurred after not more than five minutes, or the blood would have dried and would not wipe at all. We have done many experiments with blood running down different appendages, and we find that in about three minutes, the stream of blood on a living body you cannot smear. I'm saying five minutes would be the maximum time this could have happened," MacDonell said.

"Can you name any object that would have caused the wiping?"

"I can't be certain." MacDonell said. "It isn't a towel or handkerchief, it isn't bed clothing. It would more likely be a finger or hands."

"Professor, have you done any examination concerning the approximate times of the beating?" Carmouche asked.

"Yes, there are some stains that are not totally fresh blood. I'm sure everyone is familiar with clotting. In analysis of some of the spots, we find they have centers of coagulated blood."

"Is that an indication there was an interval between the two beatings?"

"Yes, there was. In order to produce blood spattering with centers of coagulated blood, the blood has to coagulate."

"Professor, with respect to the clock that was on the floor, did you conduct an examination of that item?"

"In examining the photographs and the articles made available to me, I found an inconsistency in the clock itself. The sledgehammer has bloodstains up near the head. It might have been choked up or held with two hands. This is the kind of instrument that will produce cast-off patterns, which are simply [blood] flung off as the instrument is raised. They would be cast off, going straight up over the victim, as the beating is occurring. The patterns shown on the photographs of the ceiling demonstrate the typical arc pattern you get from a heavy, short-handled instrument. A long instrument, like a pointer, can be flung rather quickly, and you get a fine line of patterns. A heavy instrument, like this hammer, is very difficult to move rapidly, so the cast-off of blood allows for larger spots to strike farther apart. The clock was not consistent, because it had one spot of blood with an essentially straight-on configuration. If it were on the nightstand, it would be in a straight line to where the victim was beaten. There was movement of the clock—it might have been knocked down, or fallen to the floor."

Now Carmouche sought to tie it all together, to show how the prosecution thought the crime had been committed, and by whom. "Professor MacDonell, you conducted some examinations of the T-shirt in this case?"

"Yes, on the T-shirt and the shorts. The first pattern [from the T-shirt] is the soaking blood pattern from the stab wound. The other stain is a replica of some angular instrument. The stain could very well have been made from an object covered with blood, and that object could have been the sledgehammer. I found no other objects from the room with the same geometric shape, but there's no way of saying it has to be the sledgehammer.

"There is another type of pattern on the T-shirt in many locations. There is the presence of fine specks of blood. There are also small spots of blood up on the right shoulder on the back. The ones on the front could have resulted from impact—spatter coming back to the shirt. The ones on the back are somewhat larger, and these are cast off. It is very common, whenever there is a beating and the instrument is raised by whoever is wearing an item like this shirt, the blood will not only spatter from impact, but goes up and over their back, and the ceiling as well."

Carmouche smiled to himself as he led his witness to the next point. "With respect to the T-shirt, and State's Exhibit 76, did you conduct an examination of this?" He wanted the expert's opinion of several fairly parallel bloodstains on Graham's T-shirt.

"There are what appear to be wiping patterns. Those patterns are consistent with someone wiping a knife. It is consistent with the knife, but I can't say it is the only instrument that could have caused it," MacDonell said.

"State's Exhibit 91 [Graham's underwear]. Professor, have you examined that object?"

"Yes, I have. I photographed the front of the undershorts, and I located the concentration of blood spots, some of which are very, very small. They seem to be more or less evenly distributed over the front of the shorts. I prepared an overlay, a tracing, of the shorts when they were stretched out and held down firmly. Some of the spots, two in particular, were photographed to show the type of bloodstain I referred to earlier. The center of those stains is darker, where there is clotting of the blood."

MacDonell continued. At Carmouche's request, he had prepared a clear plastic overlay of the size and shape of Graham's underwear, and drawn spots on it that matched the pattern of bloodstains found on the shorts.

"Those number between two hundred fifty and three hundred spots, and they are of medium-velocity impact. They are so small, the concentration of two-fifty to three hundred requires that it was very close. Whoever was wearing those [undershorts] had to be in close proximity to the [victim's] head at the time each one of the blows was struck."

Whispering broke out throughout the courtroom as the effect of MacDonell's testimony sank in.

Carmouche asked the witness to recap his opinion. "Would you tell us from beginning to end how you proceeded through this examination of evidence?"

"The reconstruction is somewhat straightforward. The victim was at one time over on the right side, looking from the base of the bed. There are spatter patterns on the lampshade and other items in the room, all consistent with two origins of spatter. There are many ways of showing she was in one position and moved, or was moved [onto her back]. At some point, she was slightly upright.

Something wiped the front of the upper breast, and that something could have been a hand. The [blood spatters] on the ceiling, when related back to the bed, are consistent with casting-off. The size of the [blood] spots suggests a heavy, dense object. The clock is inconsistent with the bloodstains on it, and it was either moved or fell from the nightstand. The bloodstain on the clothing I've examined is totally consistent with the wearer being in close proximity to the beating. The presence of clotted blood is evidence there was a time interval of five minutes [between two separate beatings]. Cast-off patterns on the back of the T-shirt are completely consistent with raising an instrument up, elbows bent, wrists bent together, and causing a whipping action. That's why blood goes straight up and extends back behind the person performing such an act."

MacDonell held up his tracing of the underwear, showing the jury and the courtroom the multitude of blood spatter.

"I have no way of knowing who was wearing this clothing. I have no way of knowing if they were involved in this beating, but everything I've examined is consistent with that, and there is nothing inconsistent with it."

"Thank you, Professor."

MACDONELL had testified for two and a half hours, and around lunchtime, Sutton and Walker wanted to break up court and consider their cross-examination.

"Your Honor, my cross-examination of Mr. MacDonell is going to be long and extensive. I suggest we might adjourn for lunch so I won't be interrupted."

During the lunch break, Sutton and Walker went over the notes they'd made during MacDonell's testimony. Back in court, making certain not to enhance MacDonell's credibility by calling him "professor," Sutton went on the attack.

"Mr. MacDonell, you mentioned your review of the photographs, as well as some tangible, physical elements from scene. Did you ever go to the scene yourself?"

"No, I have not."

"You mentioned in a pamphlet written by you in 1971, on page three, 'the examination of evidence at the scene of any occurrence of sufficient violence to result in bloodshed, should, in every instance, include a detailed study of every detectable bloodstain.' I assume you agree that should be done?" Sutton asked.

"Yes, I agree with that, ideally."

"If I could direct your attention to the master bedroom: initially, you were looking at some photographs which showed cast-off patterns on the ceiling of that room. The conclusions you expressed today—do they take into consideration a possibility of cast-off patterns going from north to south?"

"No, they wouldn't."

"Okay. On page twenty-six of the pamphlet, Mr. MacDonell, you state, 'necessity for a thorough investigation cannot be overemphasized. Everything regarding a case should be checked, as it may have an influence on an otherwise obvious but erroneous conclusion.' Now, I assume what you're saying there is, you must take everything into consideration?"

"Yes and no. You must take everything into consideration, but the conclusions based on what you do see cannot necessarily be altered by what you don't see."

"If there were other cast-off stains in the bedroom that were *not* taken into consideration, it could influence your conclusions?"

"Not at all. If there were cast-offs going in this direction, it would indicate there was an additional blow. That in no way reduces the obvious cast-off in this direction," MacDonell said.

"In your experience I presume you've made many experiments creating blood spatters."

"That's correct."

"Do you use a source, something like polyurethane or a sponge soaked in blood?"

"In some instances we do. In other instances, we use animals."

"I believe you spoke in your book about some high-velocity tests, about shooting some dogs?"

"Yes. The initial grant funds were provided to buy some animals that were being destroyed routinely. They were large dogs, and they were anesthetized, and were, in fact, already dying of an overdose. They were sheared and shot. Subsequent to that, we have done the same thing with beatings. It's not a pleasant thing to do, but it's the closest thing we can do to relate blood patterns to a natural, living organism."

"Mr. MacDonell, were you provided with the bedspreads from other beds in the house?"

"No, I don't believe I was."

"I want to show you some photographs, and if you were to assume those marks are, in fact, blood, could you make a conclusion as to the manner in which they were deposited?"

Sutton showed MacDonell several pictures taken of David Graham's bedspread, which had a few small drops of blood on it.

"There really aren't enough to form a pattern. It could easily be a transfer from something that had blood on it. It's not a drip—I think it's a transfer from something."

"You were talking about a pattern on the left portion of the deceased's chest. You said that smear was caused by a nonporous item. Could the smear have been caused by the deceased's fingers?"

"Certainly. If there was contact with the hand in rolling over or being rolled over, it is possible."

"If I'm correct, you said the wiping had to occur from twenty to thirty seconds, up to five minutes [after the blood was shed]?"

"That is an approximation. In my experience, with blood that thin on flesh, it would dry within three minutes. After that, you could not wipe it."

"You examined the photographs of, and the clock itself?"

"That's correct."

"I understood you to say, because of one spot of blood on the lens of the clock, and one on the rim, the clock could not have been [on the floor] when it received those spots?"

"That's correct. It had to be, in essence, facing the origin of the impact."

"If someone had a bloody T-shirt, and were wrestling or fighting, and they got slapped, could it produce spatter?" Sutton asked.

"It could, yes."

Sutton went after MacDonell's testimony that the T-shirt had blood patterns from a knife wiped on it.

"You were referring to the T-shirt earlier—and correct me if I'm wrong—[you said] those marks were caused by a nonporous item. I found it interesting you said they were consistent with a wiping action, as though one would wipe the [knife] blade on the shirt. How firm are you in your opinion those are wipe stains?" Sutton asked.

"Quite confident they are, because they're double as you hold onto something. There's blood on each side."

"If that T-shirt were removed when the bloodstain was wet, wouldn't it cause those stains?"

"Only if it were folded and put in a bag while it was wet. It's something of a mirror image; there is not enough blood there to transfer. Blood on cloth dries very rapidly."

Sutton wasn't gaining much ground sparring with this witness. He moved his line of challenge to perhaps the most damaging part of MacDonell's theory.

"As I understand your description of the spots on the back of the T-shirt, these spots went up, didn't quite make it to the ceiling, made their arc, and came back down and landed on the back of the T-shirt. Is that correct?"

"That's correct. That certainly is the way they could have got there."

"Suppose a person was lying flat on his stomach on the floor. Would they be consistent with that?"

"Yes, or bending over, face down."

"You made an overlay of the front of the shorts. Could the pattern on the front of the shorts also occur if the person wearing them was lying flat on his back on the floor?"

"Yes, if there was an exact point [of impact] directly above him."

"If the person wearing those shorts were standing in front of a lavatory, and he had blood on his hands, and he turned the water on and held his hand under the water, would the splashing from the lavatory cause that type of pattern?" Sutton asked.

"Not at all. There would be evidence of blood that is diluted, and the color would be totally different."

"Did you test the blood?"

"You gave a hypothetical 'If they had blood on their hand, and if they ran water, would it produce this?' The answer is no."

"Are you telling me that when you stand in front of a lavatory, and hold the hand under the water, you will never spatter the front of your pants?" Sutton asked.

"The size, shape, and distribution makes it a pattern. You cannot produce spots this small without producing a lot of larger ones, and if you would like to get a unit of blood and go to the men's room, I'll demonstrate it. It just can't happen. It follows the laws of physics."

"I understand you to say that the pattern of blood on the front of the shorts would only travel two to four feet?"

"That's correct."

"When that blood reaches four feet, it abruptly terminates?" Sutton's sarcastic tone was obvious.

"I think I said in a horizontal component, it would go up two, three, four feet, then fall down. It could *fall* a hundred feet."

Sutton pressed on. "If the person wearing those shorts were being pulled horizontally out of bed when the blow was being administered, could the pattern of blood on the shorts result while they are in close proximity to the wound?"

"The pattern is too concentrated. There are too many spots of blood. The only way that could happen would be if the wearer were lying close to the origin. There are too many spots too close together to be much farther than two feet, but I will say possibly as far as four feet."

Sutton and the blood expert battled for almost three hours. The defense counsel wanted to create at least a reasonable doubt about this expert's conclusions. Sutton asked one last question.

"Mr. MacDonell, have you, in connection with your work, ever given an opinion that later turned out to be incorrect?"

"Do you mean, have I ever made a mistake?"

"Yes."

The gray-haired, bespectacled criminologist smiled. "Certainly, but not in testimony."

Paul Carmouche addressed the court. "Your Honor, at this time the State rests."

16

ON Monday, July 27, the Graham trial entered its second week. Rarely did prosecutors, defense lawyers, judges, and court staff have to work this many days straight without a break. The jurors had seen seven intense days of testimony and still had not yet heard from the defense's witnesses. Bobby Sutton looked tired, his sharp features now becoming even more prominent, his complexion growing pale.

As a savvy trial lawyer, Sutton knew that he had to open his case with the most dramatic testimony possible. Because Graham's claim that intruders had entered his house the night Kathy was killed was central to his argument, he called a series of witnesses to back up the contention that the neighborhood around the Graham house that night was, in fact, "very, very busy."

David Breedlove, who lived seven houses down from the Grahams, was the defense team's first witness. Shortly after they took the case, Sutton and Walker had knocked on every door on Kirkwood Drive. Sutton had come across Breedlove early on and was actually happy the police hadn't spoken to him. The prosecutors were unprepared for his testimony. Sutton asked his witness about the weekend of the murder.

"Did you have any unusual experience in your home

immediately prior to that?"

"Yes, I did. Twice . . . The first [incident] was two weeks prior to March thirty-first, 1980," Breedlove said. "I had two incidents. One on a Sunday night and one immediately prior, and I don't recall which came in which order. We had just been in bed about fifteen or twenty minutes. We had some trouble getting my son, who's nine, to sleep. I heard a cabinet door shut."

"What area of the house was the cabinet located in?" Sutton asked.

"In the kitchen. I thought maybe it was my son, and I got out of bed to see if he was in bed. He was asleep. I checked my dog to see if it was her, and it wasn't, so I came back and got my pistol."

"Did you go to your kitchen?"

"Yes, I did. I found the door leading to the garage [standing] open," Despite the open door, Breedlove explained, no intruder, no one was inside his house.

"Before you go to bed at night, do you check to see whether your doors are locked?"

"Locked, yes."

"Did you call the police?"

"No."

"Why not?"

"Well, I didn't see anybody, for one thing."

Sutton walked near the jury. He wanted to be sure they understood the timing of this witness's testimony. "We are talking about two weeks prior to Mrs. Graham's death?" Sutton asked.

"This time period."

"When was the last time, prior to her death, something happened?"

"It was Sunday night, around two-thirty in the morning. The dog we have, a small poodle, woke up, and I woke up about the same time, and someone was rattling the front door," Breedlove said.

"Was your dog barking, or did the front door wake you up?"

"Both, I guess. The dog went immediately to the front

door, and I got my pistol and went to check it out. By the time I got there, the dog beat me, and whoever was there was gone," Breedlove said.

"This is the weekend prior to Mrs. Graham's death?"

"This is true."

ON cross-examination, Carmouche looked to turn the testimony to his advantage.

"Mr. Breedlove, did I understand you correctly when you said you were not sure which incident came first?"

"That's true."

"Now, the incident where the door to your kitchen was open, who did you check first?" Carmouche asked.

"I checked to see if my son was asleep."

"And who did you check next?"

"My daughter, Amy."

Carmouche wondered if the jury saw the connection he was attempting to make. "And then you got your gun, in that order?" Carmouche asked.

"Yes."

"Did you call the police after Kathleen Graham's murder?"

"No, I did not."

"Did you ever call me about it, the D.A.'s office?"

"No, I did not."

"Did your dog bark at the incident when the back door was open?"

"No."

"Do you keep tools in your garage, Mr. Breedlove?" Carmouche asked.

"Yes, I do."

"Were any of your tools tampered with?"

"Not that I know of."

THE next defense witness was ten-year-old Michael Rak, who also had something to say about unusual happenings at his house the night of the murder. After much legal discussion, Judge Bolin agreed to relax the Rules of Evidence and allow Sutton to ask questions normally considered leading. Mike held up three fingers in the Boy Scout honesty symbol as the court clerk swore him in.

"Mike, where do you live?"

"2022 South Kirkwood."

"Do you know where the Grahams used to live on South Kirkwood?" Sutton asked.

"I don't know their address, but I know where they lived."

"On March thirty-first, 1980, do you recall something happening at the back door of your home?" Sutton asked.

The young boy nodded, then answered. "Yes. I was sleeping, then I heard a noise at the back door. It was coming from the garage. I went back there, I turned on the light and saw a man out there. He looked at me and ran out."

"Was this a regular door, like the door behind you?"

Mike glanced at the door Sutton pointed to, and shook his head. "No, it has a window in it."

"Do you recall what he looked like?" Sutton asked.

"He was white. He had a black moustache and black hair."

"What do you recall about his clothes?" Sutton asked.

"A tan leather jacket and blue jeans."

"Now, after the man turned around and ran out, what did you do?" Sutton asked.

"I just ran to my mom and dad's room and knocked on the door and they came."

CARMOUCHE knew to be careful in cross-examining a child. "Mike, did you say what time this was?"

"No."

"When you woke up, did you wake up on your own, or did something wake you up?"

"Something woke me up."

"Did you hear a dog barking?" Carmouche asked.

"No."

"Do you have a dog?"

"Yes."

"Was the man at the laundry room door?" Carmouche asked.

"He was in the garage. He got through one door, and he was trying to get into the house."

Carmouche asked a few additional questions, but the boy held firm to his version of what he remembered.

To forestall any prosecution attempt to discredit Mike Rak, Sutton put the boy's physician on the stand. Dr. Harold Levy said he had given Mike a prescription for hyperactivity. The medication, according to Dr. Levy, would not unduly enhance Mike's imagination.

THE third defense witness was Brenda Alford, seventeen, the daughter of Mr. and Mrs. Otto Chandler, next-door neighbors of the Grahams on Kirkwood Drive.

"So your bedroom is closest to the Grahams' house?" Sutton asked.

"Yes, it is."

"Where is your mother's bedroom located?"

"On the opposite end of the house."

"Did anything cause you to be awakened during the night of March thirtieth and early March thirty-first?" Sutton asked.

"Yes. My dog, Toto, was outside, and she awoke me barking."

"Do you know what time it was?"

"I have one of those digital clocks, and usually when I wake up, it's the first thing I look at. It was 2:02 a.m. I looked out the front window, and the dog quit barking and I went back to sleep."

"Did the police subsequently come by and talk to your parents?"

"A few detectives. They only wanted to talk to my parents."

"Did I contact you—knock on your door, and ask you questions about it?"

"Yes."

TRADING off with Carmouche, Jim McMichael took over for the State. "Miss Alford, does Toto bark a lot?"

"She's a barking dog, yes."

"Do you think, if there had been someone out there, she

would have continued barking?"

"Unless it's one of us."

"Could it have been a raccoon she was barking at?" McMichael asked.

"Or a turtle, a frog."

THE first three witnesses for the defense had talked about strange noises and happenings around South Kirkwood Drive. But the most dramatic testimony was yet to come. Dorothy Milam was a pre-med student who used to live near Kirkwood Drive. She first contacted the police on July 15, 1981, after jury selection had begun.

She had told Shreveport Police detectives that on the night of the murder, she had seen a teenage boy standing just outside her yard. The time of the sighting roughly coincided with the times of the other neighborhood disturbances. But what made Milam's information so significant was not merely that it had occurred on March 31, but that she said the teenager she saw bore a striking resemblance to David Graham. She had called the Shreveport Police Department after seeing a picture of David Graham in the newspaper, believing that she might have information of great importance.

Bennett Kitchings was dispatched by Carmouche to verify her claim. During his visit, Dorothy Milam picked David out of a photograph of his high school basketball team that Kitchings had brought with him. Kitchings reported back to the D.A. that he believed she was a credible witness.

Whether or not Milam had actually seen David Graham, her testimony presented some interesting dilemmas for both sides. By law the prosecutors were obliged to report the information to the defense team, and Carmouche and McMichael immediately did so. But the prosecutors knew that the defense team would use her testimony to try to muddy the waters—to deflect attention away from the man they believed had committed the crime. And that is exactly what Sutton and Walker sought to do.

After the defense lawyers had a chance to interview Dorothy Milam, they had another meeting with Graham, this time more determined than ever to open up their defense tactics.

"Lew, this woman has already told us and the police that she saw a boy who looked like David," Sutton said. "Glenn and I don't think the D.A. will bring the information out at all. So you have to let us pursue that line of questioning, to let the jury see that there are many parts to this puzzle."

"I've already talked to David," Graham answered, "and he said it wasn't him. I believe him. Besides, we've discussed this a hundred times. I don't feel right about involving my children."

"We are *not* trying to implicate David. But we do think that you should trust our judgment on this, and let us use the tools at our disposal. If you don't want this woman to testify that she saw David, then let's subpoena Kitchings and get him to testify about her identification. Either way, it's vital to our defense."

Graham shook his head. "No, definitely not. We'll either win or lose on what we have. Don't say anything in court about David or Eric. Nothing."

As Dorothy Milam was sworn in, Sutton thought about the argument with Graham. He still hadn't decided whether or not to go against his client's wishes. "Mrs. Milam, have you ever lived near South Kirkwood?"

"I lived one block over, on Darlington Court."

"Do you recall anything significant happening on March thirty-first, 1980?"

"Yes. I was awakened during the night, or early morning, I should say. I had two dogs that were barking."

"Your dogs stay in the house or back yard?"

"Back yard."

"What did you do?" Sutton asked.

"I got up and looked out the window directly behind the bed. The dogs were on the right-hand corner of the yard, in the back. They were viciously barking and throwing themselves up against the cyclone fence," Milam said.

"Did you see anything else, other than the dogs?"

"Yes, I saw a person. He was standing on the outside of the fence, just standing within two feet of the fence. He was white and had on blue jeans."

"Could you tell what kind of shirt he had on?"

"No sir."

"Long hair, short hair, what?"

"It wasn't long, and it wasn't short. About average length for a young man."

"Did you attempt to wake your husband?" Sutton asked.

"Yes."

"Were you successful?"

"No, I was not. I got frightened and got back under the covers. I was afraid he would see me."

"What time did you get up?"

"To the best of my memory, it was between three and four a.m."

"When did you hear about the death of Kathleen Graham?"

"On the way to take my children to the sitter [the next morning]. On the radio."

"Did you tell anyone what you had seen that night?"

"I told my husband before I ever even heard about it! I told the sitter, because I was shaking when I walked in. I was going to call the police from work."

"When you arrived at work, did you speak to someone there?"

"Everyone. A friend I worked with had told me before I called she knew someone at the scene of the murder. From what she told me I concluded the person I saw did not fit the description of anyone connected."

"What was it that caused you to think it wasn't necessary to call the police?"

"Based on the fact the children were all asleep, and the person I saw was definitely a teenager. I understood Mr. Graham was not a teenager."

"When you say teenager, that could be between thirteen and nineteen?"

"I would say he was seventeen—in that area."

Sutton paused for a moment. He wanted to ask his witness if she had ever identified a picture of David Graham. Let Lew get mad and chew me out, Sutton thought, at least

I'll get the information to the jury.

He turned and looked Graham square in the eye and was irritated when he saw Graham shake his head no. Sutton's shoulders slumped. "I have no more questions," he said.

Carmouche asked very few questions on cross-examination, and made no mention of David Graham.

THE defense team brought in a series of relatives and character witnesses. First up was George C. "Cliff" Hall, Kathy's uncle from Mississippi. Hall was a licensed locksmith who, along with Ancelet, had repaired the locks on the back door of the house on Kirkwood Drive.

"Mr. Hall, what happens if a deadbolt is not fully extruded to the full amount of the bolt?" Sutton asked.

"If it's not fully out, you can take any flat object and work it back and unlock the door."

"After you looked at the locks, with that knowledge, could you have gone through that door?"

"I could probably get in that door without a key as fast or faster than you could with a key."

CARMOUCHE asked Hall to remember the day of the murder. "Did the defendant, Lewis Graham, point out that door to you?"

"I don't recall if he pointed it out, or if I just noticed it."

"Hadn't the family members told you they pried through that door themselves?" Carmouche asked.

"I heard that Eric went through. They didn't tell me that they [the pry marks] were there before. I presume they were made during forced entry."

AFTER lunch, Ray Parish, Kathy's stepfather, continued to describe the Lewis Graham he knew, the one Sutton wanted the jury to see.

"Mr. Parish, when did you first meet Lew and Kathy Graham?" Sutton asked.

"In the latter half of 1970, around July. I was living in Indianapolis, and they had just moved into a new home in an addition across from the church we attended."

"What was the name of that church?"

"White Harvest United Methodist Church. I was chairman of the administrative board for two years."

"Did Lew Graham ever serve in that church while you knew him?"

"He was nominated and elected to the board of trustees. He ushered and took part in work projects we had on the church property."

"Now, when did you marry Kathleen Graham's mother?" Sutton asked.

"In December of 1973."

"In the years you have known Lew Graham, have you ever witnessed him display any outward manifestation of emotion? Crying, hysteria, grief?"

"No, never. Lew is very—it's a little hard to say. He was always very stable and not excited at any time I ever saw him."

"Is Lew Graham a cold person?"

"No, no. He was not cold, no. He was reserved. He didn't discuss his affairs a great deal. In fact, I didn't get to know Lew for close to a year after I met them, because Lew didn't push himself forward. He was never aggressive in any way I could see."

"Did you see Lew Graham during the week of March thirty-first, 1980?"

"Yes."

"Were his conduct or actions in any way different from what you would have expected from Lew Graham?"

"They were in no way different, no."

The prosecution and defense disagreed on whether Lewis Graham was a killer or a victim, but they had to agree that his reactions to the murder were unusual.

CARMOUCHE seemed bored when he cross-examined Ray Parish.

"Mr. Parish, you say it took you a while to get to know the defendant, Lew Graham?"

"Well, only to the extent that Lew would not be aggressive in developing friendships. He was reserved—he just didn't talk a great deal. He was never unfriendly."

"What about Kathleen Graham?" Carmouche asked.

"Kathy was, as you might say, a contrast. Kathy had an exceptionally outgoing personality. She pursued friendships. She was genuinely interested in people and had a very broad friendship with neighbors and people in the church," Parish said.

"Did you all come to Shreveport and visit while Kathy was alive?"

"Yes. About every six months."

"Do you know what church Kathy attended in Shreveport?"

"Summer Grove Baptist Church."

"Do you know whether or not Lew ever attended that church?"

"Yes. We've gone to church with them."

Carmouche glanced at his notes. "Mr. Parish, is Lewis Graham presently attending church?"

"Yes."

"You've never heard the defendant say he didn't believe in going to church?"

"Never."

"When did you first learn he had become a suspect in this case?"

"I left Shreveport the day of the funeral. When I came back the following weekend, Lew and I had to go over to the supermarket. At that time, Lew said, 'I think I should tell you before somebody else does, I'm considered a suspect.' That was the first time."

"Did he show any anger about that?"

"No."

Carmouche shrugged his shoulders. "No emotion about that either?"

"No."

SUTTON continued the defense with Joe Thibodeaux, Jr., Kathy's brother, asking about Lew Graham's attitude the day of her murder. "Based on your twenty years' acquaintance with him, did he act any differently than you expected him to?"

"No, sir. He's just a quiet person, reserved."

"Did you ever hear him yell at either your sister or any of his children?" Sutton asked.

"I don't believe I have ever heard him raise his voice."

"Did you ever see him cry or be hysterical or in any way outwardly manifest emotion?"

"Just once. When he spoke to my dad, that Monday afternoon."

"Where was he?"

"Across the street from his house. We were in-between the Godwins' house and the Stringers'."

"He was speaking to both of you?"

"Yes."

"What kind of emotion did you see?"

"I guess he wanted to cry. His words got thick, and his eyes got watery. He and my dad, they like, hugged each other."

"Is Lew Graham a cold person?"

"No, sir. Not at all."

CARMOUCHE approached Thibodeaux. "You described him as quiet and reserved, never displaying emotion. Is this how he was acting? Emotionless?"

"Except when he talked to my dad."

"Were you aware that Kathy and the defendant had been having problems in their marriage?" Carmouche asked.

"Yes, sir."

"Were you aware Lew Graham had been having an affair?"

"No, sir."

BECAUSE the D.A. had put on witnesses who said they'd seen Kathy upset the day before her murder, the defense team found their own balancing testimony.

Tammy Warwick was David Graham's girlfriend of two years. Kitchings had told Carmouche repeatedly that Kathy Graham didn't like Tammy and often told David he should date other people. In one story Kitchings had heard, David had gotten mad and punched the wall with his fist when his mother criticized his and Tammy's relationship.

"Were you at the Graham residence on Sunday, March thirtieth?"

"Yes."

"Tell me what you did that afternoon."

"David and Eric and a couple of friends of ours went and flew a kite in the South Park Mall parking lot. We came back to the house and ate some cake."

"Who was at the house when you returned?"

"Mr. and Mrs. Graham."

"What were they doing?"

"They were measuring the walls on the sides to see how high they wanted to put those—I forgot what they're called."

"Chair railings?" Sutton asked.

"That's right."

"How late did you stay that evening?"

"Until about six."

"Do you know how to cut hair?"

"I learned that day. David washed his hair, and Mrs. Graham combed it. She would hold it where I was supposed to cut it, and I'd cut it there."

"Did you have a towel around his neck while he was getting a haircut?"

"Yes."

"How was Mrs. Graham acting those hours you were over there that day?" Sutton asked.

"She was fine."

"Did you see her crying?"

"No."

"Sniffling around?"

"No."

"Did you notice whether or not she had dark eyes?"

"She looked fine to me. She was normal."

CARMOUCHE stood up and noticed Tammy sat up a little straighter when he approached. "In March of 1980, you were in the tenth grade?"

"Yes."

"You met David Graham shortly after your family moved here. Have you gone out pretty steadily since then?"

"Since September first of '79."

"The fact that you and David were going out a lot, did this bother Mrs. Graham?"

"No."

Carmouche looked surprised. "She never spoke to you about, maybe you all should go out with somebody else?"

"She talked to me to make sure he was a gentleman. He always was."

"On the day before she was killed, that Sunday, did Mrs. Graham talk to you about you and David seeing each other too much?"

He could see he was annoying her.

"She never talked about us seeing each other too much. Not to me, or David either."

"Or at least, David didn't tell you?"

"Maybe."

"Have you ever been in David's room on South Kirkwood?"

"On Christmas when she had all their things laid out all over the room. There were about four people in there with me besides him. Mrs. Graham too."

Carmouche raised the tempo of his questions. "Have you ever seen [Lewis Graham] in church?"

"I go with them a lot."

"Before or after Kathy was killed?"

"Since then."

"Mrs. Graham wasn't upset at all that day?"

"No."

"Did you ever hear her talking about a friend of the Stringers'?"

"Yes."

"She wasn't upset about that on Sunday?"

"She was concerned."

"It didn't cause her to cry?" Carmouche asked.

"I didn't see her cry at all."

17

SUTTON and Walker now challenged the prosecution's physical evidence. William Candler, a private detective in Shreveport, was called to the stand. In the beginning of the prosecution's case, several police officers had testified that they had found water in the sink and bathtub of the Graham house the morning of the murder, thus implying that Graham had cleaned up, perhaps even taken a shower, before he called the police or checked on his children.

After the trial began, after the defense team heard that police testimony, Sutton had sent Investigator Candler to the house on Kirkwood Drive to perform some experiments.

"Did you go to 2033 South Kirkwood at my request?" Sutton asked.

Candler, who wore horn-rimmed glasses, looked nervous as he answered. "Yes, sir. The first occasion was July twenty-second, 1981." He identified four pictures he took in the Graham bathroom.

"Would you tell me the conditions under which you made the photographs?"

"On July twenty-second, at eleven p.m., I turned on the shower, creating a spray as a simulation of a person taking a shower. I allowed the shower to run for sixteen minutes.

I turned the shower off, did some photography work, left and locked the premises. I returned on July twenty-third and made another series of photographs, beginning at six-twenty a.m." Candler described taking several pictures of the chain-link fence in the rear part of the Grahams' back yard. A number of the photographs depicted bent barbs on the top of some of the fences, suggesting that someone, at some point, had climbed over the fence either entering or leaving the back yard.

CO-PROSECUTOR Jim McMichael thought the whole line of questioning was silly. "Mr. Candler, when were you retained to work on this case?"

"Sixty days, ninety days ago."

"You consider this a big case [for your company]?" McMichael asked.

"Not the biggest one I've ever had, but apparently it's important to Shreveport."

"You made some observations about the room temperature at the time the shower test was done. You said it was ninety-two degrees. This would indicate the central air conditioning was not on at the time?"

"Yes, sir. It was not on."

"Do you have any idea what effect the room temperature might have on the evaporation of water in the tub?" McMichael asked.

"No, sir, I don't."

"Do you know what the relative humidity of the bathroom was when the test was done?" McMichael asked.

"No, sir."

"Do you know what effect that might have on the evaporation of water?"

"No, I would not."

"Do you have any idea how much water may have run into the tub during the sixteen-minute period of time?" McMichael asked.

"No, sir, I do not."

"How did you arrive at sixteen minutes?"

"I took from memory approximately how long I shower."

• • •

J.C. Day, a retired fingerprint expert from Dallas, testified he had found a second, partial, unidentified fingerprint on the hunting knife used to stab Lewis Graham. Under cross-examination from Carmouche, Day said it was possible that this second print could just be a repositioning of the full fingerprint which had been matched to Graham. Day also said it was possible that it wasn't.

Up next was Dr. Irving Stone, Chief of the Physical Science Section of the Dallas County (Texas) Institute for Forensic Sciences. His opinions were a complete mystery to the prosecution, and they were nervous about his testimony.

"Dr. Stone, did you visit the Graham residence at 2033 South Kirkwood?" Sutton asked.

"Yes sir, two times. The first was May thirtieth, 1980, and the other was some time this year—I don't recall the exact date."

"By whom were you accompanied on your first visit?"

"Dr. Charles Petty. He's the Director of the Institute and the Chief Medical Examiner for Dallas County."

"Did you visit the Northwest Louisiana Crime Lab?" Sutton asked.

"Yes, sir. The first visit was February seventh, 1981, and the second was in March of this year."

Stone described how he and Petty had searched the home for signs of bloodstains. They had made their trip to Shreveport long after Graham had had the house cleaned of the blood spatters. Stone told the jury about looking at the locks on the utility room door, and of his expertise as a locksmith. Stone repeated previous trial testimony that the locks were faulty and could be opened using a knife, credit card, or other flat object without destroying the door by prying.

Then Sutton used Stone to demonstrate his theory of how Graham would have had to hold the hunting knife to stab himself and still leave a fingerprint on the handle where it was found. In the defense's demonstration, a self-inflicted stab wound appeared unlikely, awkward.

A Dallas serologist testified she had typed spots of blood found on David Graham's bedspread. In addition to bloodstains of type O, the same as Lewis Graham's, she also testified that she found some type A—the same as Kathy Graham's.

The prosecution, on cross-examination, did not ask the witness to speculate how the blood could have gotten on David Graham's bed linens.

METICULOUSLY dressed in suit and bow tie, Dr. Charles Petty conveyed the persona of a detail man. One of the best-known forensic pathologists in the South, he was an immovable expert witness. After relaying his credentials to the court, Petty leaned back in his chair, as though ready to tell the world exactly what he thought.

"Dr. Petty, are you familiar with the type of wounds Mrs. Graham received?" Sutton asked.

Petty had been allowed to study all of the crime-scene and autopsy photographs. "Yes, sir. There were several separate and distinct wounds about the head and face. The first most obviously present was just to the left of the midline of the head, on the crown. This wound was approximately two-plus inches in length. It penetrated through the entire scalp and was a compound wound made by several blows with a firm, heavy instrument. It's impossible to tell how many blows were struck here. Three, four, possibly five."

Petty continued. "The next wound area involved the forehead. This was a huge, gaping wound with multiple fractures of the skull beneath it. In addition, there was a tearing of the skin in the right eyebrow area. That was about an inch in length, involving the upper and lower eyelids. There was some stretching of the skin, and the entire area was a dark, bluish-purple-red color. A further wound was on the bridge of the nose, and the final face wound involved the outer aspect of the left nostril, consisting of a sort of irregular tearing of the skin through the entire thickness of the lip."

"Can you form an opinion, to a reasonable medical certainty, as to the possible cause of the wounds to the right eye and nostril?"

"Yes, sir. The wounds are different. First, the wound of the right eye. There was extensive fracturing and breaking of the bones beneath the forehead. These fracture lines extend in all directions, with a portion of the bone being driven into the brain itself. Within a reasonable medical certainty, the wound to the forehead caused the adjacent tearing and fracturing of the bone beneath the eye. The other wound, to the left nostril, was a special type of wound. That wound is the result of the blow forcing the head into the underlying object [the bed] and the teeth being forced up through the facial structures at that point."

Petty went on to say there was an indication the blow came from the victim's right to left. That differed from what Dr. McCormick had said and suggested the perpetrator was left-handed.

Sutton continued. "If a person were to receive the wounds such as you've described, then, during an autopsy, some blood was found in the stomach and lungs, there was the appearance of shocked kidneys, and in addition, a few white blood cells were found in a wound to the top of the head, would those items indicate anything to you about a time sequence between the wounds to the top of the head, and the forehead wound?"

Petty leaned back as if he'd never heard the question before. "Your question is very complicated. First, the presence of blood in the lungs and stomach. Blood gets into the lungs by being inhaled through the normal air passages. In this case, there was also tremendous fracturing at the base of the skull, opening into those air sinuses. Both of those things can take place very rapidly. Shocked kidneys can appear in five or ten minutes. The other factor you mentioned, I believe, was white blood cells known as polys. That would indicate a reaction to some sort of wound."

"Taking all those items together, does that indicate whether or not there was a difference in time between the two series of wounds?" Sutton asked.

"There is nothing you have given me that is a signpost to when these things occurred. I can't answer your question."

"Dr. Petty, I want to show you a copy of a photograph marked State's Exhibit 3, which reflects a bloodstain on the carpet in the master bedroom. Can you look at that and tell me approximately how much blood it might take to cause that stain?"

"Not very much. It's thick, clotted, adhering to the carpet material. I'm talking about three or four or five cc's of blood, about as much as might be contained in the smallest joint of my small finger."

"Is there any way, within reasonable medical certainty, you could give an opinion as to how long it would take a wound to have bled that much?"

"Not within reasonable medical certainty. The factors which would influence the rate of bleeding would be individual things—blood pressure, how much pressure was applied to the wound, whether the person was sitting, standing, or moving about."

"If you look at the wounds you have described, is there any way you can make an opinion as to the accuracy of those wounds?"

Petty paused a moment before answering. "No, I really can't give you an opinion on that, because I don't know what the target was in the first place."

COURT was adjourned for lunch before Petty was cross-examined. Carmouche and McMichael discussed the expert's testimony, decided he'd done nothing to hurt their case, and went back in with the intent of asking him as little as possible.

Carmouche picked up the sledgehammer. "Dr. Petty, you indicated you couldn't tell whether the blows were accurate or not. If you were going to kill somebody with a weapon like this, where would you strike the blows?"

The noted pathologist cleared his throat, and glanced at the defense team. "I would tend to strike the top of the head."

Carmouche let the hammer land on the counsel table with a loud thud. "Thank you, Doctor."

SUTTON and Walker finished out the afternoon with a series of witnesses designed to show a solid marriage between Lewis and Kathy Graham.

James Phillips, Graham's accountant, discussed the couple's sizable inheritance income and Lew Graham's desire to allow all the money to become community property.

William Levinson, Graham's insurance agent and partner in a storage company, testified about other of the Grahams' financial matters. Joe LeSage, an attorney, asserted that, if he had wanted to, Graham could have kept his family inheritance separate from his and Kathy's joint finances.

18

_____

On Wednesday, July 29, the defense continued to focus on the character and personality of Lewis Graham. A.W. Bridges, who'd worked many years as an advisor to a local Boy Scout troop, told the jury how he and Graham had worked with a troop sponsored by the Christ United Methodist Church in Southern Hills.

"Was it ever any problem for you, turning the scout troop over to Lew Graham?" Sutton asked.

"No. In fact, I was very disappointed when he gave up the troop because David, his oldest son, apparently lost interest in scouting."

"Were you ever able to observe whether or not the scouts related to Lew Graham as a leader?"

"In running a scout troop, Lew had the same philosophy I did. Mainly, you work with the older boys, the junior leaders, and the very young boys. Lew had a good rapport with the boys. He was patient, which is something you don't find in all scout leaders, and he was fair but firm."

Carmouche only had one question. "Mr. Bridges, do you have any idea what happened in the Graham residence on March thirty-first, 1980?"

"I have no knowledge of what happened."

• • •

PAUL Long, a childhood friend of Graham's, came up to the witness stand.

"In your high school years, do you know whether or not Lew Graham was active in the Boy Scouts?" Sutton asked.

"I ran across Lew in Troop 19, which was the Methodist group. I was in Troop 50. We had a lot of good, spirited competition against each other—knot-tying, that sort of thing."

"From your knowledge of Lew Graham over the years, how would you describe his personality?"

"You have to know Lew. It took me a while to get to know him. I've never heard Lew blow his cool. He is very calculative. He will weigh things and then he'll speak," Long said.

"Have you ever heard him talk bad about anyone?"

"No."

"Have you ever heard him use profanity, either to or about someone?"

"Not in my presence."

"If you were to see Lew Graham during a time of sadness, would you be surprised if there was no outward manifestation of that sadness?" Sutton asked.

"No. I remember when his father died. I could tell he was saddened at the loss of his father."

"Was there any outward manifestation of emotion on Lew's part?"

"No."

CARMOUCHE repeated himself. "Do you have any idea what occurred in the Graham residence on March thirty-first, 1980?"

"No idea at all."

BILL Simon, another old friend, came up next. "Do you know whether or not in high school Lew Graham graduated with honors?" Sutton asked.

"Yes, he did. He was very high scholastically, and he was president of the Key Club. I know he was a leader in just about everything he was in."

"After college, did you maintain contact with Lew Graham?" Sutton asked.

"Yes, I did. Jim, Paul, Lew, and myself kept in touch over the years, and we'd meet in Lafayette whenever the four of us were together. I would say that we would meet on the average of about once every five years since we graduated college."

"And the times you would see Lew Graham, as the years passed, was there ever any significant change you noticed from when you knew him in Lafayette?"

"No changes I know of. He was always emotionally very stable and someone I looked up to."

CARMOUCHE didn't stand up. "Mr. Simon, you finished college in what year?"

"1963."

"And you've seen Lew Graham on the average of once every five years since then? About four times in the last twenty years?"

"Probably so, yes, sir."

"Have you ever been to Shreveport, other than today?"

"No. This is the first time I have ever come to Shreveport."

THE defense shifted to evaluations of Graham's mind and character from two psychologists and a psychiatrist. Dr. Donald Gucker, a clinical psychologist, had the wild unkempt hair stereotypic of a professor. He testified that he had given Graham a battery of psychological tests, an IQ test, the Bender Gestalt, the House-Tree-Person Projective Drawings, Rorschach inkblots, and the MMPI personality index.

"Dr. Graham is a highly intelligent individual. His IQ was 132, which places him at approximately the ninety-eighth percentile—that means his score is better than ninety-eight percent of the population," Gucker said. Furthermore, all the test results showed the defendant to be within normal ranges. "There was no indication of emotional disturbance, or schizophrenia. Schizophrenia is a very serious emotional disorder, and one looks for it in capital cases because it involves non-logical thinking. In this case, there was none present. Both the MMPI and the Rorschach suggested some moderate depression and moderate anxiety."

"These tests were done in August of 1980?" Sutton asked.

"Correct. I should say the MMPI has three scales of what we call validity indicators. They are sensitive to any attempt to produce a fake sick or fake good profile. For example, individuals in job-applicant situations often produce what I call a best-foot-forward profile; they have *no* problems. I always get them back in, have a little talk, and they do it over again. Dr. Graham's validity scales look very open. He was very open and frank in his answers and didn't try to sway it one way or another, which I think is important."

"In these tests, is there any way you can read the question and determine whether there is a right or wrong answer?" Sutton asked.

"It depends on which test you're talking about. Some of the items on the MMPI would probably be transparent. Some of them are fakable, but we know it because there are three validity scales that show that. The Rorschach, I would think, is rather 'un-fakable,' except maybe if you were a psychologist familiar with Rorschach. His response time was so fast he obviously wasn't taking the time to think a great deal."

"In all these tests, did you reach a conclusion as to the control or aggression in Dr. Graham's personality?" Sutton asked.

"I saw no indication of any aggression in his personality, no hostility. I saw some depression, I saw some anxiety. I saw a sane individual, non-psychotic, not emotionally sick, who had a great deal of control, who was obviously a reserved person."

"Is this type of personality consistent or inconsistent with violent conduct?"

"I think it would be inconsistent," Gucker said.

• • •

JIM McMichael addressed the witness.

"You described some of these tests as self-reporting. That means the individual supplies you with the information you use to evaluate him?"

"I'd like you to understand what is involved. The MMPI comes in a booklet that has 566 true-false items in it. The individual sits by himself and responds to those 566 items. Again, let me point out this is a very sophisticated instrument, with literally thousands of pieces of research about it, especially in terms of faking it," Gucker said.

McMichael looked puzzled. "I don't think I tried to intimate that he may have faked the test. Why do you keep bringing it up?"

"It is often a question in these matters."

"Well, is it your testimony that it's *impossible* to fake the test?" McMichael asked.

"No, it's not impossible. People tend to do it in varying degrees."

McMichael looked at Graham, at the jury, then back at Gucker. "Back to my original question—to put it in a simple form. All your information *about* Lew Graham came *from* Lew Graham?"

"Yes. That's the only way to get information about a person."

McMichael walked toward the jury. "You're not saying it's impossible for him to do violent things, are you?"

"I believe it is unlikely in terms of my observation and data."

"Don't you think a biochemist, with this much contact with a medical school, would be more able to fake a test?"

"Well, when you talk about faking one of those tests, it's an extremely complex effort. I'm not sure *I* could fake an MMPI. I just think it's unlikely."

SOFT-SPOKEN, intellectual Milton Rosenzweig, the Grahams' marriage counselor in 1979, took the stand. Graham thought the quiet psychologist could give valuable testimony about the details of his and Kathy's married life.

The white-haired and balding counselor said he first met with the Grahams around the beginning of 1979, at the recommendation of Dr. Jim Smith.

"My usual procedure is to meet with each member of the couple separately at first. When I feel I have enough information to evaluate the situation, I meet with them together. We discuss what the problem areas are, and what I think the procedure should be from that point on if it's a viable situation."

"What were their problems, as you saw them?" Sutton asked.

Graham glanced at the jury, and was pleased to see them giving the doctor their undivided attention.

"When I saw them, it was after things had built up over a number of years. Kathy was feeling separated from her husband emotionally. She was struggling very hard to get closer to him, using ineffectual means that were actually making things worse. Dr. Graham was responding by withdrawing more and more emotionally, trying to keep the peace but actually getting more distant," Rosenzweig said.

"Is that what laymen commonly refer to as a 'communication problem'?" Sutton asked.

"Yes, very definitely."

"How were their problems expressed?"

"Well, Kathy would get upset, get emotional, cry. Sometimes she would raise her voice, and Dr. Graham would get very quiet and withdraw. He might leave. He is a jogger; he might go out and jog, or just leave and come back when things were quieter."

"What did Dr. Graham see as the problem in the marriage?"

"He saw it, more or less, as being unable to please his wife. He didn't directly know what she wanted from him, and couldn't honestly give her the things she was asking for, like undying declarations of love," Rosenzweig said.

"Did Kathy Graham ever tell you whether or not there was any, say, abuse in the marriage?"

"I always ask how feelings are expressed, particularly anger, depression, and anxiety. Her answer was that that was one of their problems: his feelings were not expressed."

"When you counsel with people, are there patterns that married people develop that persons such as you can recognize?"

"Yes. A marital relationship of any length of time is somewhat like a dance, with one more or less leading in some areas. People get into patterns in their interpersonal relationships."

Graham vividly recalled the yelling and silence that had occurred in his marriage.

"During counseling sessions with couples, do they just keep coming on and on—do you decide when it can terminate, or do they?" Sutton asked.

"Usually it's by mutual agreement. The situation reaches a point where I feel they've gained enough insight, and we terminate with the understanding that if anything comes up in the future, the telephone is always available."

"Did your counseling with Lew and Kathy terminate by mutual consent?"

The psychologist glanced at his notes. "Yes, on the nineteenth of April, 1979, I suggested they could stretch out the sessions to every other week. On May third, they said they felt strong enough to go on their own with one more appointment to sort of summarize what had been accomplished. The last appointment was on the seventeenth of May."

Sutton walked toward the jury. "If a couple were seeking and obtaining counseling, and at the same time one of them was engaged in a random sexual relationship outside of the marriage, is that inconsistent with their coming to see you for marriage counseling?"

"No, it is not."

"Did you reach a conclusion, as a result of your counseling, whether or not their marriage had improved?"

"Yes, I felt it had improved."

• • •

CARMOUCHE tried to poke a few holes in the marriage counselor's conclusions. "Dr. Rosenzweig, do you have any idea whether or not Kathleen and Lew Graham had gone to counseling with someone else prior to coming to you?"

"Yes, I believe they had seen Mr. Bob Rausch, and Kathy had seen Dr. William McBride for her own anxiety and he had given her some mild medication," Rosenzweig said.

"So they had seen two counselors prior to getting to you?" Carmouche asked.

"Correct."

"Did you get the impression Kathleen Graham was not volatile?"

"No, she was fairly volatile. Her voice would rise, and Dr. Graham's voice would get quieter or he would leave."

"Have you ever described that kind of relationship as 'fire and ice'?"

"No, I've never used that term."

"Part of their problem, as I understand, was the defendant was unable to express his undying devotion to his wife?" Carmouche asked.

"She wanted him to say 'I love you.' And she wanted him to say it and mean it. And she wanted him to say it and mean it forever."

"Was Lewis Graham the type of person that could say 'I love you' and mean it?" Carmouche asked.

"Yes, I think he could and mean it."

"Could he say 'I love you' to a mistress and mean it?"

"Yes."

"Did the defendant ever indicate to you, if things didn't get better, it wasn't tolerable, he wouldn't be able to continue living there?"

"Yes."

Carmouche looked at Graham. "That his wife was very sarcastic on occasions?"

"Yes."

"That when she would become more sarcastic, the more she did, the more he withdrew?" Carmouche asked.

"Yes."

"Is that the type of relationship, that if it continues to build and build for some time, it could result in violence?"

"That would depend on the individual."

SUTTON responded on redirect. "Dr. Rosenzweig, it's been asked and answered, it depends on the individual. What about Lew Graham? Is his personality such that it would cause him to react in violence? Is there anything in his [background] indicating that [violence] would be his response?"

"In my opinion, there is not."

CARMOUCHE remembered something. "Dr. Rosenzweig, would it surprise you if, on the day of the murder, a few hours after the murder occurred, the defendant stated to some people that he wasn't upset because he and his wife weren't getting along?"

The counselor arched his eyebrows. "Yes, it would."

"What would that mean to you?"

"That would mean that things had regressed from the point I'd last heard from them."

AFTER lunch, the expert testimony continued with Dr. Paul Ware. Ware was a forensic psychiatrist, well-known in the legal community, primarily with criminal defense lawyers.

Graham knew from their previous meetings that Dr. Ware had no lack of self-esteem, and hoped that the psychiatrist's abundant ego didn't come across as too cocky.

"Dr. Graham had a very clear personality adaptation of two types. One would be a little of what's referred to as a loner or daydreamer. And probably the other could be referred to as a perfectionist or workaholic. I don't consider that psychiatric illness. When I examined him in August, he was suffering from what I would diagnose as a situational reaction to extreme stress and mild depression. The reason it's situational is because once the stress is removed, the symptoms go away."

"You mentioned he was a loner—does that mean antisocial?" Sutton asked.

"No sir. He is the furthest away from antisocial, or the criminal profile, or the liar or cheat, you could get. He is completely at the other end of the spectrum."

"How does the fact of having a sexual relation outside of marriage fit into that personality?"

"It fits right in. When he was born, his father was away at graduate school. Between the ages of three and five, he lived with his grandmother. At that time, his father was serving overseas. The first five years of growing up was in a family with a father largely not present. When he was around three or four, he fell from a rope and fractured his lumbar vertebrae. As a result, he was in a total body cast from his armpits down to his ankles for six to eight weeks. The second phase of his life, he lived in Lafayette. His father was a teacher in the biology department when he was six to ten years old. Then his father went to the Korean War and was again taken out of the family. In the seventh grade, Lew developed polio. He spent six months in a polio center, and was left with a residual weakness in his right leg. For the second time in his life, he had to learn to walk, and he had to wear a spring-loaded brace to compensate for foot drop." The psychiatrist paused. "If we stop and think about what is happening, we have a man who has grown up largely without a father, very little influence from a father, who has suffered a great deal of physical illness that invites—in fact, forces—you to do one of two things: you become highly dependent on other people and have them take care of you, or you become a survivor. You are looking at the survivor."

Whispering broke out in the courtroom at the word "survivor." Graham immediately realized that the term had negative connotations with the spectators. He hoped the jury didn't take it wrong.

Sutton continued. "Based on his history and the information you have, do you have an opinion as to whether Lew Graham's personality is consistent or inconsistent with violent attack?"

Ware was absolute. "His personality profile is the *most* inconsistent with violent conduct of *any* individual I've examined in fifteen years."

Sutton glanced at the jury, trying to read their reaction.

Carmouche and McMichael exchanged glances, and the D.A. wrote "fifteen years" and underlined it on his legal pad. He was anxious to get a shot at the psychiatrist on cross-examination.

"Dr. Ware," Sutton continued, "what about the situations you hear about, particularly with quiet people, that they store up something, and all of a sudden, the dam breaks?"

Graham knew that this was what the prosecution thought—that he had lost control in a moment of anger.

"People write big books about that, but if you review the literature, as I have, in regard to dangerousness, I have not found a documented case of a healthy individual who has no previous history of instability, who has not shown any type of psychosis, who has never been violent before, who has never been treated violently, who suddenly goes berserk and loses it all. People don't turn it on and off that easily," Ware said.

"From your training as a psychiatrist, if any of us experience stress—such as the tragic death of a loved one—is there a common reaction that we all experience? Is there such a thing as a 'normal' reaction?" Sutton asked.

"If there is, I don't know what it is. Some people will overreact to stress, show their feelings, or become confused in their thinking. Some will feel they have to run away. Some will feel they have to attack. I don't know what the average reaction is."

CARMOUCHE stood up and walked toward the jury, while looking at Graham. "You described the defendant as a loner. As a loner that's not antisocial?"

The psychiatrist shook his head. "There is absolutely no way Dr. Graham can be antisocial. Lewis Graham follows the rules."

"If he comes to a corner and it says, 'Don't walk,' he doesn't walk?"

"As much as any of us."

"As a loner, he preferred not being around other people?" Carmouche asked.

"As a loner, he is shy. He does not compete with people. He's more passive than active in relationships and situations. A lot of that, I think, was related to when he was little."

"A follower rather than a leader? Is that his history too?"

"Yes. He is a combination of the loner and thinker, an overall noncompetitive type of person who is programmed to achieve and do well. The perfectionist part of his personality makes him hard on himself."

"You also took note of the fact that he had been seeing a clinical psychologist along with his wife, and while attending counseling, he was also having a sexual affair. That didn't seem inconsistent?" Carmouche asked.

"No."

"Was it okay because he was in the Boy Scouts, and his daddy went to Korea?"

Dr. Ware frowned at the question. "I didn't say anything about it being okay. I don't think *he* thinks having the affair was right. He feels guilty about having the affair. It's not unusual to see someone thirty-five years old, who's been married for ten years, starting to reevaluate his marriage relationship. As he described the affair, this was a lady he worked with, and they shared thoughts. She was smart. She could be interested in what he was interested in. Their friendship moved to include some sexual involvement. He wasn't perfect, in terms of his ability to work things out. He met someone who was understanding and caring, and maybe she was needy too," Ware said.

Carmouche walked near the counsel table and looked directly at Graham. "You also described him as a 'survivor.' Is a survivor the type of person that, no matter how much trouble they're in, they're going to survive it somehow?"

"Yes, sir. He's a thinking survivor. He's convinced that if he's clear about all of this, everyone is going to understand."

"The bottom line on all of this, Dr. Ware, is you're saying the defendant is not of the personality type to commit a violent act. You're not saying it would be impossible?"

"I'm saying it would be improbable. I can't determine whether anything is possible or not possible."

Carmouche turned and faced the witness. "It seems like, many times, we read about assassins. Somebody tries to shoot the Pope, or the President, and you always read stories from their high school teachers, who talk about what an outstanding student they were. How do you explain those types of things?"

"If you go back on those people, all I've ever examined, and you get a careful history, you will get, 'Oh, I remember that guy. He was always a good guy. But I remember once he killed a dog, or killed a cat, or I remember once he told me, "Professor So-and-so, I'd really like to get him." ' I've always found that if you go back."

Carmouche glanced at the jury. "Or killing rats—a loner, dreamer, perfectionist?"

"No, sir. That's a loaded question."

19

———

THE tenth day of the trial gave the defense its opportunity to dispute MacDonell's incriminating opinions about the bloodstains found in the murder room.

Judith Bunker, an assistant to the Chief Medical Examiner in Orlando, Florida, had been working in bloodstain pattern analysis since 1974, when she attended a workshop taught by MacDonell. At the time the defense team contacted Bunker, no one knew that the D.A. was planning to bring in his own expert in the person of Professor MacDonell.

Graham knew that his case had been deeply injured by MacDonell's testimony. He hoped that Judith Bunker would be able to balance that effect with her testimony.

Bunker had large, dark eyes and a deep-tanned complexion. She had worked many long and hard hours for Lewis Graham and was anxious to tell the jury her findings. Bunker was a confident professional who meticulously documented her findings. She had visited the house on Kirkwood Drive, interviewed Graham, and built a specially constructed room of the same dimensions as the master bedroom, in which she had several men wield a sledgehammer at a blood-filled sponge.

"Mrs. Bunker, after you performed the analysis of the blood spots on the ceiling, the walls, the bed, the lamp, and so forth, did you then have a picture of the overall pattern in the room?" Sutton began.

"Yes."

"Did you then conduct any experiments to determine if these patterns could be reproduced?"

"After looking at all the evidence that was presented to me, it became apparent the victim was struck while she was on the right side of the bed, and received a minimum of two blows on this side. She was then on the south side of the bed, where she received another blow," Bunker said.

Bunker used an architect's rendering of the crime scene specially prepared for her court appearance. The display contained four clear plastic overlays, each of which held different information. One overlay showed every blood-stain detected in the bedroom, another featured only the furnishings, another the bloodstains from the ceiling, and the last showed the dimensions of the room and the various distances from the bed to different stains.

Graham had seen the visual aid in pre-trial conferences and thought it did an excellent job of supporting Bunker's conclusions.

Bunker pointed to the drawing as she explained her procedures. "I felt it was important to position not only the victim, but also the assailant. Considering the cast-off stains on the ceiling, the stains are being cast off the weapon as it's swung overhead. There are certain experiments I needed to test the overhead motion."

Graham noticed that she was careful to maintain good eye contact with the jurors. "I purchased a weapon of the same size and configuration and constructed a room of the same dimensions to allow me to test what type of patterns we might expect to find on the ceiling and walls. We used human blood, from the blood bank.

"Considering now the initial impact point [from the foot, on the right side of the bed], in taking this hammer, and impacting it with a sponge containing human blood, liquid blood, we tried several different positions. The only one that allowed us to get staining on the wall and ceiling was when we had the person use a left overhead swing. Now, the position of the assailant has to be at least sixteen to twenty inches out, because of the nightstand. He has to be at least twenty-five to thirty inches from the wall in order to impact this area of the bed."

Bunker showed the jury photographs of the various bloodstain patterns in her recreated bedroom. In her experiments, there was substantially more blood spattered, though her testimony dealt with pattern similarity, not quantity. She went on to connect her experiments to Graham's T-shirt.

"I had the person who was taking this hammer and impacting it on the sponge raising his arm back and coming down again. Each time he did that, blood was cast off the weapon. It did hit the ceiling, and it did hit the wall. But there was no blood found on the back of this person's T-shirt."

Bunker said she placed someone on the floor, at the approximate distance and position Graham described in his story. Working with a T-shirt, she was able to duplicate the stains found on the front of Graham's shirt, the ones Professor MacDonell said had been caused by wiping a knife. Bunker recreated the stains by simply having the person remove the shirt while wet blood was on it. When the shirt was pulled up and off, it folded, creating a double, parallel staining similar to the ones Graham had. She also noted that during her experiments the person lying on the floor received stains similar to the ones on the back of Graham's shirt. MacDonell had said those stains were caused by cast-off from the hammer as the beating was taking place.

Graham was pleased with the professional presentation she was making to the jury.

"When I first began working on this case, my objective was to prove or disprove whether a person wearing those clothes could inflict those wounds, and if, using the weapon overhead, we could reproduce what we see on the T-shirt. I set up my experiments three separate times, and each time, I had three blows struck, adding blood to the sponge."

"As a result of your analysis of the police photographs, your personal visits to the scene, the examination of tangible items, and the test experiments, did you arrive at any conclusions?" Sutton asked.

"First of all, I feel the victim was first on the right side of the bed, and the impact point was fifty-three to fifty-seven inches from that door [to the hallway], thirty-one to thirty-three inches above the floor, and the victim was in a position at rest with the left side of her head on the pillow. A minimum of two blows were inflicted by an assailant who was standing between the right side of the bed and the wall. The assailant was using a left overhand motion because of the blood cast off on the ceiling and wall. After this, the victim was moved or moved from the right side of the bed to the left side of the bed. At some point, she was upright, as evidenced by staining seen on her neck. She came to rest in a supine position, face up at the time the blows were inflicted in this area."

Graham could see that the jury was attentive, and they seemed to be following the expert's narration.

Bunker began her summary. "I feel the blood on the clothing of Dr. Graham is consistent with forceful bloodshed, cast-off staining, splashed and spilled blood, and directional blood. The spatter on the front of the T-shirt is consistent with being produced from blood cast off a moving object, or it could be from medium-velocity spatter. The stains on the front part of the T-shirt are round, and their distance from the impact point is anywhere from two feet to more than four feet. The stains on the back of the shirt, I feel, are more consistent with the subject being in a prone position.

"I find the statements reported to me by Dr. Graham are consistent with my findings," she concluded.

"As a bottom line, is the pattern of staining on Dr. Graham's T-shirt and shorts consistent with his having received part on the front while he was on the floor between the window and the bed, and part on the back, while he was

on the floor on his stomach near the door?" Sutton asked.
"Yes."

Graham was pleased with the quality of her presentation. He knew it was important to his case that Judith Bunker's testimony remain solid and strong under cross-examination.

AFTER a lunch break, Graham sat back nervously and watched Jim McMichael go to work.

"Mrs. Bunker, I don't know if Mr. Sutton went into this when you were stating your qualifications. What degrees did you obtain in college?"

"I have no college degree."

"Did you go to any college?" McMichael asked.

"No, I did not."

"I think Mr. Sutton indicated you had appeared on a national television program. What program was that?"

"It was a show called 'That's Incredible.' "

McMichael used Bunker's slides during his cross-examination. "You said that when you had gone to the scene, it had already been cleaned?"

"Yes."

"This is a series of four pictures, which I believe you've indicated brought you to your conclusions as to the positioning of the victim during the various beatings. Your conclusion was there were two separate areas of impact?" McMichael asked.

"Two separate areas of impact."

"You said you determined there were at least two blows over on this right side of the bed. You wouldn't dispute testimony from a pathologist [that] there appeared to be four blows?"

"Sir, I wouldn't dispute a pathologist, because I am not a pathologist."

Graham winced.

"After you examined all pictures and made your conclusions, then you began your own independent testing or experimentation?"

"That's right."

"You said your two objectives were to determine the position of the assailant, and the overhead motion used to administer the beating?" McMichael asked.

"Yes."

"Was it not also your objective to see if you could re-create the defendant's story?"

"I did not attempt to recreate the defendant's story. I wanted to see if there were consistencies or inconsistencies with his statements."

"You had talked to him before you began your experiments?"

"Yes."

"You had examined his statements to the police?"

"Yes."

"You had talked with Mr. Sutton?"

"Yes."

"You had gone to the Crime Lab?"

"Yes."

"Examined the physical evidence?"

"Yes."

Graham wished McMichael would stop.

"Your tests included having a man lie over here on his back, and a man lie over here on his stomach?"

"Yes," Bunker said.

"Is it not one of your objectives to see if his story could be recreated?"

"I never tried to recreate his story. I tried to reconstruct a chain of events that occurred during and following bloodshed. And, in reconstructing, to see if the statements were consistent."

Graham could tell by the tone in Bunker's voice that she was losing patience with the assistant D.A.

"What type of blood did you use?"

"This is human blood, obtained from the blood bank."

"The sponge that you used. What size sponge was that?"

"Oh, it was your basic sponge, about six-by-four, let's say."

"How much blood did you put on the sponge?" McMichael asked.

"I have no idea. Just enough to get it good and bloody."

"Isn't it true that hitting a sponge with a hammer would create more spatter than hitting a human head with a hammer?"

"I don't know that that's true."

"Now, each time the sponge was hit, it was re-wetted with blood?"

"Yes," Bunker said.

"Who instructed the assailants how far back to bring the hammer?"

"I never instructed anyone. I told them to hit like they were going to kill somebody. I used a mechanic. I used a police officer. I tried it myself."

"Did you ever have your assailants strike four blows in rapid succession?"

"I had them strike three blows."

Graham looked at the jury but couldn't tell what they were thinking.

"Without stopping to re-blood the sponge?"

"I always made sure the sponge was bloody," Bunker said.

"But that took into account that you would at least have to stick your hand in there and turn the sponge over?"

"Yes."

"So each blow was a full-fledged rare-back-and-smash-the-sponge?"

"Yes."

"These spatters were produced with a sponge that had an unmeasured amount of blood?"

"That's right."

"And you're saying that a sponge would be porous, unlike a human head covered with skin?"

"A sponge is porous, but it is a vessel. It is the only way to work with human blood without inflicting someone and damaging their skin."

McMichael paused. "You've never used a coconut filled with Jell-O?"

"Oh, I have, but I was not studying blood spatter at that point," Bunker said.

"Would you describe the spatter on the front of the shorts?"

"The spatter is consistent with medium-velocity spatter. It seems to be concentrated on the left leg of the shorts."

"Isn't there a simple explanation [for why the concentration is on the left leg]?"

"I don't have one."

McMichael placed his hands over the handle of an imaginary sledgehammer, and held it down as if he had just struck someone.

"If I'm going to strike an object that will spatter blood, and I do so, my arms would be covering up a lot of the front of the shirt. Wouldn't a lot of the spatter get on my arms?"

"It could."

"Wouldn't that explain the fact that there may be a little more concentration of spatters on one leg—because it got on my arms and my hands and the hammer?"

"It could."

Using the advice of Herbert MacDonell and Ray Herd, McMichael systematically attacked virtually every conclusion of the Florida blood expert. Bunker wasn't used to such an in-depth challenge and lost patience with the young prosecutor.

After more than two hours on cross-examination, Bunker was allowed to step down.

DEE Hopkins of Indianapolis, one of Kathy Graham's oldest and closest friends, testified as to what she knew of the Grahams' relationship.

"Did Kathy Graham visit you in February of 1980?" Sutton asked.

"Yes, she and Katie came up to spend a few days, while I had a vacation from school."

"In February of 1980, do you know whether or not the marriage between Lew and Kathy was having any problems?" Sutton asked.

"I think there had been problems, but when she was [in Indianapolis], she said [the past year] had been the best year they'd ever had. She was anxious to get back because they were building a new house, and she was very excited, and she wanted to talk to the builder," Hopkins said.

"Did you speak to Kathy Graham the Saturday before she was killed?"

"Yes. She called me Saturday around ten o'clock in the morning. We had made plans at Easter for both families to meet in New Orleans, and we were going to travel to where Lew's sister lived, and she was going to show us different things."

"Did she indicate to you in any way how she was feeling?"

"Well, when she called she said she really felt bad because her period had started. And she was upset because a neighbor, Marsha, had a brother who had been killed in a plane accident. I don't think she knew the brother, but she was upset for her friend."

CARMOUCHE was brief. "Mrs. Hopkins, the new house they were planning—did Kathy ever express any reservations to you that she didn't really care for the new house, that she was happy where she was?"

"She hated the house on Kirkwood. It was just that they had had so many things happen to them at that house. There was an incident with one of the younger sons," Hopkins said, in reference to Eric's story of an earlier break-in.

"Have you ever heard the name Judith Carson?" Carmouche asked.

"Yes."

"Did you hear it from Kathy?"

"No."

"Did she ever discuss with you any knowledge of whether or not her husband may or may not have had an affair?"

"No, she didn't."

20

FINALLY the production was winding to a close, and everyone involved was glad. The trial had been a strain on all the players, from the leads to the most peripheral: the five-member ladies' sewing circle from Southern Hills that arrived at the courthouse door promptly at 6:15 every morning; the skeptical reporters, clamoring for position, anxious to hear the story, tired and exhilarated at the same time (since cameras weren't allowed into the courthouse, the six and ten o'clock news had been replete with scenes of Graham, his lawyers, and his kids walking back and forth from the car to the courthouse); the middle-aged lawyer who paid a college student fifty dollars to save him a place in line for a precious seat in the courtroom; the blind man who worked the small concession booth on the first floor of the Caddo Parish Courthouse (no telling how much he'd cleared since he started bringing sandwiches upstairs during the lunch breaks); a couple of dozen acquaintances and friends of Kathy Graham's, most of the opinion Graham was the killer; the lawyers, Paul Carmouche, Jim McMichael, Bobby Sutton, and Glenn Walker; Sutton's secretary, Debbi Ware, who was present at the counsel table every minute of the trial, and was keeping the law firm's books at night; sixty-one-year-old Senior Judge C.J. Bolin, Jr., who had canceled court the Sunday before so he could attend his youngest daughter's wedding; Elizabeth Moran, the defendant's younger sister, recently remarried, supportive of Graham from the beginning, facing the possibility that she might become responsible for raising his children; and Lewis Graham himself.

For Graham, the tension of sitting in the courtroom, listening to the D.A. call him a murderer, had increased day by day. Graham had grown weary of seeing the curiosity, the speculation in the eyes of everyone he looked at.

SEVENTEEN-YEAR-OLD David Graham was popular in school, able to make friends with a wide group of kids while being quiet and reserved like his father. He believed in his father's innocence, and his testimony conveyed it.

David told the jury about the day before his mother was killed. He and his brother, sister, and mother went to church together that morning. He said his father returned from a faculty retreat while they were at church.

David described a "nothing special" Sunday of flying kites and piddling around the house. He told the jurors about getting a haircut from his mother and Tammy, thus identifying the wet towel that had loomed like a specter over the first two days of the trial.

Sutton stepped around the lawyer's table. "David, do you recall what time you went to bed that night?"

"Eleven o'clock."

"Did you see your mom and dad before you went to bed?" Sutton asked.

"Yes, sir. She was sitting on Dad's lap, giggling. Mom said something about a romantic date she had with Dad that night."

"Were they just teasing? Is that what you're saying?" Sutton asked.

"Yes."

"And that's the way they were when you went to bed?" Sutton asked.

"Yes, sir."

David said he hadn't heard anything that night, and didn't wake up until his father and Jerry Siragusa roused him and his brother out of bed, sending them across the street to the Godwins'.

"Did you see your father about noon?" Sutton asked.

"Yes, sir. He got back from the police station, and we all met him out in the front yard of the Godwins'. We just grabbed him and hugged him."

"Did your father talk with you and your brother and sister at that time?"

"Yes. We went into Mr. Godwin's study. Dad held us all close and said, 'It's just us now.' He was almost crying when he said it."

"How could you tell?"

"His voice was thick—I just know."

Sutton paused for a moment. "Do you know what blood type you have, David?"

"Type O."

"The same as your father's?"

"Yes, sir."

Sutton returned to his original line of questioning. "Did your father spend a lot of time with you and your brother and your sister while you were growing up?"

"Yes, sir."

"Attended all your baseball games and that sort of thing?"

"Yes, sir."

"Did he attend church?"

"Yes, sir. About three times a month."

"Did you find your father to be a cold person that you can't get close to?"

"No, not at all."

"Have you ever seen your father angry?" Sutton asked.

"He gets angry whenever I mess up."

"How does he correct you?"

"We usually get put on restriction. He comes in and asks us why we did this thing, and we get punished."

"You get punished by him talking to you and putting you on restriction?"

"Yes, sir. Just to know that we let him down is enough punishment."

"Why is that, David?"

"Because I just love him so much, I don't want to let him down in any way."

GRAHAM was watching the D.A. closely, not wanting him to do anything to upset David.

Carmouche walked over to the collection of State's Exhibits and picked up the blue flashlight that had been found outside by the back fence. "David, who does this belong to?"

"Dad."

Carmouche picked up the can, found next to the flashlight. "Who does *this* belong to?"

"That's Dad's coin collection. He puts dimes in it."

Carmouche picked up the crowbar, found next to the utility room door. "How about this?"

"To Dad."

The District Attorney slowly picked up the sledgehammer. "And this?"

"It's a sledgehammer. It's Dad's, too."

Carmouche picked up the hunting knife used to stab the boy's father. "Did you ever see this before?"

"Yes, sir. I bought it for Dad." David kept his gaze fixed on the District Attorney.

Carmouche walked back toward the witness box. "After the murder occurred, did you ever look through the house to see if anything was missing?"

"There was nothing missing, not anything of mine anyway."

Carmouche moved the questions to another aspect of the family life. David said that the kids sometimes picked the locks on the utility room door when they found themselves locked out. Carmouche asked about their habits of leaving lights on inside and outside, then turned to the night of the murder.

"If there had been a fight going on in your parents' room, do you think you could have heard it?" Carmouche asked.

"Not if I was asleep."

"During your life, do you ever recall your parents arguing with each other?"

"They'd have disagreements."

"Did your mother ever nag your dad?"

Graham remembered few arguments in front of the children.

"Yes, sir."

"Do you know, during the night your mom was killed, whether anybody came into your bedroom other than your dad?" Carmouche asked.

"I don't know. I was asleep."

"Nobody waked you up rummaging through the room or shaking your bed, or anything like that?"

"The only way I would be awakened was if someone shook me."

"What about Eric?" Carmouche asked.

"Eric could sleep through anything."

DAVID stepped down, relieved it was over. Sutton and Walker asked for a short recess, and used it to visit with Graham. He was ready.

AS he was sworn in, Lew Graham looked a little stiff, uncomfortable. This was the moment everything had led to, when he would take the stage to try to convince twelve people that he was an innocent man.

A dog-tired Bobby Sutton started by asking Graham about his childhood, about grade school, junior high, about polio and high school.

Graham said he'd been voted best all-around as a senior in high school. He said he joined the Army Reserve and spent six months on active duty before starting college at the University of Southwestern Louisiana in January 1959. He talked of meeting his wife, their marriage, their move to Indiana, and ultimately Shreveport.

"Were you having problems with your position at Indiana?" Sutton asked.

"Not at all. They really wanted me to stay, but for several reasons I decided to leave at that time."

"What were some of those reasons?"

"Well, I had been in full-time research for years, and I was fortunate to get into some good research projects.

I attended international meetings, and I had a book. But along with all that comes a lot of time commitments. You can't do research in a forty-hour week, at least not at the high level of the frontier. It takes a lot of time, a lot of homework. I just decided I didn't want to spend that much time at that point. Our third child had been born and was a baby, and I thought I would rather do more teaching and less full-time research."

"Is there any reason you chose to come to Shreveport?"

"Well, generally, it was the South again, which we certainly liked. Both of my parents and Kathy's parents were from the South. LSU Medical Center was a brand-new school, and I figured it would be a good opportunity to get with a developing institution."

"When you returned to Shreveport with your wife and children, did you establish a church home here?" Sutton asked.

"Yes. At first we went to Christ United Methodist Church. It was in our neighborhood."

"After you moved to Shreveport, did your wife ever go to work?"

"For a while. She finished up her education, and got a library science certificate on her teaching certificate. She did some substituting, and taught full-time for one year."

"Did she like it?" Sutton asked.

"She had mixed feelings about it. She loved the kids and the interaction in the classroom. But there was so much bureaucracy associated with teaching. You can't just teach—there are forms to fill out and all these things to keep track of, and not enough help to do it. It kept getting to be more of a burden than a benefit."

"While you were in Shreveport, did your marriage to Kathy continue on an even keel?"

"No. We had some difficulties, particularly in 1978. We kind of got into a spiral. We were on different wavelengths. She would try to get some response from me by talking loud and sometimes even saying sarcastic kinds of things. I would back off," Graham said. "What was bothering her was my being quiet, and I sort of made it worse. We had a pattern going that made things difficult—that year particularly."

"Did you have a counselor address that issue?"

"Yes. I think it was in the fall of 1977. We went to a seminar at Christ United Methodist Church, put on by Bob Rausch on the family and Christian living. A lot of things he said made sense to me, and I suggested to her, 'Why don't we go talk to him?' "

"Did it help?" Sutton asked.

"Not really. I got along with him pretty well, but she didn't take to him too well. If we were going to solve our problems, I felt we both had to have a good rapport with the counselor we were talking to. So we didn't go after two or three times," Graham said.

"On January first, 1979, did you and your wife separate?"

"Yes, very temporarily. It was about ten, eleven o'clock in the morning, and we had kind of talked off and on, and it was obvious things were coming to a head. I was uncomfortable, and we thought maybe if we just lived apart for a while, we could get a better perspective on what our problems were."

Graham told the jurors how he packed a bag, left the house, drove around in circles and finally checked into a motel. That evening, after getting a "come home" call from Kathy, he returned, having never spent a night away.

"During that time, were you still at LSU, doing research in your laboratory?" Sutton asked.

"Yes."

"What was your lab assistant's name?"

"Judith Carson."

"During this time, did you and she have a sexual affair?"

"Yes."

"When was it you and she would get together?"

"Noon hour."

"Was this on a regular basis, like every Tuesday or Thursday?"

"There was no pattern at all. It was just random."

"Did you and your wife again obtain counseling in your marriage?"

"Yes. Shortly after New Year's Day, 1979, we were talking about how we've obviously got a problem. I don't know if I suggested it to her, or she suggested it to me. She would call a friend of ours, Jim Smith, who was in the psychiatry department and knew people in the field. He recommended Milton Rosenzweig."

"Was he able to help solve your problems?" Sutton asked.

"Oh, definitely. He really pointed out that it's not a matter of right and wrong, just different. As soon as we could appreciate the difference in our background and growing up we could focus on a problem. That's what it took. We unwound on a spiral, a vicious circle, and it ended up being the best year we had had in many years," Graham said.

"Was your relationship better or worse or the same in March of 1980?" Sutton asked.

"Oh, it was better. It was getting better all the time."

Bobby Sutton took Graham to the most important subject: the day of the murder.

Graham told the jury he returned from his faculty retreat a little before noon on Sunday, and the family had spent a quiet and normal afternoon. He told the now-familiar story of how his wife woke him up that night, saying she heard something. He described how he walked through the house and found nothing, so he went back to bed. The next thing he knew, he was jerked from the bed.

"What happened when you were on your back, on the floor?" Sutton asked.

"I started struggling out of a sleep, and for a while, I was trying to figure out, 'Is this real, or am I dreaming?' Then I felt a sharp pain. I was stabbed, and I tried to grab onto something. I must have grabbed the knife, because I got my whole hand cut."

"What happened then?"

"Well, I had the sensation of just flying. I felt like—like you would throw a puppy out the door."

"Where did you land?" Sutton asked.

"The next thing I really remember is getting up off the floor. I had my head up against the wall, over by the baseboard. I turned—you know, I was hurting, I didn't know what to do. I turned on the light and turned around. I saw my wife in the bed, blood all over the place. I felt she was dead. It was obvious, I think."

Graham said he rinsed off one hand, checked his wife, and left and locked the room. He said he never noticed the sledge-hammer, clock, and knife on the floor next to the bed. Then he called the police and Carolyn Godwin, and he and Jerry Siragusa woke the children and sent them across the street.

"When you got to the police station, did they take you into an office to record your statement?" Sutton asked.

"Well, not at first. It took a long time. Lieutenant Coker would ask questions, and I would have to go over things. Then one or the other would say, 'We'll be back in a minute.' I think at some point later they were calling back to the scene. They must have been verifying," Graham said.

"Dr. Graham, before the tape player was turned on by the police officers, do you have any idea how many times you had told them [the statement]?"

"Many. Some parts more than others. They would ask questions and go over it quite a few times."

After he got back to the Godwins', Graham said, Tony Brauchi, Jim Smith, and Bob Smith had pressed him to talk privately with them, when he wanted to be alone with his children.

"You heard Dr. Brauchi when he testified, and Jim Smith when he testified, as to the essence of a statement you made during that meeting?"

"Yes, the essence of that—I think it lost something in translation. I knew that Jim Smith knew that Kathy and I had some difficulties the year before. I said to Jim, 'You know we had problems.' What I was trying to say, and they didn't seem to get the message—I thought that would assure them."

"Did you tell Dr. Brauchi that you were not going to shoot yourself?"

"Yes."

"You heard the translation as it came out in the court-room?" Sutton asked.

"Yes, but that's not—I didn't think that's what I said, that certainly wasn't what I intended to say."

"Had you committed a crime such as this, would you have said something like that?"

"I wouldn't think so."

Sutton asked about Kathy's jewelry, still in the coroner's possession. "Did you ever make any inquiry after your wife's death?"

"Not right away. But before the funeral, I asked the funeral director, 'What about her things, her jewelry and so forth?' He told me the coroner had it. I assumed it was evidence, and I couldn't have it."

"The next day, Tuesday, did you have occasion to telephone the police?"

"Yes. Somebody in the Godwin household reminded me that Kathy used to call Eric when she got locked out to open the door, and maybe I should call the police and tell them about the door."

"Did you meet the detectives at the house that day?"

"Yes. Russell Ancelet came with me. I showed them the door didn't work. It seemed like something that should be included. The more information they had, the better."

"While they were there, did they walk you through . . ."

"One of them did. Detective Nichols said, 'Would you go through the incident and show us what you did?' So I did. And when I got all done, he said, 'There's a number of things I don't understand. Explain them.' There were a lot of points I couldn't explain. He pointed out things they were concerned about, and said, 'Well, if you come up with any explanation, let me know.' It seemed reasonable to me."

Graham said he had intended to offer some possibilities of what might have happened, and that it was the first time he started to think he might have been their chief suspect.

"Dr. Graham, you've heard a lot of testimony while you've been sitting in court about your emotional profile. Do you outwardly manifest your emotions?"

"No."

"Do you feel emotions?"

"A great deal."

"It may sound like a stupid question, but as a result of March thirty-first, 1980, did you feel any emotion?" Sutton asked.

"Yes, a lot."

"After March thirty-first, 1980, did you attend church any more or less than you did prior to that day?"

"I can't say I went every Sunday before or after, but we went regularly."

"Since the murder, have you attempted to maintain a stable family for your children?" Sutton asked.

"Yes, in every way I could."

Sutton paused, and looked directly at his client. "Dr. Graham, on March thirty-first, did you kill your wife?"

"No, absolutely not."

COURT was adjourned for lunch, and Sutton and Walker talked with Graham one last time before he submitted to cross-examination by the D.A.

"Remember what I told you. Answer his questions as truthfully as you can, but don't give him any more of a response than you have to. Oh, and one more thing. In a case like this, the prosecutors almost always want to create a mental image for the jury—don't be surprised if he walks over and hands you the sledgehammer. If he does, you take it by the head, or the side, anything except for the way someone would normally hold a hammer," Sutton said.

After lunch, Carmouche began his cross-examination. "Dr. Graham, on March thirty-first, 1980, there were some items removed from your house, or put or dropped outside. I'm going to ask if you can identify these items. State's Exhibit 87. Do you recognize that?"

"It's a flashlight. It looks like the one I used to have."

"This can, Similac can, out of the same exhibit. Do you recognize that?" Carmouche asked.

"Yes."

"The coins inside, do you recognize them?"

"Yes. Those were contained within that can, but there were a lot more in there that are not there now," Graham said.

"What kind were missing?"

"There was a hundred-fifty dollars' worth of dimes in paper rolls."

"Is this the first time you've seen it since the murder?" Carmouche asked.

"Yes."

"How many dimes go in a roll?"

"Twenty dollars, I think. I'm not sure. They were in paper rolls, stacked in there like sardines in a can. I had just recently wrapped them, that's how I know how much [was in the can]."

"Where did the wrappers come from?"

"American Bank."

Carmouche looked at his notes. "Did you own a handgun, Dr. Graham?"

"Yes. I kept it in the top dresser drawer in the master bedroom."

"Did you ever get that gun that night?"

"No, I didn't. It was an antique. It was given to me, a forty-one caliber long Colt."

"Prior to the time you went to Milton Rosenzweig for counseling, you stated you had been to counseling with someone else?" Carmouche asked.

"Yes, about a year before."

"How many meetings did you go to with Rosenzweig?"

"Oh, I don't know. Many. It was like once a week for a while, then once every other week, then maybe a month or more the last time."

"Can you be more specific—other than communication, what problems you were having?" Carmouche asked.

"That was it. I tried to describe that. Kathy was more verbal, I was more withdrawn. She used to try a verbal approach."

"She wanted you to do something you didn't want to do?"

"Just talk."

"Did you feel like you were being nagged?" Carmouche asked.

"Oh, occasionally."

"When she was sarcastic, would she belittle you?"

"Sometimes."

"The weekend retreat, the weekend of the murder, you had gone to Toro Hills?"

"Yes."

"Were there any complaints registered by the students [at the retreat] about your availability to them?" Carmouche asked.

"Some. Part of it was, I had only taken the position [as Assistant Dean for Student Affairs] about a year before. The secretary had retired. So for about three or four months there wasn't even a secretary in that office."

"That didn't make you feel down and depressed?"

"It was the nature of the job. I couldn't be in two places at the same time. I didn't take it badly at all," Graham said.

"Your lab assistant, Judith Carson, worked for you how long?"

"Since 1975."

"Did she have a great deal of interest in the research you were conducting?" Carmouche asked.

"Yes. I think to be good, you have to be interested in what you're doing."

"She was very understanding to you?"

"Yes."

"Did you all ever argue?"

"No."

"Fight? Did *she* ever nag you?"

"No."

"That statement you gave the morning of the murder. They talked to you about your statement, then they would check and talk to you again. Did you ever talk to Robert Smith during that interval?" Carmouche asked.

"Once. I know there was an interval where both of them were out and he came and stood at the door and brought me some water," Graham said.

"Did you get the idea you were a suspect at the time?"

"Not really. Lieutenant Coker explained something like this, 'We have to consider everybody that's around.' It seemed reasonable to me, but I'm sort of naive about those things."

"Did you ever tell them, 'Look, my wife has just been killed. What are you doing questioning me? Why aren't you looking for the people that did this?' "

"Not exactly. I thought I was providing background information to them about what happened."

"You were pulled or dragged from the bed?" Carmouche asked.

"Yes."

"Did you hit the nightstand with your head?"

"No."

"How much do you weigh?"

"About one-thirty-five."

"Were you in the air already when you waked up on your way out of bed?"

"I don't know. I couldn't say."

"A hundred thirty-five pounds. Have you ever lifted a hundred thirty-five pounds?" Carmouche asked.

"No, I never lift weights at all."

"Were you slammed to the floor or eased down?"

"I wasn't eased down. I know I landed flat on my back."

"You felt the knife while you were in the air?" Carmouche asked.

"No, I was on the floor."

"After that, you were picked up?"

"Raised up, sort of jostled. I was on my feet. I was standing."

"Did you still think it was a nightmare?"

"I was hurting too much by then."

"Then what happened?"

"Well, I had the sensation of, like, flying, of being in the air. And the next thing I remember is getting up," Graham said.

Carmouche used a little sarcasm. "Did you hit the chandelier on your way, while you were in the air?"

"I don't know. I don't think so."

"You assume you hit a stud or the floorboard?"

"I have no idea."

"Was the wall damaged in any way?"

"I don't think so."

"When you pushed yourself up off the floor, was it still dark in the room?"

"Yes."

"Was the door to the bedroom open or closed?"

"I think it was open."

"You turned the light on, and that's when you saw your wife?" Carmouche asked.

"Yes."

"You turned that light off, and then you went over to the bathroom?"

"Best I can remember, yes."

"Then you walked from that bathroom. Where did you go then?"

"Straight over to the bed. I remember going over there. I touched my wife's arm or something."

"Where did you stand when you touched your wife?"

"Just right there in front of this table [nightstand]."

"Did you happen to trip or kick the hammer and knife that were on the floor?"

"I don't remember anything like that."

"You didn't even notice them?" Carmouche asked.

"Didn't notice them."

"You said this morning when you got thrown in the air, it was like throwing a dog out the door. Have you ever done that?"

"Once we had a puppy that hollered at night. Every time it hollered, I'd throw it out and it would stop."

"The second, very detailed statement you gave the police, they asked about the blood on the front and back of your T-shirt and you indicated, 'There's a lot of things I can't explain.' You said the statement continued on for some time after that?"

"Yes."

"How long?"

"Oh, a half-hour or an hour."

"So there was as much left out as there is in the recording?"

"Yes."

"Was there anything significant left out?"

"The dimes being missing."

"It wasn't until after that third statement, on April second, that you finally said, 'Well, I'm a suspect, I better get a lawyer'?" Carmouche asked.

"Yes. After I talked to Nichols, I kind of got the feeling that it was [just] his opinion. I just didn't believe one detective could color a whole investigation," Graham said.

Carmouche walked to the lawyers' table, shaking his head. He sat down, finished with his cross-examination.

Sutton stood up. "Your Honor, at this point, the defense would rest."

BEFORE the attorneys for each side gave their final arguments, the prosecution presented four rebuttal witnesses.

Ruby Barton, a newspaper carrier in the Southern Hills area, testified she neither saw nor heard anything unusual the morning of the murder.

Ronald Rak, the father of ten-year-old Mike Rak, a defense witness, said he wasn't sure his son was completely truthful in telling about an intruder in the garage the night Kathy was killed. Under cross-examination, however, he conceded the boy's physical description of the intruder was the same as he had given the year before to police.

James Hood, a fingerprint expert with the Caddo Parish Sheriff's Office, told the jury he was of the opinion that the second, unidentified fingerprint found on Graham's hunting knife was merely a repositioning of the other print, found to match Graham's. The defense asked the expert for a definite conclusion, which he was unable to give.

Finally Ray Herd, director of the Northwest Louisiana Crime Lab, tried to stuff one hundred fifty dollars in rolled dimes in the Similac can as Graham said he had done but couldn't get them to fit.

Louisiana jury procedure allows for a closing argument by the prosecution, followed by one for the defense and a final rebuttal from the prosecution. With the presumption of innocence a mainstay of the American judicial system, this procedure is considered proper for a fair presentation to a jury.

21

CO-PROSECUTOR Jim McMichael began the State's closing argument, recapping their case and addressing specific defense contentions.

"Now, throughout this testimony, Mr. Sutton began to suggest through cross-examination that the police had jumped to conclusions; that is, they made a hasty judgment that the defendant was the one that killed his wife. And the defense suggests their investigation was somehow tainted from that point on and they are to be considered suspect by you.

"We submit that the police didn't jump to any conclusions. We submit the police were doing their job, and they did their job quite well. We certainly don't want the police to accept any story at face value. They are entitled to judge people's credibility just as you, the members of the jury, are. They were entitled to take into account the defendant's demeanor was mighty calm for a person who'd just been through something like that. And they were entitled to take into account the sheer improbability of his story."

McMichael walked over to the jury box. "When the police heard his story and saw the physical evidence, they just began to get the feeling things didn't add up. Burglars don't work like that. We're not talking about rookie detectives. I don't think there was one who testified that had worked less than ten years. These are policemen that investigate hundreds of burglaries and murders.

"Did the police jump to any conclusions? Were they out to *get* Lew Graham? They weren't. If they were, they would have hauled him off to jail that first morning. As it was, he wasn't arrested until months later and the police used their manpower to go out and talk to the neighbors and continue their investigation," McMichael said.

He reminded the jury of the coroners' testimony, especially McCormick's contention that Kathy Graham lived several minutes after the beating. He went on to bring out what the State saw as the significance of Judith Carson.

"And finally, in that third statement to the police, he revealed for the first time he had not really been truthful when he was asked whether or not he had engaged in sexual relations outside his marriage. He explained that he had had an affair with a lab assistant at work. He said it was nothing really serious, that it had caused no problems in his marriage, and that it had been over for some time.

"But you recall Judith Carson testified that the affair had not been terminated at the time of the murder.

"On the afternoon of the murder, the neighbors and friends of the family all gathered across the street at the Godwins' house. The defendant returned somewhere around noon. When he got there, three of his colleagues from the medical school were there: Dr. Robert Smith, Dr. Jim Smith, and Dr. Tony Brauchi, all there at the suggestion of the dean. According to their testimony, they were there to see if the defendant was going to be able to make it through this period of great sadness.

"While they were talking to him, to decide if it was okay for him to be alone, whether he was going to suffer great depression, the defendant made a statement they all remember clearly. The defendant stated, 'I'm not as upset as you might think I ought to be, because my wife and I really haven't been getting along lately.' "

McMichael went over the testimony of Detectives Nichols and Brann and the blood typing and fingerprint work done at the crime lab.

"Finally, the State presented evidence from Professor Herbert MacDonell, the leading expert in the field of blood-stain interpretation and analysis. He examined the T-shirt of the defendant, and concluded the stains on the front and back of the neck were cast-off stains, typical of the type found on the shirt of a person who administers a beating with an object like a hammer. On the front of the defendant's T-shirt, there was medium-velocity spatter, consistent with his being two or four feet away at some point in the beating. He also found a transfer pattern consistent with being made by contact with the sledgehammer. MacDonell examined the defendant's undershorts and observed between two hundred fifty and three hundred medium-velocity blood spatters, which means the defendant was within two to four feet of the victim at the time of impact," McMichael said.

"But most important was the fact that some of these spots had clotted blood, which means the defendant must have been two to four feet from his wife at the time she was beaten the last time or at least five minutes *after* the first beating occurred. That would, of course, be inconsistent with the story the defendant tells, that he was on the floor a few seconds and was then picked up and thrown over to the other side of the room."

McMichael continued. "Then the defendant presented evidence. I think it's fair to say he wanted to prove several things. First, he wanted to prove that Lew Graham's reaction on the day of his wife's murder was normal, and typical of Lew Graham. He wanted to prove Lew Graham was a good family man and is not the sort of guy who would do something like this.

"He wanted to prove the door could have easily been opened with a screwdriver or knife, or perhaps a crowbar. He wanted to prove there was a lot of suspicious activity in the neighborhood that night. And finally, he wanted to prove the physical evidence was consistent with the defendant's story. I'd like to take those points up one at a time," McMichael said.

"It's interesting to note the reactions of his friends in Shreveport, the people he worked closely with, the people that would have known him best. Robert Smith, Jim Smith, and Dean Muslow were so concerned at Lew Graham's reaction, they made a point of having Dr. Brauchi go out and talk to him. Why was that? Because even Lew Graham can't be expected to remain calm and collected through a tragic death! Even Lew Graham himself realized his reaction wasn't normal, and that's best described in the statement we've talked about—'I'm not as upset as you think I should be, because Kathy and I haven't been getting along lately.' Further, along those lines, Dr. Ware and Dr. Gucker testified they had tested the defendant, given him a battery of tests, and their conclusions were that he's just not the type of person who would do this. Dr. Ware didn't stop at that. If you recall, he said, 'I've never seen anybody in my years of practice less likely to commit a crime like this.' In judging the credibility of that testimony, all you have to do is think about what Dr. Ware said to determine that the testimony is biased and slanted in favor of the defendant," McMichael said. "You may find it unlikely the defendant would commit such a crime, but character evidence cannot destroy conclusive evidence of guilt.

"Another thing that's interesting about the character evidence is the people who *didn't* show up. Where were the people who knew him in Shreveport? Where were the people that knew him at work? Where were the people he went to church with? Where are the social friends of the Grahams? Would you not expect these people would want to come forward, too, and talk about the character of the defendant?

"Along those lines of what a good family man he was, he presented the testimony of Dr. Rosenzweig. He testified the defendant and Kathleen Graham had problems—problems of communication, problems a lot of people who are married have. But as far as he knew, they were working the problems out and didn't need his services any more.

"I think his testimony had to be considered in light of two things. One, during the time the defendant and his wife were trying to work the marriage out, the affair was still ongoing. And the defendant hadn't told anybody about that. He hadn't even told Dr. Rosenzweig! It's hard to imagine that a man who is serious about working out his marriage problems would continue such a relationship. And of course, it must be considered in light of the statement the defendant made about his wife the day of the murder. Dr. Rosenzweig himself said he would be very surprised if the defendant made that statement, because it would indicate things had regressed in their marriage. Dr. Rosenzweig stated the defendant felt trapped in his marriage at times. He felt his wife nagged him at times, and sometimes it was intolerable when she became loud and sarcastic," McMichael said.

"Now, concerning the testimony about the door—everybody who testified, from Uncle Cliff all the way through Dr. Stone from the Dallas Crime Lab, agreed the locks were faulty. What you've got to realize is they testified about this *after* they had examined the door—taken it apart. You've got to know the locks are defective, and a burglar is not going to know that.

"Judy Bunker came in from Orlando, Florida—she's the defense blood spatter expert. If she's going to testify about her findings, and if she's going to expect her testimony to stand up against Professor Herbert MacDonell, you would expect her to know a little bit about the physical sciences. You would expect her to know a sponge doesn't give the same sort of spatter that a wound in a human head would. I submit the tests Judy Bunker performed have about as much validity as the same tests one of us could have performed. She had one specific purpose in mind, to recreate the defendant's story. You stack up her testimony against the testimony of Professor MacDonell, and it's clear which one is more believable."

The baby-faced prosecutor smiled at the jurors. "After Mrs. Bunker testified, the defendant took the stand. This is the first time he's been heard from since that third statement two days after the murder. It's funny how he's still remembering things. One thing you've got to consider: nobody has any more at stake in this than the defendant. He has been described by Dr. Ware as a *survivor!* Now, what connotations do you get from *that* word? Apparently, he'll do most anything to come out of this." McMichael paused to let it sink in.

"In looking back on the evidence, there can be no doubt whatsoever that Kathleen Graham was killed on March thirty-first, 1980, at her home on Kirkwood Drive in Shreveport, Caddo Parish, Louisiana. There can likewise be no doubt that the person who did it certainly intended to kill her. So the only thing left to decide is—who did it?

"The State contends that the evidence is clear, and it's beyond a reasonable doubt that the defendant *did* kill his wife. In order to believe otherwise, you'd have to believe that burglars came to his house to break in, but they didn't bring any tools! You've got to believe that they broke in for the purpose of killing Kathleen Graham, not to steal things as burglars usually do.

"Is it reasonable to conclude that they would bludgeon her with a sledgehammer, and merely stab him in the side, causing minor injuries at best? It just doesn't add up.

"But in order to believe the *defendant* killed Kathleen Graham, you really only have to believe what the evidence plainly tells you."

McMichael used his fingers to emphasize each point. "That the defendant was within two to four feet of the victim at the time the final blow was struck. That the final blow was delivered for one reason and one reason alone. It was delivered to kill.

"It was an accurate blow.

"It was delivered unemotionally.

"It was delivered with calculation.

"It was delivered without feeling.

"And it was delivered by Lew Graham."

McMichael turned and looked at Graham.

"He could have everyone in his high school yearbook come in here and testify that he was the most talented or favorite in his class. But he can't get around the fact the physical evidence *proves* he's the one that beat Kathy Graham to death.

"I submit you have heard the evidence, and after the arguments, you will have no doubt the defendant is guilty of second-degree murder."

22

AFTER a fifteen-minute recess, Bobby Sutton got his final chance before the jury that would decide if Lewis Graham was guilty of murder.

Sutton was obviously physically exhausted. His hands trembled as he paced in front of the jury box. "Ladies and gentlemen, I want to thank you for your time. It's been a long, long trial. This case has presented a seemingly endless array of exhibits, facts, figures, opinions. There have been over sixty witnesses to testify. There have been over a hundred and fifty exhibits offered and presented to you, and you are being asked to hear all these witnesses and look at all these exhibits and make some sense out of it.

"As you know, it's the State's duty to present evidence to you in a reasonable way to prove to you, beyond a reasonable doubt, the guilt of the accused. If they fail to do this, if the evidence is insufficient for *any* reason, then you are required to return a verdict of not guilty. The absolute, overriding consideration in this case is there is *no direct evidence of the guilt of Lewis Graham*. None whatsoever.

"The law regarding circumstantial evidence was read to you. When a case is based on circumstantial evidence, then the duty of the prosecutor is not simply to prove beyond a reasonable doubt, but also to exclude every other reasonable hypothesis of innocence. That's the law.

"I'm sure you recall when you were sitting as a prospective juror, you were told the proof of the death of the person is not proof of the guilt of the accused. The fact that Kathleen Graham was killed, the fact that she was killed by the hammer that belonged to Lewis Graham, was never disputed."

Sutton continued his argument by reminding the jurors of the prosecution's assertion, in their opening statement, that no one had seen or heard anything unusual that night. He pointed to the defense witnesses from the neighborhood who *did* report several disturbances heard that night.

"If we look at the entire time sequence of all these people circling the Graham home, this is what you find: Michael Rak—the best he can say is late at night he went to his back door in response to a noise and saw an intruder inside his garage. That's across the street and up a couple of houses. Right next door, at one-thirty in the morning, Mrs. Johnston's dogs were attracted by someone or something in the back yard. Thirty minutes later, Brenda Alford's dog began furiously barking. Dr. Graham, in his statement, said, 'My wife woke me up between two and three in the morning.' Dorothy Milam, less than a block away, was awakened by her dogs after she had gone to bed. You remember Mr. Breedlove, who lives six houses down from the Graham residence, testified that on two consecutive weekends prior to March thirty-first, he had incidents occur in his home.

"I told you in the opening statement that we would prove to you the neighborhood was not quiet that night. Indeed, it was quite busy," Sutton said.

"The prosecution says, 'There is no sign of forcible entry at the Graham home.' As you recall, they did acknowledge the crowbar lying on the floor of the garage immediately beneath the back door. There were pry marks on the facing of the door. There were a number of witnesses who testified for the defense, and I believe it was made abundantly clear that no lock on that back door was in working order. Not only were the locks inferior, but you remember the gap between the door casing was so wide you could look through and see the hardware. Russell Ancelet, the state trooper, ex-brother-in-law, testified he checked the door himself, and got inside by simply taking a knife and opening the locks. Dr. Stone from Dallas also testified they were non-operable, would not lock," Sutton said.

"Contrary to the opinion of Lieutenant Nichols, you cannot determine the age of pry marks. There was some question as to whether an intruder would look at the door and know it could be opened without having to tear it out with the crowbar. I suggest to you, any time there is a gap between the door and the door casing, the logical thing to do, particularly if you're standing there with a knife, is see if you can push the bolt out of the way.

"The next point the prosecution made concerned a fingerprint found on the handle of the knife. Sergeant Blankenship, Sergeant Derrick, Officer Wood, Major Taylor, all testified the knife had been retrieved from the bedroom, had been examined for prints, and a partial print had been found on the handle. Major Taylor submitted a photograph showing . . . the position of the print on the handle. You recall it was held just the way you would hold it if you were whittling.

"Bloodstain evidence—Herbert MacDonell, Judy Bunker—you heard all of it. I think the most crucial thing about the bloodstain evidence is that after all that testimony, Mr. Herbert MacDonell said the stains found on the T-shirts and shorts were consistent with having been received when Dr. Graham was on the floor. You recall, however, that he said in his version, those stains could be received in one position, and therefore, it was a 'simpler' theory. I simply pose the question to you, whether your duty is to choose the answer which is simpler, or the answer which is correct," Sutton said.

Sutton glanced toward the lawyer's table and nodded at Jim McMichael. "Mr. McMichael said the defense attacked the police. I disagree with that. We did raise some questions about the police forming a conclusion awfully quick. Do you recall how Lieutenant Nichols made it very clear to *three* people that Lewis Graham was going to be charged the morning of March thirty-first? You recall I told you in the opening statement that once that happened, it caused the public not to come forward with evidence. It did something else: it caused Lewis Graham's every utterance, every word, every act to be scrutinized.

"When Dr. Graham was being cross-examined by the prosecution, you recall the prosecution was totally surprised to learn he had ever said anything about any coins missing from this piggy bank? All of a sudden, they said, 'Where did that come from?' Dr. Graham said it in his second statement. He told the police then, but they had already turned the recorder off!

"The police did not *know* about the incident at Mr. Breedlove's house. They did not *know* about the incident Brenda Alford reported. Dorothy Milam, you remember— *she* came forward with her information about seeing the man in the back yard during the first week of the trial! That's proof that telling the public [Graham was guilty] caused people not to come forward. How many others are out there?"

Sutton's voice took on a calm, sensitive tone as he turned and faced his client. "There was a lot of evidence put on about the character of Dr. Graham, what kind of person he is. In this case, you must look at Lewis Graham as a total person—the way he thinks, the way he works, the way he's educated. A number of witnesses describe Lew Graham as a responsible person, good father, interested in his children's activities, a quiet man who would walk away from adversity. His colleagues and part of Kathleen Graham's family testified to Lew Graham's good character. These witnesses came not only from Shreveport but other cities and states.

"The expert testimony from Dr. Gucker and Dr. Ware was consistent with that. Dr. Ware said he'd never seen an individual less prone to violence than Lew Graham in his fifteen years of psychiatric practice."

Sutton turned back, searching for a reaction from the jurors. "There are some very significant and relevant questions still pending in this case. I would like to share some of them with you.

"Why was type A blood found on David Graham's bedspread? Lew Graham has type O blood. David Graham has type O blood. Why did the serologists that took these types for the prosecution *not* find that type A blood on David Graham's bed? It was there.

"Why was one complex of wounds administered on the right side of the bed, and *then* the victim was moved over to the left and another wound administered?

"Why were bloodstains found on both sides of the door to the bedroom, indicating that the door was open at one time, closed at one time, or just happened to be in the exact perfect position to receive bloodstains on both sides?

"What happened to the money missing from the piggy bank? Do you recall that Dr. Graham signed that consent [for the police] to search his home and car? What happened to the money?

"Who was the intruder Michael Rak saw in his garage?

"Who or what caused Brenda Alford's dog to bark at two o'clock that morning?

"Who was the white teenage male Dorothy Milam saw in her back yard that morning?

"Is the fact that the timing between Michael Rak, Mrs. Johnston, Brenda Alford, and Dorothy Milam was the same as the sequence inside the Graham home—is that simply a coincidence? The prosecution has not presented any evidence to give any answers to these questions. But the questions are relevant," Sutton said.

As he moved away from the jury box, his voice grew stronger. "Most of our lives are taken up with considerations of things that are gray. We look at our daily lives, and we don't find too many things that are black-and-white choices. How important was it that you missed that elevator? There will be another coming in just a minute. How important is it that your car has a dead battery? You can always get another battery. These things happen to us each day, and they seem important at the time. But few things in our daily life require the absolute, unmitigated best that we have to offer. We can operate as average people in an average world and not be faced with having to make the ultimate choice between black and white, not presented with a choice between freedom and life in the penitentiary without benefit of parole, pardon, or probation. Ordinarily, we do compromise on a great many things in our life. We can have cereal today, pancakes tomorrow. But the problem is, you're not at the breakfast table now. You're in the jury box."

Sutton sighed outwardly. "This case demands the ultimate effort. It requires your best. I'm sure each of you recognized that the day you were sworn in. Why is Lew Graham on trial? You have a quiet man who had a wife, three lovely children. A man that spent time with his family, with his children. I don't think the evidence has shown him to be the cold, unimpassioned man it was supposed to portray. My work is finished; it's your turn. The magnitude of your responsibility is staggering. You literally have the life of Lewis Graham in your hands. You have his freedom, you have his work, you have his friends, you have his home and family."

Sutton's voice took on a commanding, theatrical presence. "I am sure that when you review the evidence and ask yourself the question, 'Is this proof beyond a reasonable doubt?,' your answer is going to cause you to return a verdict of not guilty."

AFTER a ten-minute recess, a very different Paul Carmouche stood up to give the State's final rebuttal. Carmouche and McMichael were worried, worried that they had been too civil, too polite. Looking at a twelve-member jury of Lew Graham's peers, Carmouche decided to abandon his usual restrained courtroom style and delivered the State's final argument with emotion, passion, and animation.

"When I started this case, in our opening statement, I told you in great detail exactly what evidence we were going to put on. Then the defense said they too would put on evidence. They said they would prove to you the neighborhood was very, very busy that night. They said that at the end of this trial you would wonder why the defendant was even arrested. I don't think any one of you has any doubt why this defendant was arrested. This defendant was arrested because he committed this very despicable act," Carmouche said.

The D.A. turned and picked up a crime scene picture of the body of Kathy Graham. Using the photograph as a pointer, he gestured at Lew. "That man right there committed this act. It's time to take the gloves off and not be nice. *He* certainly wasn't nice, the night of March thirty-first, 1980, when he bashed his wife's head in with a sledgehammer."

Carmouche had not been this blunt during testimony; he obviously had a different technique for closing. "This man's story occurred in a small room behind a closed door. And anybody that says they can tell you exactly what happened behind the closed doors of that room doesn't know what he's talking about. The evidence shows what we presume happened. The defense says the manner of death in this case should not prejudice you. We're not asking you to be prejudiced by the manner of this death. We're not asking you to convict this man because he had an affair. We're asking you to convict because he's guilty, and the evidence has proved it!"

Carmouche walked down the line of jurors. "He's *lied* to you on a number of occasions." His voice grew louder. "The defense said they were going to show you the neighborhood had been very, very busy. The man up the street thinks somebody came to his house. He's not sure, but he thinks it was a couple of weeks before the murder. What does that have to do with what happened March thirty-first? They put on a kid up the street, he says he saw something. His father comes in, he was very frank about it, and says, 'I don't really believe him.' The defense says Mrs. Milam had some essential evidence that didn't come into the picture until after the trial started. Well, Mrs. Milam apparently considered the evidence of so little significance she didn't come forward till a week ago! What does that have to do with anything!" Carmouche said.

"These intruders—assassins, not burglars, we are told— were they going around the neighborhood, looking for a house with a weak door that had some weapons in the garage? I don't want to sound facetious, because this is very serious, but the story sounds kind of silly.

"Bloodstain evidence. They talk about Professor MacDonell's testimony about the blood spatter on the front of the T-shirt, the front of the shorts and back of the shirt. It was very significant to me they never mentioned Judy Bunker; they are already conceding you aren't believing her. Judy Bunker is a hard worker, but I don't think she understands everything she needs to about blood. Herbert MacDonell does.

"There is some talk about the police jumping the gun and forcing some witnesses underground. I have no idea what they're talking about. Are you supposed to believe there are still witnesses out there who haven't come forward? Judge this case on the evidence. Don't start falling into that trap of saying, 'You could think this, you could think that.' When the evidence is strong, what else can the defense [do] but try to get you thinking about something else besides what's there: *the T-shirt, those shorts, the knife, the hammer, his story, his changed story, his lies!*"

Carmouche talked about defense accusations of biased police work. " . . . And Nichols went out there the next day with John Brann, and Big Bad Donnie Nichols, running off witnesses, jumping the gun, said, 'There's some holes in this story.' But this man with a 130 IQ didn't know that he was a suspect? And in his second recorded statement, he said, 'I realize I'm in a tough spot.' He knew he was in a tough spot from the time he killed his wife, and tried to figure out some way out of this thing. What would you do? You can't take something and hide it from the house because the police might find it! But you have to make it look like somebody else came in. So you put a crowbar by the door. You take some items that aren't significant. You throw it out on the ground.

"They said this case was entirely circumstantial. We don't have anybody to tell you they saw what occurred in that room that night. There were only two eyewitnesses. One of them is dead, and the other is here on trial."

Carmouche walked toward the lawyers' table. "The judge is going to instruct you that sympathy is not a part of the evidence, not to allow sympathy either for or against the defendant to affect your decision. We are not asking you to convict because it was a very heinous offense. We are not asking you to let him go because he has a pretty family, he's smart and does good work.

"They say you have the defendant's life, his freedom, his family, everything else in your hands. You also have the memory of Kathleen Graham.

"We submit Kathleen Graham lived in Shreveport. You live in Shreveport. This is your community. This is your decision. That defendant is guilty. It's your duty to find him so."

JUDGE Bolin addressed the jury. "Having heard the arguments and evidence, it now becomes my duty to instruct you on the law applicable to this case, after which you will be called upon to reach and render a verdict.

"I charge that you are the judges of the law and facts. It belongs to you alone to determine the weight and credibility of the evidence. It is for you to decide what facts have or have not been proven.

"In determining the credibility of witnesses, you may take into consideration the probability or improbability of their statements; their demeanor on the stand; the interest or lack of interest they have shown in this case; and every circumstance surrounding their testimony.

"If you believe any witness, either for the State or for the defense, has willfully and deliberately testified falsely for the purpose of deceiving you, you are justified in disregarding the entire testimony of such witness.

"I charge you that the fact an accused stands before you, charged with a crime by an indictment of a grand jury, creates no presumption against him. A person accused of a crime is presumed, by law, to be innocent, until each element of the crime is proved beyond a reasonable doubt. The State, however, is not required to prove with absolute certainty; it is sufficient if the State will prove beyond a reasonable doubt.

"In weighing the evidence, if you determine that two different and reasonable conclusions may be drawn from the evidence, one of which is favorable to the defendant, I charge that it is your duty to draw the one favorable to the defendant. If on the other hand, the State has proved beyond a reasonable doubt every essential element of the crime, it is your duty to convict the defendant.

"There are two methods by which facts can be established. These are direct and circumstantial evidence. Direct evidence is evidence bearing directly, without the aid of deduction or inference, on the question at issue. Circumstantial evidence is the evidence of certain facts, from which are to be inferred the existence of other material facts. Circumstantial evidence is legal and competent. The rule as to circumstantial evidence is: assuming every fact the evidence tends to prove, in order to convict, it must exclude every reasonable hypothesis of innocence.

"An expert witness is one who, as a result of training or experience, has acquired special knowledge. The opinions of an expert are admissible in evidence, if he states the facts on which his opinions are based. It is the duty of the jurors to consider the opinions of an expert, together with all the testimony in the case, and to give them such weight as they deem proper. However, experts are *not* called into court for the purpose of deciding the case. You, the jurors, bear that responsibility.

"If the State offers evidence of a statement by the defendant, you must first determine whether that statement was, in fact, made. If you find the defendant made the statement, you must also determine the value the statement should be accorded, if any. In making that determination, you should consider whether the statement was freely and voluntarily made, without the influence of fear, duress, threats, intimidation, inducements, or promises.

"Evidence of the good character of the accused is always admissible in his behalf and must be considered as a part of the whole testimony. But it cannot destroy conclusive evidence of guilt."

Bolin cleared his throat, took a sip of water, and continued. "The accused stands before you charged with the crime of second-degree murder, of which there are three possible verdicts. They are: guilty of second-degree murder; guilty of manslaughter; or not guilty.

"Second-degree murder is the killing of a human being, when the offender has a specific intent to kill or inflict great bodily harm. Whoever commits the crime of second-degree murder shall be punished by life imprisonment at hard labor, without benefit of parole, probation, or suspension of sentence.

"Manslaughter is a homicide which would be murder but is committed in sudden passion or heat of blood immediately caused by provocation sufficient to deprive an average person of self-control and cool reflection.

"You are further instructed that any penalty in this case is to be assessed by the Court. The penalty is not the concern of the jury.

"You are to base your verdict only upon the evidence produced in open court, and the law as charged you by the Court. You are not to be influenced by sympathy, passion, prejudice, or public opinion. You are expected to reach a just verdict.

"Ten of the twelve of you must concur in order to reach any verdict.

"Each of you must decide the case for yourself, but only after discussion and impartial consideration of the case with your fellow jurors. Do not hesitate to re-examine your own views and change your opinion, if you are convinced you are wrong. But do not surrender your honest belief solely because of the opinion of your fellow jurors or for the mere purpose of returning a verdict.

"You may now retire and consider your verdict."

23

THE Grahams went home to await the decision. Throughout
the whole sixteen-month legal process, Lew had maintained
a fairly optimistic outlook. He was reasonably confident
that once he got his day in court he'd be exonerated of the
charges. Now, with the jury deliberation under way, with
the feeling that the contest of the trial hadn't gone quite as
well as planned, he thought his chances for acquittal were
about fifty-fifty.

All along Sutton had been realistic about the possibilities.
"Lew, there's absolutely no way to predict which way a jury
is going to go. I've seen 'em where you'd just swear they
were going one way, only to see 'em go the other. The
longer they think about it, the better. Every minute they
think and argue is one minute closer to 'not guilty.'"

THE State vs. Lewis T. Graham, Jr. went to the jury a
little after 5:00 p.m. on Saturday, August 1, 1981. After
five hours of consideration, the jurors retired for the night,
deadlocked. Around 8:00 the next morning, an hour ahead
of schedule, they were back at it. At 9:30, Judge Bolin
called Bobby Sutton, who'd gone to church, and told him
a verdict was in. Sutton called Graham at home, and by
10:30 court was back in session.

Bolin cautioned the group of spectators, which had dwindled considerably since the trial began. "When the jury comes in, the written verdict will be handed to the sheriff, the sheriff will hand it to me, and I will hand it to the clerk. The clerk will then read it. When that occurs, regardless of what it is, I want no outcries, no noise. You will remain seated until I dismiss you. Let the record show the defendant and his counsel are present. Will you ask the jury to step in?"

SUTTON had told Graham that occasionally you can read the verdict in the eyes and expressions of the jurors. Graham wasn't encouraged by what he read.

"Would the defendant please rise?"

Graham stood up and faced the clerk, who was standing next to the witness box. He could feel his heart beating in his chest.

"Ladies and gentlemen of the jury, you will listen to your verdict. 'We the jury find the defendant, Lewis T Graham, Jr., guilty as charged of second-degree murder.'"

Graham was stunned. He could hear his youngest children crying in the seats behind him, but he didn't have the courage to turn and face his family. All he could think about was "guilty as charged."

He stood silent as the jury was polled, and each juror had to state his vote for the record. There were two votes not guilty, ten votes guilty—the minimum needed for conviction.

"Mr. Sheriff, will you take your prisoner?"

LEW Graham had never seen the inside of a jail before. Since his grand jury indictment over a year earlier, he had remained free on bond. He was handcuffed while standing next to the counsel table.

Walker and Sutton rode with Graham and two deputies up the special elevator to the rooftop jail at the Caddo Parish Courthouse. Graham was on the verge of tears.

The Caddo Parish Jail had a number of individual cells along with a larger holding cell. The holding cell had five bunk beds, room for ten prisoners. The cell area was painted a drab greenish-nothing—clean, but a long, long way from Graham's custom-built, 2700-square-foot home in southwest Shreveport.

Graham's lawyers watched as he was fingerprinted. His pockets were emptied of all their contents—a comb—as he was officially remanded to the custody of the parish.

The attorneys talked about the potential for appeal.

Graham said little, emotions choking back the words.

Mercifully, he was left alone in the holding cell. The huge steel door slammed shut with an ear-shattering bang.

Graham went to the lower bunk, farthest from the door, closest to the barred and meshed windows. The windows faced south, and he could see parts of the downtown skyline and a small stretch of Interstate 20.

It took twenty-six steps to walk in a circle around the cell.

Still dressed in his coat and tie from the courtroom, Graham had no pencils or papers, no books or magazines, nothing with which to share the desperation and isolation he felt.

He was touched by the instant kindness of the guards and trusties. The deputies peeked in frequently—suicide watch. Food was served promptly, and the prisoner promptly turned it down.

ON his second day in the parish lock-up, an associate pastor from Summer Grove Baptist Church brought Graham a Thompson Chain Reference Bible. It had been a few years since he had been very enthusiastic about religion. As he opened the thick book at random, his eye was caught by a verse at the top of the page:

"My grace is sufficient for thee."

Epilogue

LEWIS Graham spent a week alone in the holding cell on top of the parish courthouse. On August 24, 1981, his forty-first birthday, he was transferred to another jail. Early that morning, a sheriff's deputy picked him up at his cell, handcuffed him, and placed him in the back seat of a patrol car.

The deputy drove twenty miles out into the countryside, along a winding two-lane rural roadway, past rolling green pastures and grazing cattle, horse farms and chickens, and finally entered the grounds of the Caddo Correctional Institute. A ten-foot metal and iron gate swung open magically, operated by remote control from inside the guard's house. Graham sat silently staring out the window at his new home. He sighed, still shocked and amazed at his conviction.

As a convicted murderer, he was assigned to maximum security. He was given a cell by himself in "East Max," which turned out to be every bit as depressing and disquieting as he had expected. He silently surveyed his new home and swallowed another sigh.

Graham was alone all day, every day, in his tiny barred hole-in-the-wall. His cell was about six feet by eight feet, with a double bunk, commode, lavatory, and a G.I.-issue footlocker.

East Max was made up of two groups of cells in two levels, with all the cell doors facing the same direction. Graham's block of cells had two black-and-white televisions which were on seven days a week from noon to midnight. The prisoners could look out through the bars of their cells and watch the TV on their level.

Night was the hardest for Graham to get used to. A lot of the prisoners in East Max would sleep all day so they could "party" all night. The constant din of yelling, singing, cursing, and general noisemaking made it difficult to get to sleep. Locked up in maximum security, he smelled the sweetish odor of burning marijuana for the first time in his life.

His sister had been given guardianship of David, Eric and Katie. She and the children went about closing up the house, packing for the move to south Louisiana, putting the furnishings in storage, closing bank accounts, getting school transcripts, and otherwise putting Lew Graham's life on hold. For Elizabeth, it was as if her brother was dead. It reminded her of when she had cleared out her father's house after his death.

Sutton and Walker went to work immediately on a motion for a new trial while Graham spent each long lonely day in his cell.

Day after day Graham spent most of his waking hours reading and studying his newly acquired Bible. After a couple of weeks he put together some notes of his thoughts and studies from jail. His writings were typed, copied, and distributed to his friends and family.

Selected Verses Enjoining Quietness,
Restrained Speech, Anger, and Reserve
Compiled by
L.T. Graham, Jr.
Caddo Correctional Institute
September, 1981

These readings from the Bible may very well appear to be self-serving and prideful; in all honesty, I guess they are to some extent. I feel I must make some statement as to how I came to compile them in this manner.

Basically, this effort was in response to feelings of being severely misunderstood, rejected, and criticized for behavior which I had always felt was to be an asset rather than a liability. Yet it seemed that it was being turned against me.

To be convicted of something I had not done on the basis of not showing displays of anger and grief, not being violent, not being casually talkative, not burdening others with *my* feelings . . . result: feelings of dejection, depression, and lack of worth. Then, while reading and studying the Bible, I was led to James 1:19, which really hit me! *Wherefore, my beloved brethren, let every man be swift to hear, slow to speak, slow to wrath.* It was a comfort to me. Maybe I wasn't so worthless after all if what I could identify with as my basic personality was actually encouraged in the Scriptures. Well, one verse led to another, and after many hours I have selected these verses which have some meaning to me . . . perhaps others?

Quietness Enjoined

I Thessalonians 4:11. *And that ye study to be quiet, and to do your own business, and to work with your own hands, as we commanded you.* (Make it your aim to live a quiet life, to mind your own business, and to earn your own living, just as we told you before.)

Ecclesiastes 4:6. *Better is a handful with quietness, than both the hands full with travail and vexation of spirit.* (. . . It is better to have only a little, with peace of mind, than be busy all the with both hands trying to catch the wind.)

Restrained Speech

Proverbs 21:23. *Whoso keepeth his mouth and his tongue keepeth his soul from troubles.* (If you want to stay out of trouble, be careful what you say.)

Proverbs 10:19. *In the multitude of words there wanteth*

not sin: but he that refraineth his lips is wise. (The more you talk, the more likely you are to sin. If you are wise, you will keep quiet.)

Proverbs 29:11. *A fool uttereth all his mind: but a wise man keepeth it in till afterwards.* (Stupid people express their anger openly, but sensible people are patient and hold it back.)

Restrained Anger

Proverbs 14:17. *He that is soon angry dealeth foolishly, and a man of wicked devices is hated.* (People with a hot temper do foolish things; wiser people remain calm.)

Proverbs 15:1. *A soft answer turneth away wrath: but grievous words stir up anger.* (A gentle answer quiets anger, but a harsh one stirs it up.)

Ephesians 4:26. *Be ye angry, and sin not: let not the sun go down upon your wrath.* (If you become angry, do not let your anger lead you into sin, and do not stay angry all day.)

ON October 19, 1981, Lew Graham and his lawyers appeared in Caddo District Court for formal sentencing. Graham had drafted a statement and asked Judge Bolin for permission to read it in open court. Sutton passed out copies of the statement to the media.

"Your Honor, I understand that there is nothing I can say that will affect the verdict which has already been rendered against me, or the sentence that you must pass as required by present law. However, there are some sentiments I would like to express.

"I would like to thank Your Honor for conducting and maintaining the orderly proceedings in the courtroom during the trial, particularly in the face of so many gawking spectators. I'd like to thank my attorneys for their seemingly tireless efforts on my behalf. My attorneys don't know what I am about to say, nor have I been counseled for or against these remarks.

"I believe I stand before you in this situation because I

could not prove that I was innocent. There were simple factors that added up to weaken the doubt in the minds of the jury. But it is not my intention now to redirect the attention of the Court or anyone else to the discussion of factual issues. It is terribly unfortunate that there is some beneficial evidence, like that obtained under hypnosis, which is currently inadmissible under the letter of the law. I'm sure that it's not in the spirit of the law.

"I could not put on an emotional display for the benefit of the jury and spectators. I am not a performer. I am a logical scientist. There is no way—because they do not show—that I can tell you the feelings and acute sensitivity of a quiet man. There is certainly no way I can tell you how a quiet man suffers on the inside because of his sins.

"I have readily admitted the sins I am guilty of [the affair]. I've been bound in chains and publicly shamed. How long must this go on? Your Honor, because of my faith in the legal system, perhaps an overly naive faith in the beginning, I may have made some tactical errors in being too cooperative, at least from the defense point of view, for the first few days after my wife was killed.

"The loss of my wife was a severe tragedy. We had resolved our personal problems, and things were looking up. However, the events of the last eighteen months have seen no end to that tragedy. My children have been uprooted and moved to another community. My professional career has been irreparably damaged. My whole family has been disrupted.

"I bring all this out, Your Honor, to emphasize a point: that I *still* have faith in the system. I am confident the truth will come that I *am not guilty* of this crime. I harbor no ill feeling toward the jury. Anyone can make an honest mistake.

"Finally, Your Honor, I am sorry that I cannot stand before you now to show remorse for what I have done, because I *did not do it!* I'm here because, in spite of all the talk about the presumption of innocence, I could not *prove* I was innocent.

"Thank you, Your Honor."

Judge Bolin responded. "It is the judgment of this court, Lewis Graham, that you are hereby sentenced to life imprisonment at hard labor, without benefit of parole, probation, or suspension of sentence."

A few weeks after the trial, Paul Carmouche received the first of what would be many similar letters from Mrs. Frances "Bobbi" Parish, Kathy Graham's mother.

Dear Mr. Carmouche,

He was the happiest man I've ever seen the week after she was buried. I realized a week afterwards she was physically dead (I had been looking all day for her to walk out of her room—turning around in the kitchen, expecting to see her).

I walked out on the porch and stood by her favorite bush. For an hour, my heart turned to lead and was crying inside. Then I came in and sat in her room. Lew came in and said, "What's the matter?" I said, "I've just now realized she's dead." He patted me on the head, and said, "Oh, let's not get morbid about this." I'm not morbid, I'm grief-stricken!

When they told me he was a suspect, I began watching him. They went to pick out a burial plot. I don't know where she would have been buried if David hadn't have been there. There was one lot, in a thrown-away looking place, and he said, "This is fine, because I'm not planning on staying in Shreveport anyway." David said, "Isn't there something else?" The man had two lots up on the hill. It was real pretty, about 300 feet from the highway. David said, "We'll take those two, right Dad!" So then I pleaded for him to get her a tombstone and he put on an act of having the same place for himself, like "poor me!"

Yes, poor you, going back to lunch, back to your mistress! I'm told there were others. He wouldn't have that degree if she hadn't sacrificed and told him, "Lew, stop watching TV and study."

His face glowed when he told me about Judith Carson. Kathy was coming to tell me something serious. She said,

"Wait till I get there." He knew she'd found out about the other woman. She was afraid.

He said the children went to bed that night at 9:30 or 10:00—not true! They always waited for David. He's a boy of sterling character. He's been through a lot, and is edging towards a nervous breakdown. His mouth still trembles when he talks about his mother.

Kathy was clean, she was a gourmet cook and an educator. She loved children and was so kind to everyone, especially older people. Somebody had to take over and organize and discipline the children—she did her part and his part too!

Thank the Lord, I now have honor and respect for the law.

Sincerely,
Frances Parish

MRS. Parish has since died.

SINCE the Graham case went to trial, many of the investigators who worked the crime have left the Shreveport Police Department. Among them is Donnie Nichols, who formed a private detective agency with another former officer.

Dan Coker, who had retired by the time the case came to trial, also spent some time as a private investigator but today owns and operates a neighborhood bar in Shreveport.

John Brann now works as a public information officer with the Bossier City Police Department.

Frank Lopez retired from the department in 1986.

Bennett Kitchings is presently a captain with the Caddo Parish Sheriff's Department.

David Graham married his high school sweetheart Tammy Warwick, and their first child was born in the fall of 1989. David graduated from Baylor University with a business major and is presently a stockbroker in Texas.

Eric Graham, now twenty-two, attends junior college and works full-time in a small Texas town.

Katie Graham is a senior in high school.

Jim McMichael is a successful attorney in private practice with the Shreveport law firm of Blanchard, Walker, O'Quin & Roberts.

Bobby Sutton and Glenn Walker are still partners in a thriving legal practice. Sutton continues to handle criminal cases from time to time.

Paul Carmouche remains the District Attorney for Caddo Parish and prosecutes one or two major cases a year. He is very active in Democratic politics and is frequently touted as a prospective candidate for higher office, though he has yet to announce any intention to leave the D.A.'s office.

IN the nine years that Lewis Graham has been incarcerated, he has continued to profess his innocence, never once backing down from the story he originally told the detectives. In a prison society filled with anger, frustration, and violence, he has maintained his composure and remains a quiet, introverted man.

Perhaps because of his intellectual, highly focused personality, he adapted to jail more easily than some. Graham spent several years at the Caddo Correctional Institute— today called the Caddo Detention Center—and became one of the few "lifers" ever to be granted trusty status. In the spring of 1985 he was transferred out of the Shreveport area, ultimately finding a home at a facility in Baton Rouge. At the time he was transferred, he was still serving a life sentence.

On February 3, 1988, outgoing Governor Edwin W. Edwards, following the recommendation of the state Parole Board, commuted Graham's life sentence to twenty-five years. It was one of over a hundred paroles and commutations signed by Edwards during the final days of his administration. That action restored parole eligibility.

On November 9, 1989, Lewis Graham's first application for parole was denied by a unanimous vote of the parole board. He can reapply for release every six months.

Acknowledgments

BEFORE I began writing about the Lewis Graham case, the world of lawyers, detectives, and criminal trials was about as far removed from my own experiences as you could get. Much of my research was done as I wrote a 25-part series about the case for the *Shreveport Journal*, but I have spent as much time probing the psychological aspects of the case since the series appeared as I spent on the forensic aspects before.

Obviously, a lot of people were extremely helpful to me along the way. Early on, Judd Tooke, who is both my friend and my lawyer, encouraged me to pursue the project and opened the door with his jogging buddy, Paul Carmouche. Almost immediately Mr. Carmouche offered his complete cooperation. He gave me full access to the District Attorney's extensive files on the Graham case and even passed along a copy of his handwritten notes made during the trial. Jim McMichael, whose memory for detail is world-class, submitted to numerous lunches and interviews, and was extremely generous with his time and commentary.

Having had no previous experience with people in law enforcement, I was grateful for the patience and cooperation of the police detectives and uniformed officers who worked the Graham case. Detective Donnie Nichols was very forthcoming and gave me numerous interviews. Detective John Brann was likewise cooperative and proved to be an invaluable source for perspectives into the psyche of the investigator. Detectives Dan Coker and Frank Lopez went out of their way to help—Coker even read parts of the manuscript and helped me in reconstructing dialogue. Bennett Kitchings provided insight into the Graham family as well as supplying his point of view during the investigation and trial.

Ray Herd and Pat Wojtkiewicz of the Northwest Louisiana Crime Lab spent considerable time talking to me about the physical evidence, particularly blood spatter. To help me understand, they constructed a model room of the same dimensions as the Graham bedroom. Using white butcher paper and red ink, they drew the blood spatter on the "walls" and then explained each pattern. It was a tremendous aid in showing me what was and was not important as evidence.

I should point out that some scenes in this book feature conversations taken from on-the-record sources like trial transcripts or police records, while others had to be recreated. Scenes which contain recreated dialogue were written with the help of those involved in the conversation. A large amount of time and research went into getting the words and nuances right, again with the cooperation of the participants.

During the course of the research I conducted over one hundred interviews, most of which were recorded. I talked to people in offices, cars, and homes, as well as over the telephone. Almost every Thursday evening during late 1984 and early 1985, Bobby Sutton and I drove out to the Caddo Detention Center. There, Lew Graham and I would talk for about two hours about his life, his family, and his memories from 1980 and 1981. I found him to be open, easygoing, affable, and polite. I wouldn't say that we became friends, but we did and do have a friendly relationship.

In addition to being my escort for the prison interviews, Bobby Sutton offered several behind-the-scenes recollections that were important to the story.

Among the people who either gave interviews or otherwise helped are Detective Cecil Carter, Officer T.H. Willis, Mike and Marsha Stringer, Carolyn Godwin, Jean Johnston, Dorothy Milam, Hank Gowen, Henry Walker, Dolores "Snookie" Hall, George C. "Cliff" Hall, Judith Bunker, Bill Levinson, Al Vekovius, Russell Ancelet, David Graham, Eric Graham, Judge Gayle Hamilton, Judge C.J. Bolin, Reverend David Laverty, Jim Reeves, Linda Farrar, Gary Hines, Dale Cox, John Broadwell, Sue Webb, Dr. Jim Smith, Dr. Paul Ware, Dr. Milt Rosenzweig, Sharon Shively, Cindi Butt Chadwick, Dr. George McCormick, Dr. Don Walker, Phil Jobbe, Fire Captain L.E. Lupo, Lt. Jim Casper, Mike Staggs, John Griffith, Nick Gerdis, Elaine Brandon, Mary Durusau, Ronnie Tibbit, Bob White, Denise Copeland, Dianne Ellzey, Elizabeth Moran and Melissa Riddick. I'm sure there were others whose names escape me.

Liz Parkhurst and Hope Coulter at August House were easy to work with and had a number of good suggestions in editing. Most importantly, they believed there was an audience for this book.

Hal King has been a tennis partner, mentor, and head cheerleader through my writing career. His suggestions for dealing with both the creative and business sides of writing were invaluable.

Finally, my wife, Leeann, and daughter, Courtney, put up with me through the entire ordeal of research and writing. Their love and support are the most important thing in my life.

Craig A. Lewis
NOVEMBER 1989